D0386799   62

Virtually Dead

Books by Peter May

The Enzo Files
Extraordinary People
The Critic
Blacklight Blue
Freeze Frame

The China Thrillers
The Firemaker
The Fourth Sacrifice
The Killing Room
Snakehead
The Runner
Chinese Whispers

Other Books
The Noble Path
Hidden Faces
Fallen Hero
The Reporter
Virtually Dead

Virtually Dead

Peter May

Poisoned Pen Press

Poisoned Pen Press
6962 E. First Ave., Ste. 103
Scottsdale, AZ 85251
www.poisonedpenpress.com
info@poisonedpenpress.com

Printed in the United States of America

For Susie

Acknowledgements

My grateful thanks for all their help in the writing of this book go to Grant Fry, Lead Forensic Specialist, Orange County Sheriff, Coroner Department, California; Susan Mathews, for allowing me the use of her home in Corona del Mar; and Second Life residents Leigh Gears, Doobeedoo Littlething, Mistie Hax, Therence Akina, Mugginss Boozehound, Mikelec Criss, Anin Amat, Angel Walpole, Biglurch Habercom, Fand Flaks, Gunslinger Kurosawa, Reyne Botha, Jackycat Sands, Sable Greenwood, Iona Kyle, and Karq Flow.

"Our dreams are a second life. I have never been able to penetrate without a shudder those ivory or horned gates which separate us from the invisible world."
　　　　—Gérard de Nerval, nineteenth century French poet

"That's where we are living here, inside all the dreams of people—big and small, great and petty, beautiful and awful."
　　　　—Argent Bury, virtual world resident

There is no RL, only AFK.
　　　　—Jamie Jervil

Chapter One

This was Hell. Tombstones canted at odd angles. A Celtic cross with a skull at its centre. A huge, moss-covered tomb with an evolving message. *Evil lies ahead. You might die.*

Max could hear distant screams. A veil of cobwebs barred his way, a giant spider lurking in the shadows waiting to pounce. A pervasive, ambient sound filled this world, a sound which eventually penetrated the soul, so that if ever it were to be muted the sense of silence would be almost overpowering.

He wasn't quite sure why he was afraid, after all what could harm him here? But there had been something in the cryptic IM that spooked him. Knowledge of the account that no one should have had. And the attached Landmark to a rendezvous at the Devil's Labyrinth did not bode well.

Now that he was here, he found himself gripped by a strange, inexplicable sense of apprehension—in the dark, with the sound of water dripping close by, and those voices crying in the far distance. Chilling.

Ancient stone was barely visible in the gloom. A family portrait on the castle wall morphed from a face to a skull. He bumped into the wall in front of him, and a message appeared on his screen. *Evil wall says touch me.* Max touched it, and in an instant was transported to a room where walls and ceiling were stone carved into skulls. In the centre of the room a real skull lay on the floor. It implored him, *Touch me to return.* He did as he was bid, and instantly found himself looking down into a river of molten lava. Or was it blood? It was hard to tell. Apart from its dark, red glow, the only light came from a series of flaming torches raised at intervals along the wall. Behind him stood an ancient, arched wooden door. He clicked on it. It dropped like a drawbridge, and he went through the arch into a dark square in which jagged stone pillars pierced the ink black of the starry sky overhead.

He heard a scraping sound and turned to see a shadow moving between gothic arches. He caught the merest glimpse of a pale face. He looked for a tag above it, so that he might identify his stalker. But there was none. And he began to feel more than uncomfortable. He set to Run, and turned and hurried back the way he had come. The sound of footsteps followed in his wake, but he didn't turn around. A parapet ran above the path of the red river below, and he followed it. Foreboding had now been replaced by fear. Inexplicably, he felt threatened, and knew he should not have come. He stopped and glanced back. There was no one there. And he felt an immediate sense of relief. This was crazy. It was time to leave.

He opened his Inventory, selected *The Island* in his Landmark folder, double-clicked and was teleported home.

His island rezzed around him. Palm trees swayed gently in the warm breeze, the air filled with the sound of tropical seas washing up on silver sand. Seagulls wheeled overhead and, on the rocky outcrop five hundred yards offshore, seals basked and barked in the midday sunshine. He had moved from one time zone to another, and derived comfort and a sense of security from the daylight and familiarity.

Max loved this island that he had painstakingly created over the last couple of weeks. He loved the sweep of the steeply pitched roof of his Asian house, the red-sailed yachts berthed at the decks and landing stages he had built around his little piece of tropical paradise. Pink and blue balls stood together in couplets, scattered throughout the garden, poseballs for dance animations that he had placed so carefully, even though he had no idea with whom he might dance. He felt utterly at home here. Safe.

He clicked on the door to his house and passed from the terrace to its interior. Large windows on either side looked out on sea views. He had yet to furnish it, and he was looking forward to that with an unexpected relish. He had not anticipated that he would enjoy this world quite so much. It had an addictive quality that had taken him by surprise.

Max was portly, bald, with a small, greying goatee. It was not a look most people would have cultivated for this alternative existence. But Max had wanted to look like himself. A certain vanity, a sense of his own individuality.

A sprinkle of sparkling light around his door told him that someone outside was trying to get in. Someone not on the pass list. And he froze, his brief sense of comfort evaporating like early morning mist to be replaced once more by the foreboding that had stalked him in Hell. He called out.

Maximillian: Who's there?

There was no response, even although he could almost feel the presence on the other side of the door. He was secure inside. Without a Landmark the intruder could not enter.

Then, to his astonishment, he saw a blue poseball rez in the middle of the floor. He heard a sound like a rattlesnake, and then a figure appeared, latched on to the poseball in a strange squatting position, before standing up and turning toward him. For a moment his heart stopped, and then recognition brought an animated smile to his face, and relief surged through him.

Maximillian: Oh, it's you. How on earth did you get in?

But his visitor did not reply, simply standing staring at him, arms folded, an animated sway that seemed almost hypnotic. And then, in a single, swift movement one of those folded arms became extended, a gun held pointed at Max's chest.

And suddenly Max knew that this was no game. That he was in danger, that somehow there was real harm in this. He panicked and tried to teleport out. But instead, he hit the Fly button and began flying around the interior of his house, crashing against the walls and the roof. *Bump, bump* sound-effects thundered from his speakers. The gun followed him. He knew his assailant was now in Mouselook, targeting him. He tried to find a Landmark that would get him out of here, but he wasn't thinking straight and seemed to have lost all control, like some damned newbie. He brought up a teleport window, but missed it and double-clicked on the floor, somehow bringing up the Edit window. The house started heaving and lifting all round him. The floor canted at an odd angle. A wall detached itself from the roof and swung outwards. Whole sections of the building buckled and twisted, before finally he hit the Stop Flying button and crashed to the ground, sliding down the angle of the floor. He turned around and found the gun still pointed at him.

He heard the sharp report of it firing. Once. Twice. Three times. He saw gaping holes appear in his body. Blood. So much blood. Where in God's name was it coming from? How was it possible?

He looked up and saw his attacker, gun holstered, watching him. An animated smile, like a grimace, stretched lips across white, even teeth.

And his screen went black.

Chapter Two

Michael had been at home when the call came in, sitting on the terrace with a beer watching the moonlight shattering into a million fragments on the rippled surface of the ocean. He had been lost in his usual fog of depression, not thinking much about anything. It was a murder, they said, and he welcomed the interruption, the chance to focus his mind away from himself, even if it took another man's death to do it.

The southern California air was still warm, blood temperature, barely registering on the skin. Michael wore a simple pair of dark pants and a grey polo shirt with its Newport Beach CSI logo. He parked in the street below the house, which stood on the hill behind the coast highway, with a view out over the marina toward the peninsula. It was a big house, set on an outcrop of bedrock. Tall palms around it shifted gently in the breeze coming off the ocean. He heard the crackle of police radios. A uniformed officer stood by the open door of one of the patrol cars, and nodded as Michael hefted his tripod over his shoulder and swung his camera bag out of the trunk. "Nice night," he said, untroubled by the presence of death. He had seen it all before.

"Sure." Michael returned the nod, and loped past the white transport van that would take the body back to the Orange County Coroner's Office for autopsy. It was pulled in behind a dark blue Ford Crown Victoria and what Michael recognised as the Deputy Coroner's car.

His colleagues' white Forensic Science Services van was parked a little further up the hill.

Michael climbed the steps to the front door, stopping for a moment to take in the view. The lights of Newport arced round the bay below, the arm of the peninsula crooked protectively around the harbour and the islands that dotted its dark waters. Moonlight caught the peaks of the distant Catalina Island on this clearest of spring nights, the air infused with the heady scents of bougainvillea and honeysuckle. The view was almost as good, Michael thought, as the one that Mora had bequeathed him. The officer at the door felt compelled to comment. "I guess it takes a lot of money to buy a view like this."

Michael nodded. "It does." He stooped to pull on plastic shoe covers and snap on a pair of latex gloves. "How is it in there?"

"Messy."

He was not exaggerating. Michael followed his directions down the hall to a large study room with French windows that slid open on to a terrace that looked out on the view. Two burly gentlemen in suits, with gloved hands and a folded gurney, stood just outside the door waiting to take the body away. A large, corpulent man lay half on his side, propped in a semi-seated position by the debris of a chair that had shattered beneath his falling weight. His bald head was tipped back at a peculiar angle, eyes wide and staring into eternity. His goateed jaw hung slack, mouth open, tongue protruding slightly. There were three small bullet wounds in his chest, and three large exit wounds in his back, blood spattered in random patterns over the wall behind him, like some avant garde fresco. It had drained from his upper body through the open wounds, soaked the back of his white shirt and the cream sheepskin rug beneath him.

Michael immediately smelled the peppermint of the candies that habitually rattled around the mouth of the Deputy Coroner when he was working. Nothing had changed in Michael's three years away. Just one week back, and it felt to him like he'd never been gone. The DC had always claimed that sucking on a mint helped his concentration. And the saliva generated by the candy now slurred his words as he looked up from where he was crouched over the body. He waved a driver's licence that he had carefully extracted from the back pocket of the dead man's pants. "Photo ID matches. It's our man alright."

"Our man being who, exactly?" All the faces in the room turned toward Michael. There were a couple of homicide detectives dressed like extras from Central Casting. Ricky Schultz was fat and balding. Luis Angeloz, sometimes known as LA, was tall, thin, and pinched. Together they were known to everyone in the department as Laurel and Hardy. Then there was Janey Amat, with her straight, blue slacks and plastic covered sneakers and a flimsy black Newport Beach CSI issue jacket over a white tee-shirt. Her brown hair was pulled back in a hastily gathered ponytail, a white surgical mask hiding the lower half of a pale face devoid of make-up, tortoiseshell glasses perched on the bridge of her nose. She could hardly have made herself less attractive. Michael knew that she had all but given up in that department.

Her face lit up when she saw him. "Hey, Mike. Sorry for the home call. Jimmy's off sick." She turned back toward the dead man's desk, where she was tape-lifting a set of prints from its polished mahogany surface.

"His name is Arnold Smitts," the DC said, answering Michael's question. "Owner of the property." He was still crouched over him, leaning one hand on his gun belt, as if he thought the dead man might rise up any minute to attack him.

"An accountant." Hardy scratched his chin thoughtfully.

"Expensive pad for an accountant." Michael looked around the room. Everything about it spoke of money, from the leather-tooled writing desk to the ox-blood captain's chair and the mahogany shelves that groaned under the weight of a collector's fortune in first-edition early twentieth-century law books. Three thousand dollars worth of eight-cores standard Mac Pro computer stood on the desktop, next to a thirty-inch Apple cinema screen. The monitor displayed a landscape of rolling green fields with scattered trees sloping down to a tranquil ocean and the unfamiliar logo of a pale green open-palmed hand.

"No ordinary accountant." Laurel was expanding on his partner's cryptic description of the victim's status. "A real high flyer, Smitts. Known to us. Suspected of having connections to the mob."

Hardy said, "And you can bet your life the feds'll have a file yea thick on him." He looked at Michael. "Didn't interrupt your dinner, did we? Lobster and champagne up in Corona del Mar?"

"I don't drink champagne." Michael turned away to take his Nikon from its case.

"You're all cash and no class, Mike. Don't tell me you wash down your caviar with beer."

"Give it a rest, fat boy." Janey gave the detective a look that would have turned milk sour. "Judging from your waistline the only thing you wash down with your beer is more beer."

Hardy grinned. "Women like something to put their arms around."

"Yeh, well my preference would be an arm tight around your throat."

Laurel chuckled. "He said *women*, Janey. You don't qualify."

"Hey, guys, can we focus here, please?" The DC removed a blood-stained wallet from the shirt pocket and opened it carefully. Inside, a photograph behind a plastic window revealed two teenage girls smiling for the camera. "His kids, I guess. Do we know if he's still married?"

"Divorced," Laurel said. "Ten years ago. His girlfriend said she'd been with him for the last three."

The DC looked up. "She still here?"

"She was nauseous. Shock. Sat alone with the body for fifteen minutes before the patrol car arrived. Incoherent by the time we got here. They've taken her off somewhere to sedate her. There was no point in even trying to take a statement right now."

Michael attached a flash strobe to the hotshoe on his camera and pulled on a surgical mask before stepping into the room to start photographing the body. He moved methodically around it, first taking wide shots, then moving in tighter for detailed close-ups of the wounds, front and back, the face, the blood on the carpet, the blood spatter on the walls.

And then the room itself, officers stepping out of the way to clear his shots.

When he had finished, the DC called the two sombre employees of the body transport company waiting in the hall, and they stepped in to manoeuvre the corpse into a white zippered body bag and lift it onto their gurney.

Michael leaned on the bookcase and watched Janey dusting for prints. "Anything interesting, Miss Amat?"

She shrugged. "Nah. No weapon. No obvious calling cards. We'll have to bag the rug and a few bits and pieces. Plenty of prints, but they're probably mostly his and hers. We'll do an inch-by-inch once we've cleared the room." She glanced at him, and held him fondly in her gaze for a moment. "Howya doing, Mike?"

"Better for seeing you, Janey."

She grinned. "Yeh, that'll be right. The only time guys are happy to see me is when I'm heading out the door."

"That's just cos you've got such a cute ass."

"Hah! Mid-thirties and sagging. I don't think so, Mike."

"Hey, any guy would be glad to get his hands on your butt."

"Yeh? So how come I haven't met any of them?" She grinned and cocked a provocative eyebrow in his direction. "Unless, of course, you're offering."

He grinned. "I'm more of a tit man myself."

"Damn! And I don't have much in that department." She cupped what little she had in each hand, pulled a face and turned back to her dusting. "Speaking of large breasts, what's happening with that girl from Huntington Beach who was after your body?"

Michael's face clouded slightly, and he tried to sound casual. "Nah. Wouldn't have worked, Janey."

She turned a frown in his direction. "You mean, you never put hands on her butt either?"

He shrugged. "I figure they put the implants in the wrong place. I thought I had big hands, too. But never could get them around it."

He turned away then, his smile fading, and stared out through the French windows at the ocean view. He hadn't laid hands on anyone in a long time and couldn't imagine that he ever could again.

Chapter Three

Sunlight seeped in all around the edges of the Venetian blinds, long cracks of light falling in zigzag patterns across the furniture of the darkened room. Michael closed his eyes and saw again green, manicured lawns rising up across an undulating hillside punctuated by the occasional tree. No headstones here, just slabs engraved and laid in the ground. Plots sold, like so much real estate, with spectacular views of the Pacific, prices elevated by the proximity of John Wayne's grave just a little further up the hill. Twenty thousand dollars to lay your body down for the last time in Pacific View Memorial Park, with airplanes from John Wayne airport flying overhead every few minutes to soothe your final sleep.

It had been a fine, fall day when they put Mora in the ground here. Shirt-sleeve weather. And the mourners had gathered, uncomfortable in dark suits and coats and hats, a small group of friends and relatives, most of whom had assiduously avoided eye contact with Michael. Her late husband's children and ex-wife had arranged a lunch afterwards. A celebration, Michael thought. The chance to pick over her remains and discuss the recovery of their lost inheritance. He had not been invited, and wouldn't have gone even if he had.

He stood long after they had left, watching the gravediggers shovelling dry, loose dirt over her coffin, and turned his face up toward the sun, in the hope that it might dry his tears.

In the end he had walked back down the hill to his car and driven home to an empty house and an empty life, wondering if it would ever again be filled with anything but pain.

A sound in the room made him open his eyes, and he saw Angela's silhouette in the chair opposite. He could almost feel her impatience as she crossed her legs. "You're obsessing, Michael. Grief is a natural process for dealing with bereavement. But you are turning it into a *cause célèbre*. You are focusing on Mora's death as your loss rather than hers. And yes, of course, you suffered loss. But the dead are gone, and in the end the living must move on. You aren't moving on. You have put your life on pause, the green light winking. You're wallowing in your own self-pity."

"It's not true, Angela. I'm trying. I really am. That's why I went back to my old job." He paused, and allowed himself an ironic smile in the dark. "That, and the fact that I needed the money."

"You never told me why you quit in the first place."

"Mora wanted me to. She had so much money, neither of us needed to work. And after three years of widowhood, she wanted to play."

"And you couldn't play if you were tied to a job."

"Yes." He remembered the arguments. At first he had been dead against it. He loved his job, and he knew that without it his independence would be gone. It was her money, not his. He would be a kept man. But she had won in the end, turning those big, sad, brown eyes on him and trotting out the well-worn clichés. Life was not a rehearsal. Don't put off till tomorrow what you can do today—tomorrow may never come. And for her it had been prophetic. Such a short time they had had together, and in the end he was pleased he had quit. They had travelled the world. Italy, France, the Far East, the Caribbean. So many happy moments, now just so many memories. But at least he had them.

"So how is it going? Orange County Forensic Science Service, isn't it?"

"Yes. Originally I was at Santa Ana. But I'm based at Newport Beach now."

He heard her smile. "So you can just about walk to work."

"Just about." But he was thinking about how it had been. Those first few days back at work. People he had known for years. It wasn't that they were hostile, or even cool. Just lacking in warmth. He said, "They don't understand."

"Who don't understand what?"

"My coworkers. They can't figure out what I'm doing back there. It's like they think I'm slumming, or something. Idle rich kid just playing at it. They figure I'm worth a fortune, so why the hell would I want to work? If only they knew."

"Do you feel they are judging you in some way?"

"I'm sure of it. I'm sure they think I only married her for the money. After all, she was so much older than me."

"Not so old, Michael. Ten years is nothing between adults. And she was still in her early forties, wasn't she?"

He nodded and thought, she can't see me nodding. "Yes," he said.

There was a long silence. Then, "And did you?"

"Did I what?"

"Marry her for her money."

"Of course not!" He heard the pitch of his voice rising and wondered if he was protesting too much. If maybe there was some grain of truth in the thought and he didn't want to face it. "At first, maybe, the money made her seem glamorous. Attractive. But in the end I fell for her. She was a good-looking woman, but that wasn't it either. It was her. It was Mora. There was a beautiful, still centre to her that just drew me in and held me there. I was totally beguiled, Angela."

"And what drew her to you?"

He smiled. "At first I think it was my youth."

"And you're an attractive man."

He tried to see her face in the dark, but it was lost in shadow. "I've never had any trouble attracting women, if that's what you mean." He was a good-looking young man, tall, athletically built, with long dark hair that he swept back from a broad, tanned forehead set above ice-chip blue eyes. They were the genetic inheritance of his Celtic ancestry. Or perhaps the Eastern European gene pool that had spawned his great grandfather, from whom he had also inherited his surname. Kapinsky. Not a name he liked much. But he was the keeper of it, and the last in the line. "It doesn't matter what attracted either of us in the beginning. We fell in love. And that's what sustained us. And whatever money she might have left me, I'd trade every last penny of it to have her back."

This time the silence lasted even longer than before. Then he heard her sigh and saw her rise from her chair. Light flooded the room as she opened the blinds. He screwed up his eyes against the pain of it until his pupils contracted.

Angela's sitting room, where she conducted her sessions, was an elegant room. Framed certificates and diplomas in almost every imaginable branch of psychology, lined oak panelled walls. A soft leather sofa and armchairs stood among brass standard lamps with green glass shades on a sumptuous, thick-piled oatmeal carpet rising to crimson velvet drapes. She turned back toward him. An attractive woman herself. Thick, straight, blond hair tumbling over square shoulders. A willowy figure. Green eyes that seemed to penetrate the soul. She was not that much older than Michael, he had speculated the first time they met. Mid-to-late thirties, perhaps. But there was no wedding ring. No hint of a man around the house. She was something of an enigma.

She turned back to Michael. "Same time on Thursday?"

"Sure." He eased himself reluctantly from her sofa and braced himself to face the world again.

◇◇◇

He stepped out from the side entrance of her beachfront villa and followed the path to a high gate that opened on to the boardwalk. The houses here had narrow frontages, many of them recently remodelled. But they were deceptively large, and ran back nearly half a block to a wide access lane that serviced two streets of houses laid back to back. A wide expanse of golden, sandy beach stretched away to the cold blue of the ocean, and lifeguard stations raised on stilts were set every few hundred yards to monitor the safety of the crowds who would descend in the summer.

Tall palms and gnarled Joshua trees crowded tiny gardens where outdoor tables and chairs and huge gas barbecues, were still covered over for the season. The boardwalk was almost deserted, except for an overweight woman in a red tracksuit and straw hat walking at a leisurely pace, swinging the hand of her elderly husband. They seemed so relaxed. Comfortable with each other. Walking in silence, hand in hand, enjoying the sun. Michael envied them.

He turned and headed south toward the ferry. He and Mora had often come down here to walk the dog. Taking their time. Heading for the Crab Cooker, where they would frequently buy giant crab claws and homemade tartare sauce to carry back to the house for a lunch they would wash down with chilled, dry California Sauvignon blanc.

The ferry itself was little more than a barge that could carry three or four vehicles at a time across the few hundred yards that separated the peninsula from Balboa Island. Two of them plied back and forth between wooden landing stages. On the peninsula side, a small ferris wheel near the Maritime Museum stood silent, except for the wind fibrillating through the fine web of cable that made up its superstructure.

The shack that rented out boats and arranged parasailing was deserted, racks of sun hats and tee-shirts fluttering in the breeze outside. Michael walked down the ramp to the waiting ferry and sat on the bench beside the pilot's cabin and felt the breeze in his face as it chugged its way slowly across the channel.

As he strolled down the sidewalk of the island's Grand Canal, he let his gaze wander along the row of millionaires' homes, mock mansions built out of plyboard masked by stone facing and stucco and clapboard siding. Each one had its yacht at the door. Fifty-, sixty-, seventy-foot vessels. He and Mora had been among that in-crowd once, popular, on everyone's invitation list. Their house, after all, stood in one of Corona del Mar's most sought-after locations, overlooking all the others. But their friends had known that the money was hers, and after she died the invitations to Michael had ceased. He was not, after all, really one of them.

He cut through Balboa Avenue to Marine Avenue and bought himself a caramel machiatto at Starbucks. He and Mora had stopped here for coffee most days. He continued to come regularly with his laptop, an escape from the house. And people still remembered Mora. Retired people in running shoes and sweat pants and baseball caps. Smiles spread across age-spattered faces that had seen too much sun and too many years.

"Hi, Michael, how are you today?"

He guessed that like everyone else they thought he was still rich. Sure, he had a house worth four million—in a healthy market. But he had also inherited an outstanding home loan of three million, which was about all he might get in a sale during this period of economic downturn. And he was rapidly running out of the means to keep up the payments.

Chapter Four

It was a fifteen-minute drive from the house in Dolphin Terrace to the Lido, where the lawyer's office stood at the end of a wooden landing one floor up, opposite the marina. Michael could smell food cooking in the waterfront restaurants. Fresh fish. Garlic. The warm, yeasty scent of hot bread.

Huge yachts and seventy foot MV's rose and fell on the gentle swell, tethered to moorings that cost twenty thousand a month to rent.

Jack Sandler was smooth in every sense of the word. He had a voice like velvet, a face shaved to a shiny finish, and a bald head that seemed to have been polished to reflect the sun. Michael guessed that he earned big bucks, even for a lawyer. He had a huge desk, as polished and shiny as his skull, and an unparalleled view over the harbour. He ushered Michael into a seat by the window and sat himself down behind his big desk, peering at his client over orderly piles of files and papers.

"How are you doing, Michael?" he said as if Michael were his best friend. "You're looking well, my man." But behind the facade, Michael was certain he must be wondering if his client was going to have the wherewithal to pay the bill.

Michael had no interest in exchanging pleasantries. "What's the news, Jack?"

"Not good I'm afraid, Michael." Sandler's smile seem to fix itself on his face, before finally he allowed it to morph into something like a frown. "Looks like the judgment's gonna go against you. Best we can hope for is that they'll accept some kind of a deal and settle out of court."

Michael had a sick feeling in the pit of his stomach, like a stone slowly sinking through quicksand. He had seen this coming since the funeral. Mora had inherited her money from her husband, whom she had met when she went to work for his newspaper and magazine publishing empire in San Francisco. Originally she had interviewed for the job as his PA. He told her later she hadn't got the job because he had known immediately he would fall for her. She went to work at first for one of his executives. But she had still drawn him like a magnet, and he had spent more time in her office than in his own. In the end they had fallen in love. He had divorced his wife, made a settlement, set up trust funds for his kids, and married Mora. They should have lived happily ever after. But just five years later he died from a rare form of brain cancer, and she inherited the company.

For a year she had tried to run the operation as he had, but she hadn't the heart or the gift for it, and in the end sold up—for a staggering fifty million dollars. Which was when her late husband's ex-wife and his kids made their first attempt to grab a slice of the cake. On that occasion the courts had thrown out their case, but Mora's guilt had led her to gift cash to each of the kids, and ten million to the former wife. A mistake. For it had created a precedent, established a recognition by her that the family of her late husband had some entitlement. Certainly more than Michael. Which was the argument they were making now.

The trouble was that Mora had been no businesswoman. She had made a series of bad investments, spent money like water, and what had started out as a small fortune had dwindled to just a few million, most of which was tied up in property. Her stocks and shares provided barely enough income to cover the running costs of the house and pay the home loan.

"Well, I don't know what I can offer them, Jack. A few dodgy investments, a lot of debt."

"We'll have to do a valuation, Michael. Get a figure on what the stocks and shares are worth, how much you'll get for the house. You've put it on the market, haven't you?"

Michael nodded. "But things are slow. Real estate is in a slump right now. People are making silly offers that would put me into negative equity. I'm going to have to ride it out if I want to get the best price."

"Well, if the valuation on the property is equal to or less than the size of the home loan, they can't argue that one. Unless they want to take on the debt. But I think you are going to have to wave goodbye to the stocks and shares."

A sigh of pure frustration forced itself through Michael's lips. "That's all that's feeding the loan repayments, Jack. And the cost of running the place. You know that house costs thirty thousand bucks a year in taxes alone?"

Jack canted his head apologetically and folded his hands on the desk in front of him. "Then you're just going to have to sell it for what you can get, Michael. I'm sorry."

◇◇◇

They say that death always comes in threes. And that bad news never comes alone. Mora's money seemed tainted. It had brought only fleeting happiness to her husband, and then to her. Now both of them were dead, and it flashed through Michael's mind that maybe he was next. The third in the death cycle of three. Or maybe the money would take its death curse with it. If so, the greed of Mora's dead husband's family would bring them more than they were bargaining for.

As for the bad news. The next instalment wasn't long in coming.

Michael sat amongst the potted palms in the office allocated to the manager of the State Bank of Southern California, Newport Beach branch. It was a fish bowl looking out across an open-plan office where customers bargained with bank staff over loans and overdrafts. His meeting with Jack Sandler had been a little over two hours earlier.

Michael was not on first name terms with Walter Yuri, who liked to be called *Mister*. Mr. Yuri was a short, avuncular man with a fine head of dark hair going grey, a neatly trimmed moustache, and the bedside manner of a family doctor. He breezed into the office, a busy and distracted man.

"Sorry to keep you, Mr. Kapinsky. This subprime lending debacle is putting everyone under pressure. God knows where it's all going to end. Vicious cycle, you know. Vicious cycle." He sat down behind his desk. "I've been saying it for years. The government can't prop up the economy with consumer spending that's financed by credit. Sooner or later people have to pay back the loans. Or default on them. Which is what's happening now."

Michael shrugged. "Of course, I don't suppose the banks can shoulder any of the responsibility. I mean, who can blame them for offering unsecured loans to people who couldn't afford them?"

Yuri glanced up sharply. Michael's penchant for irony often baffled native Californians. It was something he had learned during an East Coast upbringing at the hands of an acerbic-tongued Scottish mother. Yuri pursed his lips and opened the file on the desk in front of him. "Well, fortunately, this bank had the good sense to secure your loan with the house in Dolphin Terrace, Mr. Kapinsky." He drew a short breath. "Which is just as well, since I'm going to have to call in our collateral now."

Michael frowned. "You can wait till the house is sold, surely? I mean, it's not going anywhere."

"We can't afford to wait, Mr. Kapinsky. You are several payments behind, and at $16,000 a month, we're already looking at a shortfall of over $100,000. Just imagine where we'll be in a year's time if you still haven't sold."

Michael had no answer to that.

"Which, I'm afraid, leaves us no option but to take possession of the house as soon as possible. We'll be sending someone over to do an appraisal and put a value on it."

"But I stand to drop at least a million if you do that."

Yuri adopted the sympathetic smile that doctors reserve for giving bad news to terminally ill patients. "I'm sorry, Mr.

Kapinsky, but unless you can find…" he glanced again at his folder, "…$3,173,000 by this time next week, I'm afraid we're going to have to take your house and sell it ourselves."

Chapter Five

Mora had built the house in Dolphin Terrace on one of the most sought-after plots in Corona del Mar, high up on a ridge that looked down over Balboa Island, the harbour, the peninsula beyond, and the vast blue expanse of Pacific Ocean that led the eye on a clear day to the outline, in silhouette, of Santa Catalina Island.

It was a square, single-storey building with shallow-pitched, red Roman-tiled roofs that sloped into a central open-air courtyard where they were supported on classical columns. A semicircular hot tub was built into one corner of the courtyard, and paving stones led through a profusion of shrubs and flowers in bloom to glass doors on all sides. The views into the house gave, in turn, on to views over the harbour, the entire front of the house being divided into three panoramic windows, like framed masterpieces of living landscapes.

In the central space stood the grand piano, down a short flight of steps. More glass doors opened on to a terrace that ran along the full width of the house at the front. To the left of it was the sitting room, with its own views of the harbour. And to the right, the office that Michael had shared with Mora, windows opening left and right on to the side and front terraces. It was here that they had planned their trips, mapped out their itineraries, laughing together in excited expectation of a whole world out there for them to explore.

The main impression that visitors had of the house was one of light. Light that drifted in from the central courtyard. Light that poured in through the picture windows at the front. Light that fell down through cleverly placed skylights set at angles in the ceilings. Its other virtue was its openness. The dining room gave on to the kitchen which gave on to the living room, which was open to the piano room. Only the office and the bedrooms had the privacy of doors that shut.

The courtyard, and the side and front terraces, provided unexpected little nooks where tables and chairs lurked to offer the opportunity of breakfast in the shade, or lunch in the sunlight, or dinner with a view of the sunset over Catalina, the harbour channel below glowing crimson before fading through purple to black.

Michael loved the house. He loved its curves and corners, its angles and arches and columns, the slatted trellis over the front terrace which divided the sun into long slices that fell through the window of the piano room. He loved its light and space, and the way it always lifted his spirits. It somehow captured the very soul of Mora, who had played such a major role in its design. It was her house, and just being in it made him feel close to her. It was breaking his heart to have to sell it. Like losing the last part of her, finally, six months after she had gone.

As he moved from the garage into the utility room, he could hear voices in the kitchen and his heart sank. He recognised Sherri's simpering laugh, and a couple of other voices he didn't know.

Sherri was his realtor. A blond, fifty-something, surgically perfected, large-breasted, thin-waisted, wide-eyed, thrice-married native of Newport Beach. She had been trying, unsuccessfully, for three months to sell his house. It was a wonderful property, she had assured him. People would be falling over themselves to buy it. Three-and-a-half million at least. Maybe even four.

The best offer, to date, had been two-and-a-half.

She was standing on the far side of the breakfast bar with a middle-aged couple who seemed to be scrutinising his home with a critical eye. Sherri gushed enthusiastically when she saw Michael. "Oh, what good luck. Here is the owner now. Michael, how are you?" But she didn't wait to hear. "This is Mr. and Mrs. Van Agten. They sooo love your house."

Michael glanced at the couple, whose faces conveyed a slightly different impression. But they nodded politely.

"Just take a wander round yourselves," Sherri told them. "While I have a word with Mr. Kapinsky." As she led him by the arm toward the office, she called back over her shoulder, "I'll be with you in just a minute." Immediately they were in the office she closed the door, and her smile faded. "Michael, you *have* to do something about the courtyard. It's completely overgrown. A damn wilderness. It gives such a bad first impression."

Michael wandered toward the desk where his computer's screensaver played an endless slide show of Mora. He lifted up a pile of unopened mail. Bills. Unpaid bills. Reminders. Final warnings. "I had to terminate the contract with Mo, Blow, and Go, Sherri."

She stared at him, uncomprehending. "Mo, Blow, and Go?"

He smiled sadly. "It's what Mora called the Mexican gardeners. They would descend on us every Tuesday like a whirlwind, mow the grass and weed the borders, blow away all the fallen leaves and debris with one of those motor blowers. And then they'd be gone. Mo, Blow, and Go." He looked up, but Sherrie wasn't smiling. "I couldn't afford them any longer. I've paid off the pool guy, too, the guy who serviced the hot tub and the reflecting pool. Oh, and the one who came every couple of days to feed the fish."

Mora had installed a fish tank in the wall that divided the bedroom from the hall, visible from both sides. High enough that no one could see in through it, but not so high that you couldn't stand and watch the fish darting in and out of the coral and pebbles. Feeding them was something Michael figured he could do himself now.

"Well, I wish you would do something about those boxes piled up all over the place. You should have waited until the house was sold before getting rid of furniture and starting to pack. People like to see a house that's lived-in. You're really not doing either of us any favours, you know."

"Well…" he paused for just a moment. He was going to have to break the bad news to her sometime. "It doesn't make any difference now, Sherri. The bank's foreclosing on the loan."

He watched her blue eyes turn cold as she saw her commission disappearing in a puff of smoke. "That's not fair. I've invested months of work in this place, Michael. In time and advertising. You can't do this to me."

"It's not me, Sherri. It's Mr. Yuri. He thinks the government made a mistake in propping up the economy with bad loans."

She frowned. "What?"

"I'm just telling you there's nothing I can do about it. If you can't sell the house for me before next week, you'll lose your commission, and I'll lose my home and a helluva lot of money."

They were startled by a soft knock at the door. A young man sporting a baseball cap and tennis shoes opened it and smiled in at them. He wore shorts and a tee-shirt, and a tool belt around his waist that was hung with an array of small gardening tools and a fine-spray water bottle. "Sorry to disturb you, Mr. Kapinsky. Just wondering if you had my check. You know, for the bill I left you last time."

"Oh, yes, sorry. Forgot about that, Tim." Michael opened a drawer to take out his check book, and started rummaging through his cluttered in-tray to find the bill.

"I'll go back and talk to the Van Agtens," Sherri said, and he heard the chill in her voice. "But we're going to have to talk about this, Michael."

When she had gone, Michael shrugged at Tim and pulled a wry smile. "I'm in the doghouse."

Tim smiled. "Know the feeling."

Tim had been working for Mora for years. He arrived once a week to water and tend the myriad houseplants she had collected at great expense over time.

Michael signed the check and handed it to the young man. He smiled apologetically. "I'm afraid I'm going to have to let you go, Tim."

"Is the house sold, then?"

"No, not yet. But I can't afford to keep you on.

Tim looked crestfallen. "Who's going to water the plants?" They were like his children.

Michael shrugged helplessly. "I've no idea. Me, I suppose. If I can remember."

"You'll need to work out a schedule, Mr. Kapinsky. Leave reminders for yourself. Some of these plants will be gone in a matter of days if you don't take care of them." He paused. "What are you going to do with them when the house is sold?"

"I hadn't thought about it. Maybe the new owners will take them."

"There's a few thousand dollars' worth there, Mr. Kapinsky. Maybe I could sell them for you. Some of my other clients might be interested." Like foster parents.

"That would be great, Tim. I'd appreciate that. Mora would have appreciated that."

Michael sat alone in his office for a while then, listening to Tim moving around the house, the voices of Sherri and the Van Agtens as they went from bedroom to hall, to dining room, to kitchen. And he felt depression settle heavily again upon his shoulders. Finally, he got up and slid open the door to the terrace and wandered out to stand with hands thrust in his pockets and gaze out over the view.

From the low parapet that contained the terrace, the ground dropped away steeply, eighty or a hundred feet down to the road below. Trees and bushes and shrubs and flowers grew thickly on the slope, a root network binding soft soil to prevent erosion in heavy rain. Boats motored their way up and down the harbour channels around Balboa, a couple of kayaks fighting against the swell and the sea breeze. In the distance, clusters of spindly, tall palms, like giant green dandelions swayed in the sunlight, and the water glittered and glistened beneath clear skies, jewels of light scattered across its ruffled surface. He felt emotion well from his chest and into his throat. He was going to miss this place, nearly as much as he missed Mora.

He turned at the sound of a door sliding open, and saw Tim stepping out to spray the potted cacti that stood sentinel on either side of it. A small, wrought-iron table was set beneath the trellis, two chairs facing each other across a chess board, a game in progress. Tim moved one of the chairs.

"Careful," Michael called to him. "Don't disturb the game."

Tim glanced at the table. "Oh. Sure. Who are you playing, Mr. Kapinsky?"

"Mora."

Chapter Six

"How often did you play?"

"Every morning. It was a kind of ritual. We got up at the same time and had an exercise and stretching program that we did together. Then we had breakfast in the courtyard, before moving out to the terrace to play chess for an hour."

"Who was the better player?"

"Oh, Mora was. I never beat her."

"She'd been playing a long time, then?"

"No, she hadn't. That was the irony of it. It was me who taught her to play, and right from the start she beat me every time. She had some kind of extraordinary visual memory. She could hold thousands of pictures in her head, a chess board in any number of configurations. Pure instinct. But she was unbeatable."

"So what was the point in playing, if you both knew she would win?"

Michael smiled. They had talked about that often. "It wasn't the winning, Angela. It was the playing. Time we shared together. Just us. No one else. A meeting of minds. The world simply went away."

Here he was again in the same darkened room. The same cracks of sunlight around the blinds. The same impatience with him that he felt emanating from his therapist. He wondered if she meant to convey that feeling, if it was part of the therapy. Or if she was just genuinely frustrated by him.

"But you still play?"

"Yes."

"On your own."

"No, with Mora."

"She's dead, Michael."

"You don't understand."

"Tell me."

He drew a long, slightly tremulous breath. "I make one move a day. Day One, I start. Day Two, I change seats. I'm Mora. I try to get inside her head. Day Three, I'm me again. I make my second move." He paused. "It's like she's there with me again. Sharing my thoughts, my time, the game."

"Who wins?"

"Mora, of course. As always."

There was one of those long silences that Angela seemed so fond of inflicting upon him. Then he was aware of her leaning forward in the dark. He could almost feel her disapproval. "That is literally self-defeating, Michael. You have to stop this game. You'll never get over her if you persist in giving shape and form to her ghost like this."

"Maybe I don't want to get over her."

"Yes, well, then that's the root of your problem. You have no desire to move on, to leave Mora in your memory. You don't want to start living in the present."

Michael blew air through pursed lips. "I have tried, Angela. Going back to work was a part of that."

He heard her sigh. "Well I suppose it was at least a step in the right direction."

"No. The key's in the words. Going *back* to work. Trying to pick up where I left off before meeting Mora. I can't. I'm not the person I was. It's not working for me, Angela. I don't know what I'm going to do. Probably pack it in when my contract's up. Head back east.

"There's that word again, Michael. Back. And you're right. Back is not good. We have to find a way of moving you forward."

Michael took a deep breath. "Not we, Angela. Me. I'm going to have to find a way to move forward on my own. I'm afraid I've got to bring our sessions to an end."

He heard the concern in her voice. "Because you don't feel we're getting anywhere?"

"Because I can't afford you anymore."

"Oh."

More silence. Michael wondered how much each minute of silence was costing him, and if it had ever been worth the money. Eventually she stood up and tilted the slats of the blinds to let in the day, and turned to face him across the room.

"Well, I can't help you with your financial problems. But you could continue in therapy."

"I told you…"

She cut across him. "At no cost, Michael. Well…nominal."

"I don't understand. How is that possible?"

She eased herself back into her chair and looked at him earnestly. "I've been experimenting with a new form of group therapy, Michael."

"Group therapy? You mean a bunch of people sitting around telling each other their problems?"

She smiled. "In a manner of speaking."

He shook his head. "I couldn't do that, Angela. In many ways it's hard enough just talking to you. I couldn't face the idea of unburdening myself about Mora, sharing my inner thoughts with a group of strangers."

"It wouldn't be like that. In fact, you wouldn't really be there at all. You'd send an emissary to speak for you."

He frowned. "What?"

She laughed. "Oh, Michael, I know it sounds crazy." She grinned. "But, then, that's my field."

"Explain."

"For some months now I've been conducting group sessions with patients in a 3D virtual world called Second Life. Have you heard of it?"

He shook his head.

"It's a simple concept, really. You download a piece of software. Free. Install it on your computer, and then access the virtual world through the internet. It is a completely parallel world, not unlike the real world in that its residents create everything in it. Buildings, roads, shops, products. And do all the kinds of stuff that real people do in real life. Buy things, sell things, gamble, listen to music, buy property, flirt, play games, watch movies, have sex. There are whole continents, seas, islands. It is already populated by nearly 14 million inhabitants."

Michael shook his head. "It really doesn't sound like something for me, Angela. I've never been interested in computer games."

"It's not a game, Michael. Most definitely not a game. Any more than life itself is a game. There is no manufactured conflict, no set objective. It's an entirely open-ended experience. Literally, a second life." She chuckled. "Although for some people it has almost become a first one."

He stared at her across the room, hardly able to imagine it. "You said I would send an emissary. What did you mean?"

"To go into Second Life you have to create an avatar. A virtual representation of your real life self. You can make it look like you, or you can create your fantasy self. The point is, that nobody knows who is really behind your AV. The beautiful blond who asks you to dance might be a fat old man. Who cares? In SL you are who you want to be."

Michael shook his head, still doubtful. "I don't know…"

"Look, Michael, just try it. It'll cost you nothing, and if it doesn't work for you, then you can drop out. But I have to tell you, my experience so far suggests that people find it much easier to express themselves freely from behind the anonymity of their avatars. And I'm breaking new ground here. Using my SL experiences in virtual group therapy to write a book. So I'm not charging my patients." She smiled. "In a way you're my guinea pigs. But we can all benefit."

Michael sat thinking about it. He had enough problems to deal with in his real life without having to worry about a virtual one. Angela looked at her watch and stood up.

"I have another patient coming." She walked to her writing bureau and checked her diary. "Why don't I come round tomorrow evening, show you where to download the software, and help you set up your AV. Are you free?"

"I might be on call, but yes, I guess so."

"Okay, about seven then."

And somehow, it seemed, he had agreed to it. She opened a drawer and pulled out a sheet of paper, holding it out toward him.

"Your final account." She smiled. "I hope you can still afford to pay me."

Chapter Seven

The sunset had been glorious, turning the horizon the colour of blood. As its luminosity faded, a red moon rose slowly into the gathering darkness, and the sounds of revellers rang out across the island of Revere. A DJ was playing music from the Lost Frontier sound stage, and a crowd had gathered to line dance across the open area below it.

Out on the river, people stood on the deck of a yacht to watch and to listen to the music.

Couples had gathered on wooden platforms built into huge trees with spreading branches that overlooked the stage. Some were making out, others dancing, some communing in silent conversation.

On the far side of the island Quick was engaged in her second sex act of the evening. 1000 Linden dollars already paid into her account. Of course, she didn't do it for the money. But that gave it a little extra thrill. She simply enjoyed the fantasy of selling herself for sex. Of being in complete command of a man, any man, and making him do whatever she wanted in total security.

She had met Gray Manly at the club where she was employed as a pole dancer. But that was boring, taking your top off when a mere two hundred Lindens were dropped into the tip jar, a bunch of horny men sitting on stools watching in silence, occasionally IM-ing to suggest a private rendezvous.

Of course, there was the lapdance chair in the room behind the stage, or the sex room in the skybox for those customers who wanted more than just a blow job. But her employer took twenty percent, and that seemed unfair. So she had set herself up here on Revere. A private house, her own rate card, and the promise of fabulous sex if the customer guaranteed confidentiality. She would lose her job if the boss found out, and jobs in SL were at a premium these days. Competition was fierce. There were a lot of beautiful AVs out there. And she needed the job to pull in the customers.

She had spent a long time furnishing this house as she imagined a whorehouse might look. Cheap, flashy, gaudy colours, porno pics on the wall. She particularly liked her sex bed. It had nearly a hundred animations, and she had sole charge of the control hud, the window with all its menu options appearing in the top right corner of her screen.

For the moment she was sitting astride the client, naked apart from a flimsy top that barely covered her large, perfect breasts, and the animation she had chosen was making her slide slowly up and down on his very erect penis. She was barely aware of the banalities he was uttering in open chat.

Gray: Yeh. Yeh. Fuck me, baby…

Her mind was somewhere else altogether, creating the future she dreamed of with all that money. Discreetly, and over time, so as not to arouse any suspicion. She could transfer some of it through PayPal to an offshore account in Europe. Take out a dollar debit card. Who would ever know?

Gray: Oh, baby, you turn me on.

She looked at the menu, and selected an option to flip them over into a missionary position. Time to make him do a bit of the work. She uttered some words of encouragement.

Quick: Oh, I'm so horny, lover. Go faster. Gimme all you got.

Gray: Going faster baby. Giving it to you big time.

And she returned to her fantasy, unaware of the female figure lurking in the twilight outside, a shadow against the night sky, hovering on a level with a second floor window that was blacked out so no one could see in. But the hovering figure picked a spot on the outside wall of the house, zoomed in and swivelled left, swinging her POV beyond the wall and into the bedroom, affording her an unfettered view of the sex act being performed on the bed, unseen by either of the participants.

Gray Manly was surprised by the message that appeared suddenly in his IM box, from an AV called Green Goddess. It wasn't a name he recognised.

> *Green Goddess:* Hi, Gray

Manly's sexual concentration was broken, to his annoyance.

> *Gray:* Who the fuck are you?
>
> *Green Goddess:* I'm your worst nightmare, Gray. I know who you are in RL. I know where you live. The name of your wife. Her email address. I don't think she's going to be very happy when I tell her you've been fucking other women in a virtual world. Or show her the proof. All the photographs I have of your AV in action. She helped you create it, didn't she? When you first came into SL. She'll have no doubt it's you."

There was a time lapse of nearly half a minute before he responded. Panic apparent in his silence, as he took in the implications of this threat.

> *Gray:* What do you want?
>
> *Green Goddess:* Simple. Just TP out of here. Now. No questions. Just go.

Manly didn't need any second telling. He teleported out.

Quick barely had time to register his disappearance before Green Goddess clicked on the vacant blue poseball and adopted the departed Manly's missionary position on top of the hooker. The animation had previously placed Quick's hands on Manly's chest, as if pushing him away. Now they were holding on to the swell of Green Goddess' ample breasts.

Quick: WTF?

Green Goddess detached herself from the poseball and stood at the end of the bed. And as Quick sat up the intruder's arm extended toward her, an elaborate-looking handgun held in a steady hand. A single shot rang out, tearing a large hole through Quick's nearly naked torso. Blood spattered all around the bed and across the wall behind it. And Quick's screen went black.

◇◇◇

Jennifer Mathews had lived the life of the millionairess she had been destined to become. Then a single bullet had torn a hole through her chest, passing through her second life into her first, and bringing her prematurely to that place where all lives end, for both rich and poor.

She lived in a luxury apartment block high on the hill overlooking the marina. Her red Porsche 911, parked in its private slot close to the entrance, was almost completely obscured by the accumulation of police and forensics vehicles in the lot. Unlike the whorehouse on Revere, this three bedroom condo was filled with expensive, Swedish-designed furniture and scattered with oatmeal linen cushions. Signed, limited-edition, Vettriano prints hung on the walls, and thick-piled woollen carpets covered the floors. This was a $10,000-a-month apartment, with a west-facing balcony that looked out over the Pacific sunset. In the sumptuous master bedroom, where walls displayed tastefully erotic Helmut Newton photographs, the white silk sheets of her unmade four-poster bed were stained red by her blood.

The cops had no idea who she was when they first arrived at her apartment, following a panicked 911 call from the maid. When Michael came to photograph her, spreadeagled naked on the bed, she was just another murder victim. A clumsy uniformed officer had already tripped on the power cable that connected her computer to the electric supply, so the screen was dead. And the pale green, open-palmed logo in its top left corner was long gone.

Chapter Eight

It was one of those classic Newport Beach sunsets that began with a reddening sun sinking beyond the mountains of Catalina, and ended with rivers of blood flowing around Balboa Island.

Angela stood on the terrace outside Michael's office and gazed upon it with wonder. "I get great sunsets from my house, too," she said. "But nothing like this. It's the elevation you have here. It's just spectacular. I feel house envy coming on."

Michael emerged from the interior with a bottle of chilled chardonnay and two wine glasses that he set on the parapet to fill. He handed one to his therapist and they chinked. "We used to watch it almost every night when we were here. It was a kind of ritual. Sunset, sunrise. The best times of the day."

They sipped in silence from their glasses, and she raised an eyebrow. "Mmmm. Wonderful wine. Toasted oak. Very subtle."

"It's a Bourgogne."

"Oh? Is that in Napa or Sonoma?" But she could only hold her face straight for a moment, and he grinned.

Michael said, "Mora was something of a connoisseur. It was a kind of passion passed on by her husband. There wasn't much she didn't know about wine, and hardly any limit to what she would spend on it." He shook his head. "Before she met Tom she hadn't known the first thing about the stuff, except that she liked it. He was really well connected in the wine world, a friend of the Mondavi family. He used to take her to France and Italy and

Spain, wine-tasting in all the best vineyards. Teaching her about the different varietals, the best vintages. How to smell a wine, how to taste it, how to differentiate the various flavours."

He sipped thoughtfully on the buttery white chilled liquid and let it slip slowly over his tongue.

"There is a large wine cellar attached to the garage, kept at a constant 12 degrees centigrade. And she had a room in a wine storage facility in Newport. Between the two there must be thousands of bottles. Tens of thousands of dollars worth of wine."

"Well, if you're short of cash, Michael, why don't you just sell it?"

"They won't let me, until the question of inheritance has been settled in court." He held up his glass to the sky and saw it flush pink in the sunset. "This is the first bottle I've opened since she died. But I don't see any reason why it should be the last." If he couldn't sell it, he could at least drink it.

Angela slipped a hand around his upper arm and turned him gently toward the door. "Come on, let's get started."

She pulled up a chair beside him at the computer and told him to enter the Second Life URL. Up came the welcome page. A sequence of photographs of young, beautiful avatars in a variety of settings. An orange banner urged him to GET STARTED.

In the top left-hand corner of the screen was the Second Life logo. A pale green hand held up, palm facing out, fingers spread. It doubled cleverly as an eye, with the pupil in the centre of the palm, the raised fingers like eyelashes. Michael thought there was something familiar about it. He knew he must have seen it before. But where?

"Just click on the Get Started banner and you can choose a name." Angela sipped on her wine as he followed her instructions and chose the surname Chesnokov. Something to do, perhaps, with his Eastern European ancestry. Then he tapped in C-H-A-S. Charles had been the name of his Scottish great grandfather. "Chas Chesnokov," Angela said out loud. "I like the alliteration. Now you can choose your avatar."

Michael chose a poser with a black shirt and charcoal jeans, and a mop of long, dark hair swept across his forehead. He clicked to the next page to activate his account.

WELCOME, CHAS CHESNOKOV

It took only a few minutes for the software to download and establish its icon on his computer desktop. The small green hand/eye. He sat looking at it, that strange sense of familiarity striking him again, accompanied this time by an odd feeling of anticipation. This would, after all, be another world. A world he had never shared with Mora. A world where she had never existed and never would. A world where he could be someone else altogether. And there was a feeling of comfort in that, of freedom, and escape.

"Don't go in right now." Angela's voice broke into his thoughts. "It's a disorienting experience at first. It's something you need to do alone. Set aside some time, and enjoy the experience."

She drained her glass and stood up.

"I have to go. Let me know when you're in and found your feet, and we'll arrange a session. My AV name is Angel Catchpole. Do a search for me and send me an IM."

Michael stood up. "IM?"

"Instant Message." She smiled. "You'll pick up the shorthand in no time. SL, Second Life: RL real life; OMG, WTF…" He grinned and she said, "See? You're catching on already."

By the time she had gone, so had the light. Michael sat in the dark with the remains of Mora's bottle, sipping on the wine she had so carefully chosen and never tasted. The computer screen cast a pale, ghostly light around the room. He turned toward it and wondered about taking his AV into Second Life straight away. But decided to do a little research first.

Google presented him with a choice of thousands of articles and blogs on SL. He picked a couple at random and set them to print, then searched his desk for his reading glasses. They were small, round tortoiseshell glasses that Mora had bought him. She said he would get prematurely wrinkled if he kept screwing his eyes up to read. He had never even noticed that he did. He had no idea what they might have cost, but Mora had expensive tastes. She would never buy anything at a knockdown price if there was something more expensive available. He hadn't liked to tell her that he didn't much care for them. Especially when she told him that they made him look cute, a young intellectual. And so he had kept his mouth shut and always used them when she was around.

Now he couldn't do without them.

But he couldn't find them anywhere. They were nowhere to be seen on the desktop, and not in any of the drawers. He frowned, wondering where else in the house he might have laid them down. He had just stood up to go and look when the phone rang. He checked the time. It was after eight. The Caller ID panel told him it was his office. He lifted the phone and hit the green button.

"Yeh, it's Michael."

He wandered off into the hallway. Lamps in the courtyard, operating on a timer, spilled light through all the glass into the front of the house. He headed for the kitchen, wondering if he had laid his glasses down in there.

"Mike we got a shooting in Laguna Beach. One fatality. There's a team on the way. Can you meet up with them?"

"Sure. What's the address?" He switched on the kitchen lights and blinked in the sudden brightness. Then froze where he stood as the dispatcher read out the name and number of the street.

"Fuck," he said. And his voice was smothered by the emptiness of the house. "That's where Janey lives."

Chapter Nine

A phalanx of police and forensics vehicles was parked in the street at the foot of the steps leading to Janey's bungalow. This suburban street ran parallel to the highway that followed the line of the ocean, but several streets back and well up the hill. There were more vehicles than he would have expected. Several unmarked cars and only one patrol car. Three forensics vans were drawn up side by side, which was unusual. But, then, maybe not, given whose address this was.

The van hadn't yet arrived to remove the body, which gave Michael fleeting hope that perhaps it wasn't a fatality after all. He grabbed his gear from the trunk and leaped up the steps in twos, breathless by the time he reached the wooden veranda that ran along the front of the bungalow.

Two uniformed cops stood smoking just outside the front door. They turned as he hurried up the last few steps on to the veranda. "What's going on?"

"Looks like murder, Mike." The cop regarded him grimly.

"Who?"

The officers exchanged uneasy glances. "You better go take a look."

Michael felt sick now as he hurried into the house. He had been here often. Everything about it was familiar: the worn carpet, the scuffed kickboards, the smell of stale cooking that came from the kitchen. The hall seemed to be full of people, but he was barely aware of them. He heard someone say, "Take it easy, Mike."

He turned into the doorway of the sitting room at the front of the house. Someone had already rigged up lights, and the scene was thrown into sharp contrast by the glare. More people congregated here. Faces he recognised, some half obscured by surgical masks. The deputy coroner was crouched over a body, and stood up as Michael came in. A silence fell on the room.

The body of a young woman lay twisted in the middle of the floor, hair fanned out across the carpet. She wore jeans and sneakers, and her white tee-shirt was soaked in blood. It was Janey.

Michael felt his legs almost give way beneath him. A wave of nausea rose from his stomach. Someone grabbed his arm. And he knew there was no way he could take photographs of her. He had known Janey for nearly fifteen years. They had started the same week at the FSS offices at Santa Ana. She was a couple of years older than him, and they had become good friends. Not in any sexual way, although it had been clear from the start that she found him attractive. There was, however, nothing attractive about Janey except her personality. But few men had got to know her well enough to find that out. Her hair was a straight, mousy brown, plain cut, usually drawn back in an untidy ponytail. She had a thin face with a nose like a blade and eyes set slightly too wide behind her thick glasses. She had a boy's figure, with no waist, and an almost flat chest. There was nothing very feminine about her. She wore no make-up, and Michael had never seen her in a skirt, only jeans and sneakers and, when she was working, a pair of plain, dark-blue pants. Almost from the start her co-workers had dubbed her Plain Jane. Except when Michael was around. Everyone knew he had a soft spot for her.

The DC stepped toward him and took his arm. "Better take a look, son." And he led a numbed Michael across the room to the body. "Seems like someone left us a message."

Michael saw a blood-stained note pinned to her chest, but he couldn't read what it said, and in a moment of bizarre incongruity remembered that he had misplaced his reading glasses. Slowly he crouched down and glanced at her face. There was a peaceful serenity about it, and he thought for the first time ever that there might actually be something quite beautiful in its plainness. Something like a smile rested on her pale lips.

He turned his head to look at the note and had to screw up his eyes to read it. WELCOME BACK, it said. And Janey sat up, lips stretched back across her teeth in a roar of mirth. Michael let out an involuntary exclamation and teetered backwards, stopped from falling by the steadying hand of the DC.

For a moment he was incapable of grasping what had happened. He could hear laughter ringing in his ears, and Janey reached out to place both her hands on his face, amusement and sympathy in her eyes all at the same time. "Oh, my poor baby, I'm so sorry." But she didn't sound sorry. She could hardly stop laughing. "Welcome back to the fold. This is your party, Mike."

Suddenly music was blasting out, and more people were crowding into the room. Someone put a bottle of beer in his hand. "Hey, Mike. Time to get drunk."

◇◇◇

There must have been a hundred people or more in the house now, and more still arriving. Loud music pounded out across the hillside from open windows and doors. None of the neighbours was going to call the police, since half the police force was already here.

Someone had taken a video of Michael's moment of zen, when Janey had sat up and startled the hell out of him. It was playing on a loop on Janey's widescreen TV, and everyone coming in crowded around to look at it and laugh. It had taken Michael some time to see the funny side, and he was still not sure that he did. "You cruel bastards!" he had roared at the assembled, only to elicit more laughter.

He sat now in Janey's big leather armchair in the corner of the room, a beer in his hand. He had lost count of how many he'd had. Someone was going to have to drive him home. Janey had changed out of the red-dyed tee-shirt and was draped across the arm of his chair, leaning against him, an arm around his shoulder, a beer in her free hand, swinging one of her legs like a child. She'd had more than a few herself. "You don't know how good it is to have you back, Mike. I really missed you, you know that?" And he remembered telling Angela just the day before how he intended quitting as soon as his contract was up. A contract he'd signed less than a week ago. He felt a stab of guilt. But Janey was oblivious. "Hey," she said, suddenly sitting upright. "Nearly forgot. I found some pics on an old memory stick that I took of you and Mora just after you got back from your honeymoon. Forgot I even had them. Wanna see?"

Michael had thousands of pictures of Mora, but there could never be enough. He was excited by the thought of new ones. Fresh images, new insights. "Yeh, I would, Janey. Can you give me copies?"

"Of course." She jumped up. "Come on through to the den."

He followed her through the partying crowd to a small room at the back of the house, where she kept her computers and all her media equipment. She had a video projector in here for watching movies that she projected onto the far wall, and a state-of-the-art, five-speaker sound system. She unlocked the door to let them in and closed it behind them. A small desklamp burned on the desktop next to two computer screens, and she dropped into a chair in front of them.

"You can never have enough screens," she said. "I'd have eight or ten, if I could afford it. Different stuff running on each one. So that whatever I wanted access to, all I'd have to do is turn my head."

Michael took in the comfortable recliner strategically placed for watching projected movies and picking up the best sound. The fact that there was only one spoke volumes about Janey's social life. Michael felt a surge of pity and affection for her. She was, he knew, a lonely soul. And she deserved better. He pulled up a chair beside her at the desk as she opened her iPhoto software from the dock at the foot of her screen. All of her most commonly used programs were lined up along the dock. As she scrolled through them, magnifying each in turn, he noticed the green hand/eye of the Second Life logo.

"Second Life," he said.

She turned to look at him. "You've heard of it?"

He smiled. "I'm going in."

Her face broke into a girlish grin. "You're kidding me. I've been in SL for over a year."

He looked at her blankly. "Why?"

She laughed. "I love it! That's why. I probably spend 90 percent of my nonworking, nonsleeping time in there. It's totally addictive, Mike." She paused and her smile faded a little. "What are you going in for?"

He avoided her eye for a moment. He hadn't told her about being in therapy. "I've been seeing a therapist, Janey. To help me get over Mora's death. It's been a lot harder than I ever imagined."

She put a hand over his and squeezed it. "I know." And after a moment, "But what's that got to do with SL?"

"My therapist has been experimenting with virtual group therapy sessions in Second Life, and she's talked me into trying it."

"Wow. Cool. Michael, you'll love it."

But Michael was still doubtful. "I don't know, Janey."

"Mike, you will. You haven't been in yet?"

"No, I just set up my AV tonight."

Her face flushed with excitement. "Oh, God, then you gotta let me help you. You're going to go in there and walk into walls and wave your arm around like an idiot. It's easier if you have someone to take your hand and walk you through it."

He grinned. "Like you."

"Exactly like me. What's your AV name?"

"Chas Chesnokov."

She repeated it aloud, as if trying it out for size. "Hmmm. I like it, Chas. I'm Twist O'Lemon."

He laughed out loud, and it felt good to be laughing again. "You're what?"

She grinned. "I know. Stupid, isn't it? Doesn't matter. Just call me Twist. Oh. My. God. Mike, this is so exciting." She put a hand on each of his shoulders and made him look at her. "Now, this is what you do, okay? As soon as you're in, you send me an IM, and I'll take it from there."

"What if you're not online?"

"Well, if I'm not at work, chances are I will be."

He looked at her. "What do you do in there all that time, Janey?"

Her grin widened. "Oh, you'd be surprised what you can do in Second Life, Mike. But I think you'll be even more amazed when you find out what it is I do. It'll be my little surprise." She swivelled back toward her screens. "Okay. Mike and Mora." She double-clicked on an iPhoto folder and selected the slideshow option."

Immediately, Mora's face filled the screen. Smiling, enigmatic. Those soft brown eyes. And Michael felt the pain of losing her all over again.

Chapter Ten

It was his other favourite time of the day. When he and Mora would sit under the trellis on the terrace and play chess, the taste of coffee still in his mouth. The light was crystal clear, so luminous, as it slanted across the island below, cutting sharp shadows among the palm trees. He sat there now, the players ranged across the checkered board in front of him, contemplating his next move.

But, somehow, today his concentration was less than absolute. He had spent an hour when he got in the night before, drowsy and maudlin from too much beer and lack of sleep, going through the photographs that Janey had burned for him on to a CD. He had found his focus shifting from Mora to himself. Only three years had passed, but he looked so much younger. Perhaps he had simply aged more in the six months since her death than in the previous thirty. But it brought home to him with a sudden clarity that his life was slipping away. All the more rapidly since he had affixed himself to a place in the past that he could never go back to. He knew he needed to haul anchor and move on, to catch up with his life and take control of it again before he lost his hold on it completely.

And now, as he sat looking at the chess board, he realised, almost for the first time since she'd gone, the futility of sitting here pretending she hadn't. Fantasizing that they were still playing. And Angela's words came back to him. *That is truly self-defeating, Michael. You have to stop this game. You'll never get over her if you persist in giving shape and form to her ghost like this.* He felt tears well in his eyes, and he swept his arm across the board in a sudden gesture of defiance and frustration. Chessmen went tumbling across the terrace like so many lost dreams. It was no good. He simply couldn't go on this way.

He got up and wandered back through the house, weaving among the packing cases and extraneous pieces of furniture. Soon this would all be gone, and he would have to find himself an apartment somewhere. Just ordinary old Michael Kapinsky, with an overdraft and a credit limit like everyone else. No more money, no more Mora, no more house.

On an impulse he went into his office and sat down in front of the computer. The eye of the Second Life icon seemed to be staring back at him from his computer desktop. What the hell! He had to go in sometime. He loaded up the software and was presented after a few moments, with the Second Life welcome screen.

He stared at it, with a strange sense of déjà vu. A scattering of trees across a rolling green coastline, an expanse of dark blue ocean. He *had* seen it before. And now he remembered where. On the computer screen of the murdered accountant in Newport Beach. Arnold Smitts. Had Smitts been in Second Life, too? It seemed like an extraordinary coincidence. And yet Angela had told him that there were 14 million inhabitants in SL, so was it really that much out of the ordinary? What struck Michael as odd, he realised, was that a man like Smitts would spend time in a virtual world. It didn't seem in character with either the man or his profession.

He shrugged the thought aside and tapped in his name and password and hit the Enter key. He was in.

He stared at the screen, fascinated as a whole other world began to take shape in front of his eyes. A blue sea coruscating off to a clear horizon. Buildings to left and right. Trees swaying on a spit of land extending into the water.

A figure in jeans and a white tee-shirt stood, hands at his side, head tipped forward. Above it was a tag with his name. Suleman Perl (Away). He certainly didn't look all there.

There were other figures wandering about, gazing left and right, up and down. They were the standard avatars from which Michael had made his choice the night before.

And there he was, Chas Chesnokov, standing with his back to the screen, stark naked and bald, before suddenly he grew hair, and a black shirt and charcoal jeans covered his modesty. A message appeared. *Welcome to Orientation Island, a special place where new Residents can learn several basic skills.*

More AV's started appearing in the same space. Bumping and jostling, eager to take those first few steps. More newbies being born. More new residents logging in every minute. A population explosion that mirrored the real world.

A pop-up window was now offering Chas a simple exercise. To walk to a flashing red target using the arrow keys on his keyboard. He made the walk, and did a little involuntary dance of joy when he got there. *Great, you made it!* said the window. *To learn more about other ways to move in Second Life, walk across the bridge to the city where you will find out how to drive a car and fly!*

Chas set off across the bridge. He passed a young girl in jeans and a white top standing with her arms and legs spread. Her tag said, *Yuno Orly*. She ignored him, and Chas carried on across the bridge, walking straight into the brick pillar at the far end of it.

Yuno: Hahahaha

Her name and laughter appeared in text at the bottom left of his screen. He turned around to see Yuno Orly laughing at him.

Yuno: It's lag.

Chas: Lag?

Yuno: The computer can't keep up, and you go crashing into walls and falling off buildings. Hahahaha.

She made a little jump in the air.

Yuno: You learn to compensate after a while.

Then she turned away

Yuno: C ya.

And she walked briskly back across the bridge. Chas watched her go, then looked around. He was in a city street, a skyscraper towering over him. He saw a sign with an arrow on the other side of the street, next to a fire hydrant. *Flight Training Institute.* Steam was issuing from a manhole cover in the middle of the road, and further along a steam roadroller and an orange buggy lay in an odd tangle, half on the sidewalk.

Almost for the first time, Chas became aware of a strange, droning, ambience in the air. Like the sound of a breeze blowing through the winter bare branches of trees in a wood. He swivelled to look around. Across a short stretch of water, at the far side of another bridge, was a huge glass dome. The Search Center, a large sign told him.

Abandoned in the middle of a pedestrian crossing, he spotted what he recognised as a Segway. Chas clicked on it and immediately found himself riding the vehicle. He turned left, then right, then tried to head back across the bridge. But he missed it, veering across a stretch of grass and out over the water. It was a strange, disconcerting feeling, like floating on air. He came to a stop and hovered for a moment.

A notice appeared on his screen. *Vehicle is outside city limits. Deleting.*

And suddenly it was gone. Chas dropped like a stone, through the water, to the sea bed. Above him he could see the reflection of the city distorting on the rippled undersurface of the water. How the hell did he get out of here? Another notice appeared, as if reading his mind.

Don't worry, your avatar won't drown. Walk back onto land or click the Fly button to levitate your avatar.

He looked down to a toolbar at the bottom of his screen. He clicked on fly and found himself rising until his head broke the surface of the water. He flew clear of it, then headed for the glass dome.

Flying was a truly exhilarating experience, something he had only ever done in dreams. He soared across the water, arms reaching back behind him, the wind whistling in his ears. From up here he had a clearer view of where he was. A series of islands linked by bridges to the central point where he had first landed. Each island provided lessons in mobility, searching, changing appearance, communication. Molten lava was erupting in bursts from a thermal lake at the top of a rocky outcrop. When he reached the dome, he clicked to stop flying and landed with a thump at the entrance.

Inside were huge detailed maps of the region into which he had been delivered: a bewildering array of islands with names like Robinson, Capelli, Tharu. He had no idea how to get to any of them or what to do if he got there. There were more instruction windows appearing on his screen, but he was growing impatient now and scrutinised his toolbar again to find a search option.

He typed in *Twist O'Lemon*. Up came a profile with a picture of a male AV with long, straight, red and blond-streaked hair and a bare chest. He frowned, wondering if he'd entered the name wrong. But it *was* the name Janey had given him, and he'd made no typos. The information on the profile told him that this AV had been "born" almost exactly a year ago. There was a window listing Groups of which Twist was a member, and a short paragraph about her.

Here to have fun, it said. *Check out my agency if you need help. Just IM me for a fast response.*

What agency? Chas wondered. He opened the Send Instant Message window.

> *Chas:* Hi, Twist. It's Chas. Are you there?

After a moment a reply appeared.

> *Twist:* Chas! You're here!! So cool. I'll send you a TP.
> *Chas:* A what?
> *Twist:* Teleport. Hang on.

A blue window appeared in the top right of Chas' screen. *Twist O'Lemon has offered to teleport you to his or her location. Join me on Jersey Island.* He clicked to accept. There was a loud whooshing sound. He dropped to his knees and stood up, and found himself in what appeared to be a large office lined with bookcases. Huge blue windows all around cut high up into brick walls that rose to a wooden ceiling. Paintings hung on some of the windows: a fist with the middle finger raised, followed by a large U; a strange, multicoloured eye that peered back at him from within its frame. Below stood a sofa and several soft arm-chairs. A grand piano separated two desks, each with computers. Behind one of them, bubbles rose through turquoise water in an aquarium where colourful tropical fish drifted languidly by. Above it hung a large gold crested logo for the Twist of Fate Detective Agency.

Outside, through the blue-smoked glass, Chas could see a sandy island landscape, sun shining on a glittering sea in the distance. There was a row of shops. Across a narrow waterway, several mansion houses. A railway track ran past, then somehow rose up into the sky and looped around, heading off toward an enormous shopping mall in the hazy distance.

Whatever Chas might have been expecting of Second Life, he could never have imagined any of this.

Twist: So what do you think of my office?

Chas turned to see the long-haired, bare-chested young man from Twist's profile sitting at the piano, hands drifting up and down the keyboard. He became aware of soft piano music in the air.

Chas: Who are you?

Twist: LOL. Can't you read? It's me. Twist.

Chas: But you're a man!

Twist: In SL, yes.

Chas: But why?

Twist: Cos I got fed up being harassed all the time. Guys in here are much bolder than they are in RL. A good-looking girl never gets a moment's peace—and all the girls in here are good-looking, Chas. So I decided to be a man. And anyway, this way my clients take me much more seriously. Even if I do go around with a bare chest.

Chas looked down and realised that Twist was also barefooted.

Chas: What clients?

Twist: Of the agency. Didn't you see my logo?

Chas: You're not seriously telling me you're a private detective?

Twist: Sure, I am. Get lots of work, too. Harassment cases. Stalking. Fraud. Infidelity.

Chas: Infidelity?

He couldn't keep the incredulity out of his voice.

Chas: Who's being unfaithful to who?

Twist: Hahaha. Chas, SL is just like RL. People have relationships. Get married. They also cheat. And jealous partners come to me to find out who with.

Twist stood up from the piano.

Twist: Anyway, now that you've come into SL, you can be my partner in the agency. We can be a team.

Chas: You're kidding!

Twist: No, I'm dead serious, Chas. Here…

An invitation appeared inviting him to join a Group called the Twist of Fate Detective Agency. He accepted, and immediately the tag above his head read, *Private Detective Chas Chesnokov.*

Twist: Great. Welcome to the agency, Chas. You are now officially a detective.

A pop-up asked permission for Twist to animate his avatar. As soon as he agreed, Twist advanced toward him, and the two AVs put their arms around each other in an intimate hug.

Chas: Hey! What are you doing?

Twist: Giving you a hug.

Chas: I'm not in the habit of hugging men.

Twist: LOL. Don't worry, it'll be our secret.

If Chas could have frowned, he would have.

Chas: What's this LOL you keep saying?

Twist: Laughs out loud, Chas. LOL. Anyway, now you're part of the Group, you can set this office as your Home. It's where you will log in from now on. If I'm not here, you just click on the door to get in and out. Or you can TP. Come on, I'll show you a little trick.

Twist opened the door and Chas followed him outside. It closed again behind them. He glanced down the row of shops. One was selling furniture. Another sold Skins. A third was peddling animations. And yet another had its windows filled with hair and clothes. AVs were drifting in and out of the stores or standing chatting in groups.

Chas turned around and bumped into Twist.

Twist: Pay attention Chas! This is important.

And Twist described a maneouvre with mouse and alt key that enabled Chas to move his POV from the exterior of the building to the interior, swinging past the outside wall. Chas did as instructed and found that he could see inside the office as if he were there.

Twist: Now click anywhere inside to move around. Magic, huh? You can see through brick walls. Very handy for a PI. Oh, and you can actually go inside, too. Even if the door is locked. Right-click on any of the chairs inside and you'll get an option to Sit. Click on it, and abracadabra, you'll be sitting in that chair. You'll see a Stand Up button on your toolbar. Click that and you're in.

Again, Chas followed Twists' instructions, and in an instant found himself sitting in one of the armchairs inside the office. Twist came back in through the door.

Twist: See? Just like magic.

For a moment he stood looking at Chas, to the point where Chas almost began to feel uncomfortable. It was odd how he was projecting his insecurities into the expressions of an expressionless avatar. But somehow they seemed real.

Chas: What?

Twist: I was just thinking, Chas. You look like such a newbie. We're going to need to get you a whole new look. And a whole new wardrobe. A weapon would be good, too.

Chapter Eleven

The huge brownstone building that housed the Body Doubles shopping mall stood on the edge of a lake bordered by trees that swayed in the breeze. Twist and Chas TPed into an arrival point just outside. Large posters of seductive AVs on the wall advertised the store as image consultants. A ramp led across a moat, guarded by a tiger, to the main entrance. Just inside the front door, a scantily clad blonde wearing a bra, a Stetson, and not much else stood on a circular podium welcoming shoppers to the store. Beyond, a vast two-tiered gallery displayed images around four walls of glamorous-looking men and women, film and rock star lookalikes.

Chas gazed around in amazement. He recognised AV doubles of Josh Duhamel, Halle Berry, Jessica Alba.

Chas: What on earth is this place?

Twist: This is where we're going to buy you a new body shape, and maybe a skin.

Chas: Skin?

Twist: LOL. The outside bit. Just like on real people. The stuff that makes you look the way you are. Come on.

Chas followed Twist up a flight of semicircular stairs and along the length of a catwalk populated by Body Doubles models, one sporting a new Dita Von Teese shape, another the double of Scarlett Johansson. None of the models paid them any attention as they walked past and climbed a long flight of stairs to the upper gallery.

The whole right-hand wall was devoted to male sports stars, actors, and singers. Tiger Woods, Tom Cruise, Mick Jagger.

Twist: So who would you like to be?

Chas: I don't want to be anyone. What's wrong with how I look now?

Twist: Well, for a start there will be thousands of others who look just like you. And anyone who's been in here for five minutes can spot a newbie at a hundred paces. What about Russell Crowe, like he was in The Gladiator?

Chas: No.

Twist: Elvis Presley.

Chas: Definitely not!

Twist: Enrique Iglesias, then. He's sexy.

Chas: Twist…

But Twist interrupted.

Twist: Brad Pitt! Oh, yeh. Gotta be, Chas. I have always fancied Brad Pitt. He is soooo gorgeous.

Chas glanced around to see if anyone was listening to them.

Chas: Hey, keep it down, Twist. People'll think you're gay.

Twist: LOL. Listen, Chas. You'll find out pretty fast. People in here don't give a damn what you are.

Twist led him along the gallery to the Brad Pitt poster. The lookalike AV was posing bare-chested, and from another POV, wearing black jacket and blue jeans, arms folded high across his chest.

Twist: Look at him, he's adorable. Do you have any money?

Chas: Not that I know of. How can I tell?

Twist: Top right hand side of your screen. Small green letters. Tells you how many Lindens you have.

Chas: Lindens?

Twist: Linden dollars. SL has its own economy, Chas. A real economy with its own currency and a fluctuating exchange rate with the US dollar. Currently around 245 Lindens per dollar. People have made millions in here, literally. Mostly buying and selling virtual land.

Chas laughed.

Chas: You mean, people are making millions buying and selling nothing? Pixels?

Twist: You'd better believe it. And no way to trace the transactions. The money can come in from anywhere, pass through any number of hands completely undetected, and go out the other end with no way of tracing it back. And I'm not just talking millions of Lindens, I'm talking millions of dollars, Chas.

Twist swivelled to look at him.

Twist: I'll transfer some cash to you right now. You can pay me back. Next time you go on to the website, register a credit card and you can buy as many Lindens as you like.

A cash register sounded, and a confirmation appeared that Twist had just paid Chas L$5,000.

Chas: Jeez, Twist. Five thousand?

Twist: LOL. That's about twenty bucks. I'll want it back tomorrow. So, go ahead. Buy Brad. He's only five hundred.

Chas did as he was told, and a cash register rang again to confirm the sale.

Twist: Okay, that's gone into your Inventory folder. Everything you have and will ever own is going to be stored in there.

Chas opened up his Inventory and saw the folder of Brad Pitt items he had just bought.

Twist: A notecard should tell us where to go for the rest of you. Skin, eyes, clothes. LOL. You are going to be such a hunk by the time I've finished with you.

◇◇◇

The classy indoor mall where Twist and Chas shopped for the recommended skin, hair, and eyes to go with the Brad Pitt body shape was called Naughty Island. The skin was labelled Gabriel, Golden Tan with Facial Hair 4, and a picture of it showed a pretty boy who looked pretty much as you imagined the archangel might look. They found poster displays of it on a wall in the Naughty Store.

Twist: Goddamn! It's 1500 Lindens!

Twist was incensed.

Twist: It's a ripoff. Five hundred for the shape, then you have to fork out another fifteen hundred for the skin. God knows what the hair and eyes will cost!

As it turned out, the Paris Blue Eyes cost L$500, and the Untamed in Golden Bay Multitonal III hairstyle, available in the Influence Store right next door, cost another L$300.

Twist regarded Chas speculatively

Twist: Okay, let's try it all on.

Chas: What, here?

He looked around. The place was full of customers.

Chas: People will definitely think we're gay!

A shop assistant called Queen Akina approached. She was stunningly beautiful, with long silken brown hair, a low-cut blouse, and baggy plus-four shorts above the curve of shapely calves that were stretched taut on extremely high heels. She ignored Chas, and some animation she possessed made her bare her teeth at Twist in what she imagined was a seductive smile.

Queen: Can I help you?

Twist: Well, if you're free this evening, that could probably be arranged.

Queen Akina giggles.

Chas' IM dialogue box opened up and a message appeared in it from Twist.

Twist: See, men in here just come right out and say it. And, by the way, don't worry. IM's are private. Just between us.

Chas: Twist, you aren't a guy!

Twist: Hehehe. I am in here. And she has no idea. She'd be all over me given half a chance. Sometimes I am really disappointed by my own sex. But it's okay, she won't give you a second look until you're Brad Pitt. Right now you're just a goofy newbie that no chick worth her salt would give a second glance.

Twist turned back to the shop assistant.

Twist: So what do you say, babe?

Queen: Well...I finish here about seven. So if you want to drop me an IM...

Chas: This is embarrassing.

He moved away to find a quiet corner and walked into a display rack laden with boxes of hairstyles. He tried to correct and walked smack into a wall. Heads turned in his direction.

> *Twist:* Jesus, Chas! You're the embarrassment. Let's get you out of here.

◇◇◇

Back at the Naughty Store, there was a corner partitioned off for customers to try on demo skins, or skins they had just bought. Chas was about to make the whole transformation. Twist followed him behind the screen.

Twist: Better if you take your clothes off. We'll get the full effect that way.

Chas: I'm not stripping off in here, Twist.

Twist: Oh, don't be so modest, Chas. No one's looking. LOL. Except me. And in any case, you don't have any dick to cover up.

Chas: I don't?

Chas was unaccountably disappointed.

Twist: No. If you want a penis you're going to have to buy yourself one. I would recommend a multisized, tintable, with and without foreskin, and a side order of nipples. But that's for another day. Now, come on, strip off.

Reluctantly Chas did as he was told and was soon stark naked, standing only in his shoes. It seemed odd to have nothing dangling between his legs. If he could have blushed, he would.

Twist: Right, now just drag and drop everything we have bought on to your AV. Body shape, skin, eyes, hair.

Chas watched in amazement as he transformed into a tanned, muscular young man with startling blue eyes, a shock of blond hair, and just the hint of a light goatee. He particularly liked his six-pack. No matter how much he worked out in RL, he had never managed to produce muscle tone like that.

Twist: Wow! Baby, you are HOT!

Chas blushed beyond his screen, quickly found his clothes in his Inventory, and put them back on.

Twist: Spoilsport. Oh, well, never mind. Time to get you a gun.

Chapter Twelve

Gunslinger Armaments, Ltd., was located in a seedy corner of SL called Excalibur. Twist and Chas teleported into a car park surrounded by a protective mesh fence topped with razor wire. Weeds poked up through cracks in the tarmac. Thick, black smoke rose from an oil drum filled with garbage in a corner piled high with discarded boxes and old packing cases. An empty Coke can rattled about in the wind, and green security laser beams tracked back and forth across the yard from the other side of smoked glass windows. Beyond the fence lay a few rundown houses in a copse of trees and a deserted-looking tower block.

A brown guard dog called Jaeger came out and sniffed around them. Jaeger and Twist seemed to be on speaking terms.

Twist: Hey, boy. Good dog.

Twist walked straight through the glass of the sliding door, and Chas followed.

A sandpit and target shooting area, with a bullseye transposed over the head of Osama Bin Laden, opened up on their left. A display of the five models of handgun created by Kurosawa presented themselves for sale on the wall in front of them. A staircase off to their right led up to his office. Chas followed Twist up the stairs.

Twist: He handcrafts these weapons himself you know. Faithful replicas of the Colt 911. Writes his own scripts, too. Ever want to know anything about guns, Gunslinger is the man to talk to.

Kurosawa sat behind a green glass-topped office desk, a cigarette burning between his middle and fourth fingers. An animated sketch of a Colt handgun fired relentlessly on the wall behind him. A huge metal safe stood in the corner and a digital counter on the wall charted sales. From his office Kurosawa had a panoramic view over the carpark. It didn't quite match up, Chas thought, to his own RL view over Balboa Island.

Kurosawa himself was younger than Chas had been expecting. He had a shock of auburn hair with a pair of sunglasses pushed well up into it, and a half-grown beard. A leather holster belt hung across the shoulder of a black shirt. He wore blue jeans and boots with stirrups that chinked as he put both feet up on the desk, one crossed over the other.

Kurosawa: Hey, Twist. Howya doing?

Twist: I'm doing good, Kuro. This is my partner, Chas. We need to get him a gun, so I thought we'd ask your advice.

Kurosawa swivelled in his seat to take a look at Chas.

Kurosawa: Brad Pitt, huh? You been at Body Doubles?

Twist: LOL. How'd you guess, Kuro?

Gunslinger Kurosawa smiles.

Kurosawa: So you'll be doing the same sort of work as Twist, then, Chas?

Chas: I guess I will.

Kurosawa: Well, you couldn't do much better than the 1911A1 Custom. It's got great detail. Hud-driven.

Twist turned to Chas.

Twist: That means a menu will come up on your screen.

Kurosawa: Oh, a newbie, huh? Well, all the better. The Custom's idiot-proof.

Chas wasn't certain that he enjoyed being called an idiot

Kurosawa: It's got a speed holster, smoking shell casings, tracking smoke, an invisible trap, standard damage and push, and six shield-crushing bullets. A bargain at a mere 1000 lindens.

Chas glanced up at the green figure in the top right of his screen to see that he had just enough left to cover it.

Chas: Okay. Let's do it.

So they went back down to the store and Chas made the purchase. He attached the holster to his right thigh, then dragged the gun to the holster. A red hud appeared at the top of his screen.

Kurosawa: Make your choice of bullet, and use mouselook to line up the sight with your target and shoot.

Chas: Mouselook?

Twist: Yeh. The whole screen becomes your POV. Moves with the mouse. Click and fire.

Kurosawa: Try it out on the shooting range. Get in a bit of practice.

Kurosawa headed for the sandpit to set it up for a practice session.

Twist: Hang on guys, I'm getting an IM.

Twist seemed lost for a few moments. Then,

Twist: Shit, sorry Kuro, we've gotta go. Harassment case I've been working on at a nightclub. The guy's there now. Gotta go get him.

Twist turned to Chas.

Twist: Come on then, big boy. Your first job.

Chapter Thirteen

Sinful Seductions night club was a skybox 595 metres up above a mall and a small colony of houses on Lancelot Island. Access to the club was through a transparent image of a fiery dark-haired woman sporting a sword and pistol. Twist and Chas just breezed right through it. The blue velvet dance floor was crowded, AVs animated in dance by a central ball that hung from the ceiling. Exotic dancers were pole dancing on the stage. Four of them. Each with her own tip jar. Chas stood for a moment, watching them, open-mouthed, as they removed items of clothing in response to cash paid into their jars by salivating male customers. These were the most sophisticated AVs he had seen yet. Beautifully sculpted, with tanned, shiny skin and such fluid animation that he could almost believe they were real.

The predominant colour scheme of the club was blue and grey, punctuated by odd flashes of a fiery red. A sign behind the stage read *Sin Is a Seduction of the Soul.* A flight of stairs led up to a honeycomb of private rooms and a gallery that ran the length of the club. From here there was a view of the dance floor and the DJ's podium on the opposite stage. Torches flamed in the dark, throwing shadows across the dancers, and Chas felt the beat of the music pounding through his AV.

The crowd parted as a large, bald-headed avatar, covered from head to foot with elaborate tattoos, ran through the crowd swinging an axe above his head. His name tag identified him, appropriately, as Tommy Tattoo. He had an enormously erect penis that was clearing a path ahead of him, and he left a trail of obscenities in his wake. Anyone who got in his way just seemed to vanish.

Twist: That's our man, Chas. He's got an orbiter.

Chas: A what?

Twist: It's a gadget that sends anyone he targets flying into space. But it's okay. I'm wearing a shield. He can't do anything to me.

Chas: What are you going to do to him?

Twist: Cage him. Then fire him straight to the other end of SL, and file a report with Linden Lab to get him barred inworld. Come on. Get your gun out.

They drew their weapons and pushed through the dancers toward the advancing AV, and suddenly Twist stopped dead.

Twist: Oh, shit!

Chas: What is it?

Twist: I'm gonna crash.

Chas: Goddamnit, Twist, you pick your moments!

But Twist was already gone, in a twinkle of fading sparkles. Chas turned around to face Tommy Tattoo, gun swinging unsteadily in his direction. He fumbled to get into Mouselook. But before he could, Tommy took off. Lifting right up over his head. And as Chas turned, he saw him landing on the stage, next to one of the dancers. He immediately activated some dance animation and began circling her, gyrating his hips lewdly. Chas managed finally to get himself into Mouselook. A small gunsight appeared in the centre of his screen, and it immediately became apparent to him that lining it up with a moving target was a lot more difficult than it sounded. He swung left to right, overreacting, then under-reacting, until finally the tattooed man was in his sights. He pulled the trigger and somehow managed to shoot the dancer.

She let out a startled yell, and great clouds of black smoke started issuing from the hole that Chas had just shot through her middle, very quickly enveloping her entirely. He watched in horror as she started running about the stage, the smoke following her everywhere she went. Tommy Tattoo put his hands on his hips and roared with laughter.

Chas was aware of a figure materialising at his side. He turned to find a young woman standing there. She had long, dark hair, and an elfin face with rich, chocolate brown eyes which she fixed on him with a look of patent disbelief. Her name tag revealed her to be *Sinful Sensations Dancer Doobie Littlething*. Except that she wasn't dressed like a dancer. She wore a low-cut grey camouflage top and shorts, a pistol strapped to her thigh, an equipment belt laden with tools and a water flask, and armoured pads protecting her hips and shins.

Doobie: Did you do that?

Chas: Do what?

Doobie: Shoot the dancer.

Chas was getting used to blushing by now.

Chas: It was an accident.

She looked at his tag.

Doobie: Private detective, huh? Are you with the Twist agency?

He nodded.

Doobie: Where's Twist?

Chas: Crashed.

Doobie: Fucking useless!

For some reason Chas was shocked by her language. But she was already on the move. Striding toward the stage. She sprang up in a forward somersault, and landed right next to the tattooed troublemaker, her weapon drawn. And some dissociated part of Chas thought how incredibly attractive she looked: her hair swept back from her face, a slash of crimson cupid for her mouth, the tiny heart-shaped birthmark high on her cheek next to her right eye. He even noticed the streaks of red in her dark hair.

The dancer was still running around the stage, bleeding smoke. No one was dancing any more. The music had stopped, and everyone stood in silence waiting to see what would happen next.

Tommy Tattoo turned toward Doobie and leered at her.

Tommy: Orbit, you bitch!

A sprinkle of lights appeared and disappeared. But Doobie remained where she was, her handgun held up next to her head, pointed at the ceiling.

Tattoo: WTF?

Doobie: I'm shielded, shit-for-brains! Prepare to crash and burn in hell!

Her handgun was suddenly extended at arm's length, pointed straight at Tommy, and Chas knew that she had gone into Mouselook. But before she could fire, Tommy Tattoo vanished in a flash of light.

Doobie: Shit!

And she too, vanished, leaving the stage empty, apart from the smoking dancer. Chas barely had time to resurrect his sense of guilt before an offer appeared on his screen. *Doobie Littlething invites Chas Chesnokov to join her in Crack Town.* He accepted, and in a whoosh his screen went black, before he found himself dropping to his knees on the decaying wooden porch of a grim derelict brick building in the heart of a dark, oppressive cityscape. He stood up and looked around. This condemned building had been fenced off. But one section of the fence had been broken down and the door of the building ripped open.

He was in a long, gloomy street. Immediately opposite, a police patrol car with flashing lights was drawn up in the entrance to a covered parking lot that seemed to be occupied by down-and-outs and prostitutes. A uniformed officer stood by a fluttering black and yellow Crime Scene tape, and watched him with casual indifference. Chas could hear static and a dispatcher's voice coming across the police radio.

Further down the street, beneath a poster of a Rottweiler bearing the logo MAKE MY DAY, an AV sprawled in the street in a pool of fresh blood. A gun lay next to his head. A hooker stood, arms folded, outside the doors of the Carnal City Police Department. Some youths sat on a wall, dangling their legs, indulging in idle conversation. But there was no sign of Doobie or Tattoo Tommy.

Chas turned back to the derelict building and peered apprehensively inside before taking a few tentative steps into the semi-darkness.

To his left, a tattered settee and two old armchairs were gathered around a 1950s TV set. An old packing case served as a table. The space was littered with what Chas now recognised to be poseballs. They were everywhere in SL. Pink for females, blue for males. A right-click on a poseball attached you to it, and your AV would be animated by its script to do almost anything. Sit, chat, have sex, play a piano. And so much in SL seemed sex-oriented. *Give blow job. Receive blow job. Wallfuck.* Two poseballs that said *Love* seemed somehow incongruous. On the wall hung a painting of Jesus dressed as pirate.

The room to his left was a bathroom. Above the bath were two poseballs. *Drowned* and *DrowningHold.* Pornographic posters covered brick walls.

The next room along the corridor was a filthy kitchen with cockroaches running around the floor. Off to the left, a room with a mattress. Rats scuttled about the place, disturbing the drifts of litter that had accumulated there.

At the end of the corridor, Chas emerged into the gloom of a stretch of waste ground, where a pile of burning tires belched oily black smoke into the night sky. A hobo wrapped up in old newspapers huddled nearby for warmth. Graffiti on the wall opposite read, *Religion is not the opium of the masses. Opium is.*

Chas climbed a ramp to the street above. Next to a scarred blue tenement door opposite, a sign advertised apartments for rent. And he wondered who in their right minds would want to rent an apartment in a place like this. It was like the worst nightmare of social urban decay. In an alleyway further down the street, two poseballs against a colourfully graffitied wall read, *Strangle* and *Strangled*.

He turned left and crossed a bridge over a stream of chemical green sludge. He could hear the sound of distant traffic flashing past on the freeway, the constant wail of a police siren, before a shadow flashed across his screen. A startling explosion of light sent multicoloured particles flying in every direction. When they cleared, Tommy Tattoo was crouched in front of him in the middle of the road, a maniacal grin on his face. He stood up and seemed to tower over Chas as he raised his axe high above his head. Chas was rooted to the spot by fear, even though he was nearly certain that this avatar could do him no damage. All the same, he fumbled and clicked on the hud to activate his handgun. But too late. The axe was descending on him. No time to move, or to TP out.

But Tommy Tattoo froze in midstroke as the black bars of a tightly meshed cage closed around him, and held him immobile inside it.

Tommy: FUCK!

Doobie Littlething dropped out of the sky and landed beside them. She turned to Chas.

Doobie: So you decided to put in an appearance after all.

Chas: Well, with an invitation from a gun-toting dancer

to join her and a tattooed maniac in a place called Crack Town, how could I resist?

Doobie stared at him for a moment, then burst out laughing.

Doobie: Well, you may be incompetent, but at least you have a sense of humour.

Tommy: I hate to break up this cosy little mutual admiration society, but would someone like to tell me exactly how long I'm going to be stuck in here?

Doobie turned around.

Doobie: Just as long as it takes to blow a hole in your brainless head, set your AV on fire, and crash you so hard it'll take you a week to get back in.

Tommy: Yeh, right.

Doobie: Watch me.

She drew her weapon, cocked it, held it at arm's length and fired twice into the cage, blowing holes right through Tommy's head and chest. She recocked it and fired again, this time setting him on fire.

A stream of abuse and profanity issued like smoke from the stricken Tommy, before Doobie recocked again and shot AV and cage straight up into the sky. Chas swivelled to look up, but Tattoo Tommy had already gone.

Chas: Did you destroy him?

Doobie: No, Mr. Chesnokov. You can't destroy an AV. You can damage him, make him crash. Nothing permanent. But he'll think twice about messing with Doobs the next time.

Chas took a step back, sudden excitement rising through him, and drew his weapon again, this time selecting Damage from his menu. He spun around to point it at Doobie and went straight into Mouselook.

She was so startled she had no time to react.

Doobie: WTF!

Chas fired three times and Doobie spun out of the way, turning in time to see three AV's running around with smoke escaping from huge holes blown straight through the chest of each.

Doobie: Great shooting, Chas!

Chas allowed himself a small smile of self-congratulation.

Chas: I know how to handle a gun, Doobie. I came first on the practice range in training.

Doobie: Good for you. Just one little thing. Why did you shoot these guys?

Chas: They were sneaking up on us, Doobie. Pretty unsavoury looking characters. I thought they could be friends of Tommy Tattoo.

Doobie threw her head back and roared with laughter.

Doobie: People like Tommy Tattoo don't have friends, Chas. They were just three AVs out for a bit of fun. Role-playing probably. LOL. That's the fourth innocent AV you've shot the fuck out of in the space of ten minutes. We'd better get you out of here before you get reported and Linden Lab ban you for life.

Before he could open his mouth to make excuses, Doobie was gone. And an invitation appeared to join her at the Armory Overstock in Shepherd. Chas accepted and glanced at the time. He had been in Second Life for less than two hours, and it felt like two days.

Chapter Fourteen

Spread over the vast indoor floorspace of a huge, brick warehouse, the Armory Overstock sold everything from armoured vehicles, helicopters and troop carriers, to personal weapons, bugging devices and gridwide radar systems.

Chas landed with a thump next to Doobie, in front of an enormous welcome board and a water fountain. He looked about as the store began to take shape around him.

Doobie: It's taking a while to rez today.

Chas: Rez?

Doobie: For things to upload and become focused. SL is responsible for introducing a lot of new words to the English language.

Chas: If only they made things any clearer. I have so many initial letters going round my head, I'm beginning to feel like a walking acronym.

Doobie Littlething: Oh, good word, Chas.

An invitation appeared. *Doobie Littlething is offering you Friendship. Accept or Decline.* Chas hesitated for only a moment before clicking to accept.

Chas: So that makes us friends now, does it? It's not that long ago I was "fucking incompetent".

Doobie: Hahahaha. Yes, well, that probably hasn't changed. Though maybe we can do something about it. But you know, Chas, I haven't met that many people in here who would know what an acronym was. That makes you a little unusual. And maybe worth knowing.

Unexpectedly, she did a little backward flip, landing on her tip-toes and holding out her arms for balance, like a ballet dancer.

Doobie: Follow me.

Chas struggled to keep up as Doobie strode off across the floor, dodging banners and stands.

Chas: What are we here for?

Doobie: To get you an AV radar tracking system. You clearly have no idea what's going on around you. Which is something of a disadvantage for a private investigator. Where is your partner, by the way? Did he ever show up again?

Chas: Twist? No, he never did.

Doobie: Must've been a bad crash, then. Sometimes it can take forever to get back online.

They walked past giant billboards advertising weapons and bugging devices. One promoted a mosquito, which it claimed was SL's smallest weapon. Each one, it promised, would target the person of your choice and keep attacking until you called it off. It also offered the opportunity to rez multiple mosquitoes for swarming attacks.

Another described itself as a Covert Ops Clock.

Chas: Innoculous-looking clock (and scripts) spy on the unsuspecting. Shouldn't that be "innocuous"? Unless of course it's some kind of clock that injects its victims. Maybe its hands are hypodermic syringes.

Doobie Littlething laughs long and loud.

Doobie: You are a funny man, Chas.

Chas: LOLOL. But really, Doobs, there are all these clever people who can write complex software scripts but can barely spell, or conjugate a verb. Makes you wonder where the world of communication will finish up.

Doobie: Probably in a bunch of acronyms that nobody understands.

In the end, Doobie selected a simple radar hud that would provide Chas with a permanent display, letting him know exactly who was within ninety-six metres of him at any given time, with the option of caging or orbiting anyone who seemed threatening.

Doobie: Just 500 Lindens

Chas checked his Linden total.

Chas: I don't have enough, Doobs.

Doobie Littlething sighs.

Doobie: Okay, here, I'll lend it to you. But in return I'll expect you to take me out to dinner.

A cash register sounded, and 500 Lindens were paid into Chas' account. He purchased the radar and filed it in his inventory for later.

Chas: How can I take you out to dinner, Doobie? Man cannot live by pixels alone.

Doobie: Hahahaha. Don't worry, Chas. I know the very place. And their deep-fried pixels in batter are excellent.

◇◇◇

Chas followed Doobie's TP and found himself on a breezy island filled with flowers and trees, jagged green rocks rising up to pierce the purest of blue skies. They were in a garden with pink petals falling all around them like snow. Parasols shaded circular glass tables. Slow-dance poseballs were scattered around a lush, green lawn. Finger food and a bottle of champagne chilling in a bucket were laid out on a buffet table.

Doobie: You see, not everywhere in SL is seedy or violent.

Chas: Where are we?

Doobie: Midsomer Isle. This place is known as Puck's Hideaway. Quite romantic, really.

Chas turned around and saw that Doobie had changed out of her armour and camouflage and was now sporting a black beret, black scarf, and a cream chiffon top, with tight, black, three-quarter length pants.

Chas: So why did you bring me here?

Doobie: Because you made me laugh. And because you owe me 500 lindens. I always believe in looking after my investments. Come on, take a look at the island.

And she soared up into the sky. Chas followed and they hovered together for a few minutes looking at the view spread out below them. It was spectacular. Chas could never have imagined that something like this might exist in a virtual world. Waterfalls and minarets, hidden terraces, domed pavilions, and private houses tucked away in hidden coves, rocky pinnacles rising on all sides. He looked again at Doobie's name tag.

Chas: So why do you dance?

Doobie: For money, of course. I have to finance my shopping sprees somehow.

Chas: What do you buy?

Doobie: Well, when I'm not buying guns or weapons, it would be clothes, or hair, or new skins.

Chas: You change your appearance, then?

Doobie: From time to time. When you're a dancer, you have to keep up with the rest. Got to look good or you lose your job.

Chas: But you're really more of a stripper than a dancer. If what I saw at Sinful Sensations was anything to go by.

Doobie Littlething shrugs.

Doobie: Sure. What's wrong with that? I'm also an escort.

Chas: Really? What does an escort do?

Doobie: Hahahaha. You're kidding me, Chas. What does an escort do in RL?

Chas: You're a prostitute?

Doobie: I prefer "hooker". It's a little sluttier, don't you think? LOL. Yeh, sure. I have sex for money.

Chas gazed at her in amazement. Then remembered his own missing parts.

Chas: How on earth does an AV have sex?

Doobie Littlething laughs till she's fit to burst.

Doobie: My God, you really are a newbie, aren't you. Let's have a look at your profile.

A brief pause.

Doobie: OMG! You only came in today! No wonder you know sweet FA.

Chas called up Doobie's profile and saw that she had been "born" nearly three years ago. There was a picture of her, and her info panel described her as an escort, model, and exotic dancer. *IM me for my rate card*, it implored potential clients. Chas clicked the 1st Life tab, but that window was empty.

Chas: You have a rate card?

Doobie: Sure. I'll give you my rates. Are you interested in having sex with me?

A blue window appeared to let him know that Doobie Littlething was making him an offer. He declined it hastily and felt himself blushing again.

Chas: No, I do not want to have sex with you.

He paused.

Chas: And anyway, I don't have a penis.

Doobie: LOLOLOLOL! Well, that would make it a little difficult. Let me take you to my favourite spot.

She turned and soared off into the gathering gloom, and as Chas followed, he saw the sun setting on the horizon, sending jewels of claret sparkling across the darkening ocean. A domed, circular terrace surrounded by painted columns was perched on the edge of the cliff, looking directly out across the sunset.

Doobie dropped like a stone, landing right on the edge of the terrace, and Chas followed. For a moment he held his breath. For set in the middle of the terrace, on a Persian rug, was a large, square chess table laid out with a full complement of chessmen, chairs facing each other across the battlefield. The sunset was lined up perfectly with the four rows of squares between the opposing players.

Doobie: You probably don't play. Not many people seem to these days. But I love the mental challenge of it. And I love a man who can push me to my limits. In all sorts of ways. I sometimes come here on my own and play against myself. LOL. That's a unique kind of challenge.

Chas: I know. I've played against myself many times these last months.

She turned to look at him.

Doobie: Have you: why?

Chas: Because I have no one else to play with.

She seemed to think about that for a moment.

Doobie: Would you like a game?

Chas: I'd love a game.

And so they sat with the sun setting between them and made their first few moves across a virgin board.

Chas: It's strange, I haven't been here that long today, and yet it seems to have been light and dark, light and dark.

Doobie: Well, SL like RL, has time zones, and we've been teleporting back and forth across them. But a Second Life day is only two hours long. So we cram a lot into a day here. And we don't waste time walking or driving or taking airplanes. Or eating and sleeping. It makes the whole SL experience that much more concentrated, that much more intense. Things come and go more quickly, including people. And all their human emotions—love, hate, jealousy, envy—are like the light that burns twice as bright but only half as long. If you stay in SL, Chas, you'll experience much more than you ever expected.

They played, then, in silence, a game so evenly balanced that they were each down to their last few players before she finally chased his king into a corner and forced his surrender. He was glad that Doobie couldn't see the tears that moistened his eyes behind the screen. She played just like Mora. Not with great flair, but with a relentless, intelligent pursuit that finally ground down her opponent. And he was reminded so strongly of Mora that it almost hurt.

They sat for several minutes without talking.

Doobie: Bad loser?

Chas: LOL. No, Doobie. Just replaying the game to figure out how to beat you next time.

Doobie Littlething smiles.

She stood up suddenly.

Doobie: I promised you could take me out to dinner. I'll send you a TP.

And she was gone in a sprinkling of fairy dust.

◇◇◇

Chas followed Doobie's TP, and found himself in a circular terrace just like the one they had left. Except that the chess board had been replaced by a dining table for two, with candles and a chocolate and strawberry fondu, and white wine chilling in a bucket. There was no sea view here. They were almost completely enclosed by tall conifers, and the columns supporting the dome were draped with wreaths of pink and white roses. Somehow, in the time it had taken to teleport from one location to another, Doobie had changed her clothes again. Now she wore a flowing, full-length black dress with a daringly low cut neckline revealing full, sensuous breasts. Chas found his eyes being drawn by them, and wondered how he could possibly be turned on by a cartoon. But somehow the personality behind the image was transcending the visual. He thought that Doobie was incredibly attractive.

He glanced down at his own newbie clothes.

Chas: I really need to get myself a new outfit.

Doobie: Need to get yourself some money first. Then you can build as big a wardrobe as you like. I have so many clothes in my inventory, collected over nearly three years, that I know I'll never ever wear them all again.

They sat down and were immediately animated to eat from the plates of steaming virtual food in front of them. Chas seemed to be carving his way through a thick steak.

Two *chings* in rapid succession drew Chas' eye to the fact that he had an incoming IM. It was from Twist.

Twist: Goddamned SL! I only just got back in. What happened?

Chas: Oh, me and a beautiful exotic dancer chased Tommy Tattoo to Crack Town, caged him, shot him, and sent him crashing into orbit.

Twist: Jesus, Chas. How on earth did you manage all that?

Chas: Easy, Twist. When you know how.

Twist: Pfffff!

Chas: Anyway, I'm kind of busy right now. Having dinner with a lady.

Twist: What!?

Chas: I'll explain later. But just to let you know, Twist, I'll be looking for my share of the fee for getting rid of Tommy. Fifty-fifty, although I'm not sure it shouldn't be more, given that you weren't even there. How much do we charge, by the way?

Twist: 100 a day, plus expenses

Chas Chesnokov: Lindens?

Twist: LOL. What else?

Chas: Gees, Twist, it's hardly worth showing up for that.

Twist: Well, big shot, maybe you should take it up with your union rep. I have to log off now. I'll see you at work.

Chas looked up to find Doobie watching him.

Doobie: IM?

Chas: How did you know?

Doobie: Well, when someone takes nearly a minute to answer a question, I have to figure they are a little distracted.

Chas: Oh, I'm sorry, Doobs. It was Twist. What was the question?

Doobie: I was offering you Landmarks to stores where you can pick up decent clothes at reasonable prices. You interested?

Chas: What's a Landmark?

Doobie: A teleport link. There's a folder for them in your Inventory. I'll look out some LMs for interesting places for you to visit in SL. Pass them on to you next time. And I know there'll be a next time, because you still owe me 500 Lindens.

Chas looked at her speculatively.

Chas: How much time do you spend in here on an average day, Doobie?

Doobie: Pretty much all my waking hours. Except when I'm eating. Although sometimes I eat at the computer, too. LOL.

Chas: Well, what does your family say?

There was quite a long silence.

Doobie: I don't have any family, Chas. None to speak of, anyway.

He decided not to probe any further. It was odd how it was possible to divine reluctance, hesitation, embarrassment, amusement, without ever really seeing someone, or hearing their voice.

Chas: So what else do you do with your time? I mean, when you're not dancing or…entertaining clients?

Doobie: I hunt griefers.

Chas: What's a griefer?

Doobie: LOL. Well, what does it sound like, Chas? It's someone who causes grief. You get them in RL. Troublemakers. Vandals, criminals, people who infect computers with viruses…Folk are just the same in the virtual world as they are in the real one. Only here, it's gloves off. They get what's coming to them. If Linden Lab don't deal with them, then citizens take the law into their own hands. We go after them where they hide and gather. Free damage areas where there are frequent pitched battles. That's why I have my armour and my weapons. I usually go griefer hunting at a place called Sandbox Island. Anything goes there. And you know what? It's fun.

She suddenly stood up.

Doobie: I'm not hungry any more. Do you wanna dance?

Chas felt that he had barely begun his meal. But Doobie was clearly restless. She didn't seem to want to remain in one place for more than a few minutes at a time. And, besides, he was curious to know what it would feel like to dance with her.

Chas: Sure.

He stood up.

Doobie: I'll TP you.

And she vanished.

◇◇◇

The poseballs for Slow-dance v3 were set in the centre of yet another terrace ringed by columns. Petals fell here, too. The night sky was only just visible through the trees that grew all around, swaying in the cool night breezes that blew across Midsomer Isle from the ocean. Discreetly placed lamps threw the long shadows of the columns across the dancefloor, and Doobie was already attached to her poseball, waiting, with arms extended, for her partner. Chas clicked and joined her.

The dance began formally enough. Chas had his arm around Doobie's waist. Their left and right hands extended together.

Doobie: On your toolbar, at the bottom right, you'll see a musical symbol. Click on it.

Chas did as he was told, and immediately soft, seductive Celtic music filled his ears, transforming the atmosphere of the night.

Almost at the same time, Doobie's arms slipped up around his neck, drawing him closer, and he watched as his hands slid behind her to glide over the curve of her buttocks. He felt a strange, unaccountable thrill. How was it possible for animated pixels on a screen to have such an effect on him? The AV's gazed at each other in the night, a strange intensity in their eyes, and Chas felt the beginnings of butterflies in his stomach.

Doobie's hands slid over his chest, and she buried her head in his shoulder as his arms moved around her waist to hold her tight. Chas felt a stirring in his loins and had the oddest urge to kiss her. An urge frustrated by the limitations of the animation.

Chas: This is nice.

Doobie: Mmmm. Yeh. Can you feel my breath on your neck as you hold me?

Chas: Yes, I can.

And he almost believed that he could.

Doobie: Then feel my hands as they glide over your chest, slipping beneath the cool cotton of your shirt to touch the heat of your skin.

Chas: OMG Doobie, should we be doing this? I hardly know you.

Doobie: Don't worry. You'll get my bill tomorrow.

Chas: Hahahaha.

Doobie: He laughs!

Chas: You're not serious?

Doobie Littlething smiles.

Doobie: Of course. Not. LOL. Thank you for brightening up my day, Chas.

She paused.

Doobie: So, tell me, how does a newbie get to be so good-looking on his first day in SL?

Chas: I had inside help.

She was silent again for a while, and they listened to the music and wrapped themselves in each other's arms.

Doobie: Will you play chess with me again sometime?

Chas: Well, as long as you hold my marker for 500 Lindens, I guess you can ask me to do anything you want.

Doobie Littlething smiles.

Doobie: I like a man who plays chess. Never yet found one who could beat me, though. And never will fall for one till I do.

Chas: I'll have to practise, then.

Suddenly she detached herself from her poseball.

Doobie: I have to go.

Chas was disappointed. He clicked to stand up and detached himself from his now solo dance, standing awkwardly, wondering how to say goodbye, and how he would ever find his way out of here.

Another invitation appeared. This time Doobie was asking permission to animate his AV. He consented, and she advanced toward, him, placing her arms around his neck and giving him a long, slow kiss. It was bewilderingly exciting. Then she stepped back.

Doobie: I'll look for you next time. You'll find me on your Friends List now, if you ever need to IM me. Bye.

A shower of lights flared and died in the night. And she was gone.

◇◇◇

Michael sat staring at Chas on the screen, and made the slow transition from night-time Second Life to the morning sun of real life streaming through his office window. He looked at the clock on the wall. He had spent nearly three hours in this other world, where he had become someone else. For the first time in months, the pain of losing Mora had not been the foremost thing on his mind. What surprised and disturbed him most, however, was how Chas had in some way taken over, like some hidden part of himself that he barely knew existed. He was not Chas, and Chas was not him. But they shared feelings, and memories, and pain. They were one and at the same time two. It had been an extraordinary, whirlwind experience, and it was a little scary.

Chapter Fifteen

It was the following day before Michael had the chance to dig out the photographs he had taken at the Arnold Smitts crime scene. He sat in what had once been the darkroom, from the days when they still used film, and scrolled through the digital images downloaded onto his computer.

They brought back very vividly the warm scented air of that California night when morose thoughts had been interrupted to call him out to a murder. He looked at the images of the dead man with a new eye. Here was someone who, like him, had been a denizen of Second Life, and Michael wondered how a bald, ageing accountant, rumoured to have connections to the mob, had spent his time in there. Had he danced, like Chas, with an exotic escort, or chased griefers through Carnal City? Michael found it difficult to imagine that the experiences of Chas' first few hours in SL had been in any way typical. So what had drawn Smitts to this virtual world? What had there been there for him?

Eventually he came to a shot that included Smitts' computer monitor. And there it was. The Second Life welcome screen. That now disturbingly familiar green hand and eye. He gazed at it thoughtfully, then made several prints of shots he had not previously turned into hard copy. He slipped them into an envelope and left the darkroom to make his way through an office divided and subdivided into open-plan cubicles where fellow

CSI officers huddled over desks and surrounded themselves with personal knick-knacks and family photos.

Janey's head popped up from one of them. "Hey, Mike." She smiled, as if at a fellow conspirator. "Will you be 'in' later?" Her special emphasis on the word 'in' conveyed its meaning clearly enough. He understood why she would not want to confess openly to her coworkers that she spent all her free time in an online virtual world as a private dick.

He nodded. "Maybe tonight."

"Catch you then, then." She winked and grinned, and disappeared from view.

◇◇◇

Michael found the Hardy half of Laurel and Hardy at his desk in the detectives' office. He watched Michael approaching with a distinct lack of enthusiasm. "I'm busy, Mr. Getty; what do you want?"

Michael stopped by his chair and dropped the envelope of photographs on Hardy's desk. "That's a few extra prints I ran off, Ollie. From Smitts' house." He saw the Smitts file open in front of the fat detective, spread across an untidy avalanche of paperwork that looked as if it might have been accumulating there for months. "Any progress?"

"Well, maybe there would have been if you guys had come up with something better from the crime scene."

"Can't give you what's not there, Ollie. Did you establish a mob connection?"

"Hah! Turns out the FBI had a file on him as thick as the bible. He was bookkeeping for the Mafia out here for at least twenty years. They're pretty damned sure of that."

"How come he wasn't behind bars, then?"

"A little thing called proof, sonny. You know: evidence? What we need to take to court to get a conviction? Best they could get him on in all that time was a couple of unpaid parking fines. He was squeaky clean."

Hardy pulled Michael's prints out of their envelope and gave them a cursory look. "Nothing much new in these." He tossed them to one side. "Why did you think I'd be interested?"

Michael shrugged. "More's better than less." He paused, and then added casually, "I noticed the Second Life welcome screen on his computer."

Hardy glanced up at him, one skeptical eyebrow raised in surprise. "What would *you* know about Second Life? Goddamned refuge for sad fucks and perverts." And then he managed a leering sort of grin. "Unless, of course you're in there yourself. Which wouldn't surprise me. And if you're not, then maybe you should be. I'm sure you'd feel right at home."

Michael ignored the barb. "I know someone who spends a lot of time in SL." He paused. "So was Smitts a citizen, then?"

"Well, yeh, as far as we can figure. But, then again, no. Because there is no record of him on the Linden Lab database."

Michael frowned. "How do you mean?"

"Well, he had an account. An AV called Maximillian Thrust. Jesus, these people give themselves some stupid fucking names! Anyway, that was the name entered on the welcome screen for logging in. And we found mails in his computer forwarded to his email address from IMs and Group Notices issued from within Second Life."

"What Groups was he in?"

"Aw, jees, I dunno." He riffled through some of the papers in his file. "Nothing that makes much sense to me. Black Creek Saloon. AAA Club. DJ Badboys Fans. Gurls Rock. Virtual Realty. Whatever the hell any of these might be. But here's the weird shit. When we asked Linden Lab for access to Smitts' account, they said there *was* no such account. And never had been. No record of it in their computers."

"That *is* strange."

"Damn tootin' it is! Because there's no doubt he had an account. It's as if someone just erased all record of it from the server."

Chapter Sixteen

Chas crouched for a moment and then stood up. Twist's office began to rez slowly around him. He could see green text hovering above the Agency sign outside the door. *Twist O'Lemon is offline. Click to leave an IM.* A blue pop-up informed him that Doobie Littlething had offered him Inventory items in his absence. They were the LMs she had promised him, and when he accepted, they went automatically into his Landmark Folder. They were teleport links to various locations around SL, and one of them, he saw, would take him to Sinful Seductions Night Club.

He saw, too, that Doobie was online. He thought about sending her an IM, but decided instead to try out one of his new Landmarks. He double-clicked. His screen went black, and a sound like wind rushing through a tunnel transported him across Second Life continents to the walkway that ran around the exterior of Sinful Seductions Night Club. A rail prevented him from falling off. He peered over it to the tops of clouds far below, and the distant glitter of sun on sea. He walked through the woman with the sword and into the club. It was empty. Not a soul there. He checked the time next to his Lindens total. It was 7.32PM, SLT, which he knew to be the same as Pacific Daylight Time, and he wondered when things got going at the club. It was early for California, late for Europe, and he had no idea which nationality of clientele the club catered for.

Then he remembered the radar system that Doobie had made him buy the previous day. He found it in his Inventory and installed it on his screen. Two names immediately appeared. *Doobie Littlething* and *Jackin Thebox*. Both, apparently, exactly ninety meters away. But where? Not in the club, it seemed. He went back out on to the walkway. Twist had told him that the club was in a skybox 595 metres up. So the chances were that Doobie and Jackin were either somewhere above or below.

Chas craned to look up and saw the underside of another building floating some way above the club. He took off and soared skywards, arms pressed to his side, until he was on a level with the building he had seen from below. In fact, it was just a large, grey box. There appeared to be no doors or windows in it. But Doobie and Jackin now showed as being just eight metres away. So, somehow, they were inside it. They must have teleported in.

Chas recalled Twist's first lesson in Second Life private investigation. He pointed at the nearest wall, zoomed in and then swivelled to the side so that he bypassed the wall altogether and suddenly had a view of the interior. Floor, walls, and ceiling appeared to be covered in thick-piled crimson plush. Lamps on the walls cast muted light around the room. Cushions were scattered across the floor, multicoloured, multisized. Among them pose balls offering any number of sexual activities, some odd-looking furniture, and some scarier-looking BDSM contraptions.

Two figures lay naked among the pillows. Doobie was on her back, her legs apart, while Jackin lay between them, his pink bottom rising and falling to a steady, rhythmic beat. Chas clicked among the cushions for a closer view, confident that he was quite invisible to them, and watched with a certain amount of horrified fascination, and an odd, distant, feeling of jealousy.

The dialogue of the sex partners was visible on his screen in open chat, and he was almost shocked by the mundane crudity of it.

Jackin: Yeh. Yeh. Fucking you, baby. Fucking you.

Doobie: Fuck me, Jack. Fuck me.

Jackin: Bite my nipples, you bitch. Bite them!

Doobie: Mmm. Biting your nipples, Jack. Sucking them hard.

Chas selected Doobie from his Friends List and sent her an IM. Watching her closely, as if he might actually be able to discern some visual reaction.

> *Chas:* Hey, Doobie.
>
> After a moment...
>
> *Doobie:* I'm working right now, Chas.
>
> *Chas:* So I see.

There was a long silence, during which Chas could almost feel Doobie absorbing the implications of that.

> *Doobie:* Where are you?
>
> *Chas:* Right outside.
>
> *Doobie:* Damned Peeping Tom!! Where'd you learn that trick?
>
> *Chas:* Actually, I'm trying very hard not to look. The sight of Mr. Thebox's flaccid pink bottom flapping up and down is not exactly compulsive viewing.
>
> *Doobie:* No. Well, I'm not looking either. I've got my eyes closed. He thinks it's ecstasy. What do you want, Chas?
>
> *Chas:* I'm looking for some SL advice, Doobie. It's kind of important.
>
> *Doobie:* Well, that's okay. Fire away. He doesn't know we're talking. And I'll throw him the odd titbit to keep him excited. LOL. How can I help?
>
> *Chas:* How well do you know Twist?

> *Doobie:* Not at all, really. I saw him when he came to talk to Sable, the owner of the club, about the harassment problem. That's about it.
>
> *Chas:* Well, I don't want to say too much, but Twist and I are colleagues in RL. Crime scene investigators. I specialise in photography.
>
> *Doobie:* Oh, wow! Cool. Real-life detectives.
>
> *Chas:* Not detectives, Doobie. We just collect evidence. That's all I'm going to tell you about who and where we are, but a few days ago we were at the home of a murder victim who turned out to have an account in Second Life.
>
> *Doobie:* Hey, Chas, this is getting exciting. Hang on a sec…

Doobie: Yeh, baby, gimme more. Yeh, that's it.

Jackin Thebox's bottom was still rising and falling between her legs.

> *Doobie:* Okay, how can I help?
>
> *Chas:* Well, somehow or other, all records of this guy's account got wiped off the Linden Lab database, so we know nothing about who he was in SL.
>
> *Doobie:* Do you have a name?
>
> *Chas:* Maximillian Thrust.
>
> *Doobie:* Do you know if he was in any Groups?
>
> *Chas:* Yes, he was. I don't know all of them.

He thought back to the names Hardy had rattled off from the file.

> *Chas:* Black Creek Saloon. AAA Club. Virtual Realty.
>
> *Doobie:* Tell you what, then. I'll do a little checking on these Groups, ask around a bit, see what I can find out for you. Oooh, this is exciting Chas!
>
> *She paused.*
>
> *Doobie:* I thought you said you weren't detectives.
>
> *Chas:* We're not, Doobs. Just…interested. You know?

Jackin: I'm cumming, baby, I'm cumming.

> *Doobie:* Oh, God. Duty calls. I'll let you know if I find anything. And leave now, please! No more peeping. I have to get rid of this guy, and I can't go before he cums. So to speak. LOL.

◇◇◇

Back at Twist's office, Chas saw that his partner in crime was still offline, and he wasn't quite sure what to do with himself. He wandered around, trying out different chairs and then the grand piano. He had never played a piano in his life, but suddenly he was a virtuoso.

He was distracted by the sound of a train hooting in the distance, and he went to the window as a miniature steam train hauling half a dozen open carriages chugged past. There were two passengers, who looked very much like giant pink dildos. They had name tags above them. *DJ Rob* and *Mistie Hax.* So they were clearly avatars. Chas frowned in confusion as the train dipped down under water, before emerging a minute later to follow the tracks up into the sky.

He turned around, then, and clicked to sit behind the desk in Twist's chair, fish drifting past his head in the aquarium behind him. He had barely time to register the Third Life welcome page on the computer screen when a double *ching* alerted him to the arrival of an IM.

> *Jamir:* Chas. You are a private detective?

Chas supposed that since his name was now on the Group list, people would see he was online and assume he was indeed a private detective, and that he knew what he was doing.

> *Chas:* Er…yes.
>
> *Jamir:* I need to talk to you. Can you send me a TP?

Chas began to panic. He had no idea how to send a TP. He saw that Jamir's full name was Jamir Jones and brought up his profile. Immediately he spotted an option to *Offer Teleport*. He clicked it and felt a certain amount of self-congratulatory satisfaction as he sent an invitation to Jamir to join him in the office on Jersey Island.

> *Chas:* The limousine is on its way.

After several seconds, a flash of light cleared to reveal a grey shape that gradually rezzed into what looked like a small orange dragon on the floor in front of his desk. The tag above its head read, *Pilot Jamir Jones*. Chas looked at the creature in astonishment, and when he had regained some composure typed a greeting.

> *Chas:* Hi, Jamir. How may I help you?
>
> *Jamir:* We've been threatened, Chas, and I'd like you to do something about it.
>
> *Chas:* Who threatened you?
>
> *Jamir:* A griefer called Nevar Telling. He's based on Sandbox Island.

Chas cocked an eyebrow. Sandbox Island. That's where Doobie had told him yesterday that she went griefer-hunting.

> *Chas:* Okay, why don't you start from the beginning, Jamir. Gimme a rundown.
>
> *Jamir:* Ok. Well. We were flying a jet, Roger and me. Then…
>
> *Chas:* And Roger is?
>
> *Jamir:* Beside me.

Chas was startled, dragging his eyes away from the dialogue box to see what appeared to be an identical creature on the floor beside Jamir, except that this one was blue. And was called Roger Showmun. Jamir, it seemed, had sent his friend a TP, and Chas hadn't noticed his arrival. Chas had the sense that he had somehow slipped out of the real, or even virtual, world into some surreal netherworld beyond any horizon known to man.

> *Chas:* Hi, Rog.
>
> *Jamir:* We heard a big crash on the wing. Then a hippy-hair-looking man called Nevar Telling told us ridiculous things. Here is a Notecard I recorded of our conversation.

Jamir passed Chas a Notecard, which opened up on his screen. It seemed to be a cut and pasted record of everything that had passed between the dragons and Nevar Telling. But made very little sense to him.

> *Chas:* What is it you'd like me to do, Jamir?
>
> *Jamir:* Well, if you look at the conversation, it was in caplock and was threatening me and Roger.

Chas was beginning to feel a sense of despair.

> *Chas:* So he just landed on the wing of your jet and bombarded you with these threats.
>
> *Roger:* Yes, and shot one of our passengers.

> *Chas:* What are you guys anyway, dragons?
>
> *Jamir:* Geckos.

Chas shook his head. He was having a conversation with giant geckos.

> *Chas:* And you were flying a jet?
>
> *Jamir:* Yes. Modern, luxury.
>
> *Chas:* Where to?
>
> *Jamir:* Nowhere. Just practising.
>
> *Chas:* You don't often find geckos flying jets.
>
> *Jamir:* Hehe. No
>
> *Chas:* So, to sum up, this Nevar Telling character threatened you, and shot one of your passengers?
>
> *Roger:* Yes, me and Jamir was shocked.
>
> *Chas:* Well, you need to take whatever it is geckos take to calm down, and let me look into this.

Ching-ching. Another IM came in. It was from Angel Catchpole.

> *Angel:* Hi, Chas. I'm just about to start a group session, if you want to join us.
>
> *Chas:* Two secs, Angel

He turned to the geckos.

> *Chas:* Listen, guys, I have a pressing appointment right now. Why don't you let me go and have a word with our friend, Nevar Telling, and I'll get back to you?
>
> *Jamir:* Okay. Thanks, Chas. Here are our cards for when you need to get in touch.

Offers of friendship arrived from each of the geckos, and he added them to his Friends List. A cash register sounded, and Chas was notified that Jamir had just paid him five hundred Lindens.

> *Jamir:* That's on account, Chas. We'll look forward to hearing from you.

And with that, the two geckos were gone, leaving Chas looking at the five hundred Lindens clocked up in green figures at the top of his screen. He had just earned his first fee as a private investigator. He sent a brief account of his meeting to Twist in an IM that would be waiting for him when he logged in. Then he remembered Angel.

> *Chas:* Hi Angel. Sorry to keep you waiting. How do I get there?

A window appeared almost immediately on his screen offering him a teleport to The Blackhouse, Poison Island.

Chapter Seventeen

Chas landed in full sunlight on a flat, empty stretch of sand that faded off to a blurred horizon as far as he could see in every direction. He immediately had a sense of something not quite right. Some primal instinct at work. The sand seemed divided by shallow waterways into square parcels. To the south he could see water, but no shoreline. Just a sharp division between the two. Tall, red FOR SALE obelisks spun in slow motion over several parcels, and as he stood, a large, black building began slowly to rez on the neighbouring plot.

He started walking toward it. He could have flown, but he felt as if he had less control in the air than on the ground, and something was telling him that he needed to stay in control. He waded through the waterway that separated the two parcels, and emerged closer to what was clearly The Blackhouse.

Gradually, as he got nearer, detail began to form. It seemed as if the building were constructed from some kind of black steel, welded together and studded with huge, round-headed rivets. Enormous double doors, three or four times Chas' own height, stood wide, and as he approached them he saw that giant, demonic heads with short, curling horns had been carved into each of them, glowing red opals in the place of eyes. He hesitated and peered inside. It was dark, in stark contrast to the white, dusty glare of the midday sun on the outside. He took several cautious steps through the doors and stopped.

There, in front of him, on a floor as black as the rest of the building, was a large pool of blood. Chas had seen blood left by murderers at many crime scenes over the years, but there was something chilling about this pool of it here in the middle of a virtual floor somewhere in the ether. He knew, of course, that it wasn't real. That he had no cause to be afraid. And yet, without reason, he felt uncomfortable. He tapped into Open Chat.

Chas: Hello?

And waited. There was no reply. Why had Angel sent him a TP to this place? It made no sense. He took several steps further inside and heard a loud creak, the sound of metal grinding against metal. He turned quickly, in time to see the giant doors close behind him. They shut with a resounding clang. And his discomfort turned to something very much like fear.

This was insane!

He fumbled to open up his Inventory and the Landmark folder within it. There, he found all the LMs Doobie had given him. He clicked on one and selected Teleport.

Nothing happened.

He tried again. The same. He tried another. Still nothing. Something about this place was disabling his ability to teleport out. He was trapped. There were no windows here, and he wondered how he could see. There was a light source somewhere, but he was unable to locate it. The blood on the floor seemed to glow in the dark. Carefully, he worked his way around it, anxious not to step in it, the crime scene investigator in him fastidious about not disturbing evidence. And as he reached the far side, he saw that someone, or something, had not taken the same care as he. There were trails through the blood, and tracks led out of it into a corridor that curved away out of sight. But they weren't footprints. They were clawmarks, as if some huge creature had feasted here amongst the blood and then dragged itself off down the corridor, leaving a bloody trail in its wake.

Chas supposed he still had the option to quit the program, to simply log out. But that, he reasoned, would be foolish. What could possibly happen to him? He tried to rationalise the tension he felt tightening across his chest. He was simply projecting real-life fears on to Second Life fantasy. None of this was real. He forced himself to relax and take deep breaths. And he started off along the corridor, following the trail of clawmarks.

As he rounded the curve, he saw light ahead, and moving further along, a row of small windows appeared, opening to the outside. Light fell into the building in long, misty yellow shafts. And the blood on the floor glowed even more vividly, caught in the beams. Chas forced himself on, keeping close to the wall, until finally the corridor opened into a vast, square arena, light pouring into it from tall windows on all sides. The bloody clawmarks led into the centre of the arena, where an even larger pool of blood reflected the light from the windows, steam rising from it into the gloom, as if the air were chill and the blood still fresh and warm.

Angel: Welcome.

Chas was momentarily startled, looking up to see a small group of people seated in a circle on a low stage at the far side of the arena.

Angel: We've been watching you. Well done. You were faster than most.

Chas walked toward the stage.

Chas: I don't understand.

Angel: A little psychological test. Had you failed it, I would have deemed you unsuitable for therapy in Second Life.

He saw her clearly now for the first time and knew that he would not have recognised her were it not for the tag above her head. She was dressed, head to foot, in deep purple, a long, flowing dress with a neckline cut almost to the naval. A silver-chained red pendant hung between ample breasts, a mirror of the earrings that hung like drops of blood from each lobe. Her face was the purest white, crimson lips cut like a deep slash across its lower half. Her eyes were the coldest, palest blue. Husky eyes. Black hair streaked with silver hung down below her waist, and in the crook of a very pale arm, she held open a large oxblood leather-bound tome, with the word *Spellbook* tooled into its front cover.

Chas: Well, what was the test?

Angel: The virtual world, Chas, affects different people in different ways. In spite of knowing that what we experience here is not real, some people are very deeply affected by it. They transfer real fears and feelings from the real world to the virtual, where the very nature of the experience is rooted deeply in our imaginations, tapping into the hidden depths of our psyche. Everything can seem more profound. More intense.

And Chas remembered Doobie's words from yesterday. *Human emotions—love, hate, jealousy, envy—are like the light that burns twice as bright but only half as long.*

Angel: And for some people that intensity can be dangerous. They become overtaken by their own emotions, in a way that neither they, nor I, can control. The experience is damaging. We require a certain inner strength to survive this second life intact.

Chas: So some people fail your test?

Angel: Oh, yes. Quite a number.

Chas: And how do they fail?

Angel: Some of them simply never cross the threshold. The very act of moving from bright sunlight into the dark unknown is too much for them. Then there are those who retreat at the sight of blood. Blood is symbolic, you see. Of life, and death. Of our own mortality. So many people go through life failing to come to terms with the fact that, in the end, they will die. Religion has, since the dawn of time, facilitated mankind's need for denial, faith feeding a belief that, after all, death can be defeated. It is the ultimate example of man's great capacity for self-deception. Then there are those who simply panic when the doors close. Some think to try to teleport out, some don't. But the brain freezes, paralysed by an irrational fear. After all, what harm can really become them here? All they have to do is log out. I'm sure that thought passed through your mind.

Chas: Yes.

He did not like feeling that he was so predictable, that every emotion he had gone through had been carefully choreographed, his responses to them falling into preordained categories. A psychologist's boxes ticked and checked.

Angel: But still you proceeded to the arena. Which demonstrates a depth of character that tells me you are mentally strong enough to join our little group.

Chas felt unaccountably annoyed. As if he had somehow been manipulated against his will, subjected to scrutiny, tried, tested and judged.

Chas: I suppose I should feel privileged then.

Angel: Yes, Chas, you should. You are already proving yourself stronger than your RL counterpart.

Chas realised that there was some truth in that. Not stronger, necessarily, but more confident. More like the man he had been before Mora's death. As if Chas was the part of himself that had died with her, and his ghost was in some way being resurrected here in Second Life, as in some virtual afterlife. It was a confusing and unsettling thought. After all, who would he be when he logged out again? Michael or Chas? Or was it possible that, with time, more and more of Chas would return with him to RL?

Angel: Come, take a seat. And I will introduce you to the group.

Chas climbed up on to the stage, where a single, empty seat awaited him. He clicked on it and sat. The others all had their heads turned toward him, watching in silence. There were five of them. He felt very self-conscious.

Angel: Laffa Minit has been attending our sessions for nearly six months now.

Laffa Minit made a small bow. She was a furry. A voluptuous female body with a rabbit's head and red, cupid lips.

Angel: Laffa has been involved in an extra-marital affair for over a year. She is trying to come to terms with conflicting emotions of guilt and addiction. Guilt, about the betrayal of her husband, and a hopeless psychological addiction to her lover. Unfortunately, the only progress we seem to have made—if we can call it that—is that Laffa now has another lover. In Second Life. Something we were debating before your arrival. But we'll come back to that.

Seated next to Laffa was a Goth called Demetrius Smith.

Angel: Demi also has a problem with addiction. Demi's addiction is sex, and I'm not so sure it wasn't a mistake introducing him to Second Life. Rather too many opportunities to indulge that addiction, am I right, Demi?

Demetrius: LOLOLOL!

Angel: And then there is Dark. Dark Daley. Dark has troubled, hidden fantasies, that we have still not persuaded him to share with us.

Chas looked at Dark. Of all the members of the group, he seemed the most normal, a young man with an untidy shock of brown hair. He was bare-chested, with a ring through his left nipple and a tattoo on his right shoulder. He wore baggy black trousers and no shoes.

Angel: And Tweedle Dum and Tweedle Dee are twins.

These were two dumpy, unattractive girls, with pigtails and identical blue pinafore dresses. Their feet didn't quite touch the floor, and their legs swung free, like bored children.

Angel: But only in Second Life. In real life they are lesbian lovers, each victims of child abuse at the hands of male relatives.

Chas shifted uncomfortably. This was clearly a group of very disturbed people, and it disturbed him to think that he was included among them.

Chas: Hi

No one replied.

Angel: So where were we? Ah, yes. The question of betrayal. I think that everyone accepts that by taking an RL lover, Laffa is betraying her husband, and compounding that betrayal by lies and deceit. Now, here is the moral question which has been testing us. Is she commiting the same act of betrayal by taking a lover in SL? Betraying, in fact, not only her husband, but her RL lover as well?

Dark: How can you betray someone in the real world by humping a cartoon in the virtual one? It's patently absurd.

Demetrius: No, it's not. Betrayal is in the mind. Betrayal of the flesh is only an extension of the mental treachery. So to take an SL lover is just as much of a betrayal as having an illicit partner in RL.

Dark: Crap!

Angel: No, it's an interesting point, Dark. It could be argued that all betrayal begins in the mind. Long before it ever turns to flesh.

Tweedle Dum: Depends whether you want to call it betrayal, or not. Just because you fall out of love with someone doesn't mean you're betraying them. It happens, that's all.

Tweedle Dee: Up to a point, maybe. But the betrayal begins, surely, when you start to lie. The betrayal is the deceit.

Dark: Oh, gimme a fucking break!

Chas was startled by this sudden lapse from the intellectual to the profane.

Dark: Take it to a fucking court, for Chrissake! What do you think they'd say? That she's been commiting adultery with a bunch of electrons on a computer screen? I don't think so. The fact that she's fucking some guy in RL, that's a different story. That's cheating, plain and simple, and if I knew who the poor husband was I'd fucking tell him.

Angel: One of Dark's not so hidden fantasies, Chas, is his desire to one day construct an entire sentence made up only of profanities. What do you think about it, Laffa?

Laffa: If I could stop crying for a moment, I might tell you.

Dark: Jesus Christ!

Tweedle Dum: Oh, grow up, Laffa. If you go around fucking everything on three legs then you gotta expect to field a bit of flak.

Laffa: Okay, since you're all so frigging perfect, let me tell you what I think. I think the only reason I've taken a lover in SL is because I'm so unhappy in RL. And because my SL lover makes me happy, I am able to carry some of that happiness with with me back into RL. And both my husband and my lover benefit. So they should be grateful.

Dark: Yeh, like you're doing them such a favour.

Laffa: Why do you always have to be so negative? You're a sarcastic bastard, Dark. Always happy to talk about others. Never about yourself. And your secret fantasies. You're probably just some perv child molester!

Chas felt the tension in the group ratchet up another few notches.

Angel: What do you think, Chas?

Chas was startled. He had not expected to have to contribute.

Chas: Er…I don't know. To be honest, it's not something I've ever given any thought to.

Demetrius: You don't have to think about it. You hear an argument. You get a gut feeling. What's yours?

Chas: Well, probably I'd be with Angel on this. The first betrayal is always in the mind.

Tweedle Dee: That is just so much shit. So you've got a lover, right? And you're out on your own somewhere for the night without her. And some chick hits on you. Your hormones kick in, you fuck her. You never see her again. It's a one-night stand. You never thought about it beforehand, you never think about it again. Means nothing to you. Purely physical. But do you think your lover's going to see it that way? Will she, hell! Betrayal's just as much physical as it is mental. It can be one, or the other, or both. It all counts.

Tweedle Dum: So is that what happened with you and that girl at Twinkle's?

Tweedle Dee: What?

Tweedle Dum: What was her name, Rachel? The one with the implants.

Tweedle Dum: Aw, for Chrissake, don't start that again!

Angel: No, let's not. I'm not sure that we've exhausted the subject, but maybe we should come back to it another time. Chas, why don't you tell us why you're here?

Chas stiffened. Immediately tense, and glad that no one could see his discomfort beyond the screen.

Chas: I'm here because you asked me to be.

Dark: LOLOLOL! Good avoidance technique, Chas. Almost as good as mine.

Angel: Okay, let me kick this off for you. Chas is having difficulty dealing with the death of his wife.

Demetrius: How long since she died?

Chas: A little over six months.

Dark: Oh, for Chrissake, man! Get over it.

Laffa: Yeh, who're you grieving for? Her or you?

Tweedle Dee: People die, Chas. Didn't you know? Happens to us all someday. Nothing we can do for the ones who're gone, except get on with the living.

Chas was startled by the brutality of this response. Angel had always trodden gently around the subject, getting him to explore his feelings, suggesting ways that he might be able to come to terms with his loss.

Demetrius: I never did hold with this grieving thing. The death of a loved one is always a shock. But we get over shocks. Personally, I think the Irish have got it right. Hold a wake. Have a party. Celebrate the life that's gone. Grief, in the end, is nothing more than self-pity.

There was a long silence then. And Chas felt that all their eyes were on him.

Angel: Well, Chas. Was that the kind of response you expected?

Chas: I didn't know what to expect. Not abuse, certainly.

Dark: Well, you won't get much sympathy from this lot. We've all got our own problems, bud. And there probably isn't anyone here who hasn't lost a loved one. So get your head out of your butt and get on with your life.

Angel: Okay, okay. I think you've made your views clear enough. We have all, at one time or another, had the opportunity to tell our own stories. So next time, we'll listen to Chas. And he can tell us exactly why he's having such difficulty coming to terms with his wife's death.

But Chas knew there was no way he was going to tell these people anything. Exposing his soul to them would be like throwing meat to a flock of vultures. It was clear that they would simply pick over the remains of his love for Mora without any regard for his feelings or any attempt at understanding them.

He told Angel as much when the session drew to a close. The others had drifted off, and he was left standing with her in the arena on his own. She shook her head.

Angel: It's hard, Chas, I know. But people are like that in SL. Maybe not just SL. Maybe it's the Internet. People are never face-to-face or eye-to-eye. And somehow they seem to think that frees them from all the usual social obligations of politeness and tact. Look at any of the online forums. Bloody, brutal battlegrounds sometimes, where bile flows freely and people give expression to things they would never say to your face. Here they have their AV's to hide behind. They are anonymous and say what they like.

The sun was sinking low in the sky now, and red light fell in long slabs across the arena floor, light reflecting in the large pool of blood, steam still rising like smoke into the evening light.

Through the window, Chas saw the sun almost on the horizon, sending yellow diamonds sparkling across the broken surface of the ocean toward them.

Chas: Maybe that's true, Angel. But I don't have to put myself in the firing line.

Angel: Don't be so touchy, Chas. The group approach is a very different kind of therapy. You need to let go. Of whatever emotion it is that's messing with your mind. Whether it be anger, pity, hurt…Let those feelings out. Direct them at others. Because they will direct theirs at you.

Chas: I noticed.

Angel: But don't you see, Chas, it's a release for everyone. Of all that tension that builds up inside us. It's all we ever really need. Tension is like pressure contained without any means of escape. If we can't find a release valve, in the end we will either blow up or implode. And remember, these people don't know who you are. And you don't know them. You would pass each other in the street without recognition. So there is no past, no future, only the present, when we are all together in the group. Give it a chance. If you're still not happy after the third of fourth session, then call it a day. But you've come this far. Don't turn back at the first hurdle.

Chas noticed a blue banner flashing on and off the foot of his screen. Twist had just come on line. He decided to change the subject and looked around the vast interior of the black metal building. For the first time, he noticed a grilled staircase spiralling up to another level and wondered what was up there.

Chas: What is this place, Angel?

Angel: It was owned by a group of graphics programmers, Chas. Used to be a Goth club, I believe. I bought it from them. It was ideal for my purposes. They wrote the scripts for me, for the pools of blood and the claw marks. Pretty realistic, huh?

Chas: Scarily so, Angel. And I've seen some blood in my time.

Angel: LOL, Chas. So you have.

A teleport invitation appeared from Twist.

Chas: I have to go, Angel.

Angel: You'll come to the next session?

Chas sighed.

Chas: IM me with a day and time, and if I can I'll be there.

Angel Catchpole smiles.

Angel: Good. Well, TC then, Chas.

Chas: TC?

Angel: LOL. Take care.

Chas clicked to accept Twist's teleport, and in a rush of sound his screen went black.

Chapter Eighteen

Chas dropped to the ground, crouching to keep his balance, and then stood up as a grey figure before him rezzed into the grinning Twist. He still hadn't got used to seeing Janey as a man, with long red and blond hair and a bare chest. He looked around, as a large floor area divided by tall partitions took shape around him. Promos for combat systems and teleporters and object scanners covered the walls.

Twist: Hiya.

Chas: Hi. Where are we?

Twist: The TalTech Weapons store at the Galleria.

Chas: What are we doing here?

Twist: I got your IM. About the geckos. LOLOLOLOL. Very SL. Hahahaha. If you're planning to go to Sandbox Island to talk to Nevar Telling, we need to get you some protection first.

Chas: I've got a gun.

Twist: Not enough.

Chas: And a radar system. Doobie made me buy that yesterday.

Twist: Who's Doobie?

Chas could almost feel the jealous aggression in the question.

Chas: Doobie Littlething. She's one of the dancers at Sinful Seductions. She was the one that dealt with Tommy Tattoo.

Twist: And the one you took to dinner?

Chas: Yeh.

Twist: Hmmph. Well, you still need more than that. What you really want is a shield and weapons system combined.

Chas: Do I?

Twist: Yes, you do. And I've found two things here that I think you should buy.

He turned toward the wall.

Twist: These two. The Immortals Combat System, and the gKill HUD. They should provide you with protection against just about anything, as well as giving you a whole range of attack options. A blinder, a trap, a trasher and several kill versions. You'll need to familiarise yourself with it all before you go in the field, though. Don't want to be fumbling with a menu when someone's bearing down on you all guns blazing.

Chas: I'm not sure I like the sound of any of this, Twist. Doobie took me to a beautiful island yesterday, with mountains and trees and waterfalls. Not a weapons system in sight.

Twist: Yeh, well, just like the real world, Chas, SL has many sides to it. But if you want to go to Sandbox Island you need to be prepared. Just like when you have sex for the first time, it'll be helpful if you have a dick.

Chas looked at the weapons systems that Twist wanted him to buy. The gKill HUD claimed that it would break through shields and attack a target from anywhere on the grid until told to stop. The Immortals Combat System allowed you to deform avatars with a trasher. He sighed.

Chas: How much for all this?

Twist: A grand total of twelve hundred and fifty. Cheap at the price.

Chas: I don't have that much Twist. I haven't had a chance to set up a credit card yet.

Twist: How much you got, then?

Chas glanced at his green Lindens total and frowned. And kept staring at it for a full fifteen, maybe twenty seconds.

Twist: Well?

Chas: There must be some mistake.

Twist: How much?

Chas: According to this I have 780 million Lindens.

Twist: Hahahaha. Yeh, right. Must be a screw-up with the server. That would be around three million dollars. You don't have three million dollars, do you, Chas?

Chas: No, I do not.

Twist: Hey, I thought you were rich.

Chas: If I was rich, I wouldn't be back at work having to put up with people like you.

Twist: Hahaha. So what happened to all Mora's money?

Chas: Gone, most of it, Twist. And Mora's first husband's family look like getting most of the balance. The house is worth a few million, but there's a home loan on it that I can't pay, and the bank's foreclosing. So chances are I'm going to walk away without a penny.

Twist: Shit, Chas, that's rough. And there was me thinking I could seduce you and marry into a fortune. But, hey, maybe I still can if you've got three million in your SL account.

Chas: How is that possible, Twist?

Twist: It's not. It'll be a phantom figure, Chas. A glitch. It'll probably be gone when you relog.

Chas: Well, I know that at least 500 of it's mine. From the geckos.

Twist: So get the gKill HUD and we'll come back for the Immortals another time.

Chas paid for the weapons system, and the SL cash register rang up the expenditure. Almost at the same moment, an IM came in from Doobie.

Doobie: I found out a bit about your murder victim, Chas. Well, about his AV anyway.

Chas: Great, Doobs. What did you learn?

Doobie: Well, I learned that this guy was a bigshot dealer in SL land sales. Virtual Realty was his Group. Massive turnover in the purchase and sale of offshore sims.

Chas: Sims?

Doobie: Short for simulators. A sim is just a parcel of virtual land. People buy and sell property here, and some of them make a fortune.

Chas: Wow!

Doobie: But there's more. He owned property himself, Chas. A tropical island called Pitaya in a group of islands known as the Fruit Islands. Beautiful. Absolutely gorgeous. He'd just built a house on the island. A stunning asian home. I'm there right now.

A pause.

Doobie: Chas?

Chas: Yeh?

Doobie: This guy was murdered in real life, yes?

Chas Chesnokov nods

Doobie: How was he killed?

Chas: Shot three times in the chest

There was a long silence.

Chas: Doobie, are you still there?

Doobie: He was killed the same way in SL, Chas.

Chas frowned.

Chas: I don't understand.

Doobie: Someone shot his AV three times in the chest at the house here in Pitaya.

Chas: How can you possibly know that?

Doobie: Well, someone might have erased his account from the database, but his AV's corpse is still here in the house. Lying where it was shot.

Chapter Nineteen

Chas and Twist teleported into the house almost simultaneously. Doobie, dressed in a sober, tailored grey suit, her hair tied back, stood in the middle of the shambles that was the interior of the house. Sunlight streamed in through enormous picture windows on either side.

Twist: Is someone going to tell me what's going on?

Chas: Arnold Smitts was in Second Life, Twist. He had an AV called Maximillian Thrust. He was a bigshot land dealer in here, and this is his house,

Twist: So?

Chas looked around for the body.

Chas: Where is he, Doobs?

Doobie climbed over a jumble of beams and planking, disjointed sections of floor and wall, and through a moongate that led to the bedroom. They scrambled after her. Maximillian Thrust lay in an oddly twisted heap between two sections of floor that had been pushed up, as if by an earthquake. There were three gaping holes in the centre of his chest. There was animated blood all over his torso, and it was pooling on the floor beneath him.

Twist: Jesus Christ! How's that possible? He must have been logged out for days.

Chas: Even more impossible, Twist. There is no record in the Linden Lab database that he ever existed.

Twist: So how's his AV still here?

Doobie: Because it's not his AV.

They both turned to look at her.

Chas: How do you mean?

Doobie: Well, it can't be. It has to be a clone.

Chas: Explain.

Doobie: Not an explanation, Chas, just a guess. His AV was shot with a scripted gun of some kind. Most weapons in SL fire scripts at their targets that generate the desired graphic effect. Smoke, fire, a cage, whatever. My guess would be that the script in this gun actually destroyed the original AV, but made a clone of the victim, showing the damage and the blood. And that's what we're seeing here.

Twist: That makes sense, Doobie. I'm Twist, by the way. Since Chas doesn't seem to be going to introduce us.

Doobie: Hi, Twist.

Chas: What we have here, then, is a virtual crime scene. Undisturbed. So we should be able to piece together at least part of what happened.

He looked around.

Chas: How the hell did the house get into this state? It looks like it got blitzed by something at the top end of the Richter Scale.

Twist: Something pretty close to that, I'd say. The only

way you could do this amount of damage, Chas, would be if you were in Edit mode.

Chas: What's that?

Doobie: A mode you go into when you are building, so you can move stuff around.

Twist: Thrust must have panicked when he was attacked, and hit the wrong button. If he went into Edit, everything he touched would have started shifting around with him. Just like a real earthquake.

Everything had been moved or dislocated. Whole sections of floor and wall buckled out of place. The ceiling was dragged down almost to the floor in one corner.

Chas: So how come none of this has been disturbed since it happened?

Doobie: Because the whole place still belongs to Maximillian Thrust. If you click on the name of the property—it's written in blue at the top of the screen—it will bring up the Land Window. That tells you who owns the property, and how many prims it supports.

Chas: Prims?

Twist: Primitives. The name given to the bits that go to make up everything in SL. It's a kind of measurement of processing power. Every object has a prim value in here.

Doobie: Anyway, the Land Window shows Maximillian Thrust as the owner. And there's a rock out there on the beach where you pay your tiers. Thrust was paid up for several weeks to come, so no one would have been coming to reclaim the property for some time.

Chas sighed.

Chas: One of these days we'll get back to speaking English. What are tiers?

Doobie Littlething smiles.

Doobie: Even though you own a property, Chas, you still have to pay a kind of rental on it. Land-use fees. They're called tiers. How do you think Linden Lab make their money?

Twist: Better take some pictures, Chas. You are the photographer, after all.

Chas: How do I do that?

Twist: There's a Snapshot button on your toolbar. You can work it out yourself from there.

Chas found that he could easily line up the shots he wanted to take, just like using a real camera, uploading to his Inventory and then downloading to his desktop, so that he had RL and SL copies of each.

He took pictures of the body from various angles and of the interior damage to the house, and was able to give copies to Twist and Doobie by dragging them on to their AVs.

Chas: How about we take a look outside?

He clicked on the door. But it wouldn't open.

Doobie: Both doors are locked.

Chas: How did you get in, then?

Doobie smiles knowingly.

Doobie: Same way we're going to get out. An old griefer's trick.

Twist: You know it, Chas. It's almost the first thing I showed you.

Doobie climbed over the broken floor to the door and zoomed in, swivelling tight on it to get an exterior perspective. Chas did the same and watched as Doobie rezzed a couple of poseballs from her Inventory onto the wooden deck outside.

Doobie: Just click on the blue.

Chas right-clicked, and his AV immediately appeared out on the deck, standing legs astride, arms open wide. Doobie clicked on the pink, and her AV ran to Chas, throwing herself into his arms, crossing her legs behind his back, and the two turned two full circles before locking together in a long, passionate kiss.

Twist stood watching impatiently from inside.

Twist: When you two are finished, would you mind vacating a poseball so I can get out of here!

They both detached themselves, and Twist materialised out on the deck, disentangling himself quickly from the animation. Chas stood breathing heavily.

Chas: Wow! Wasn't expecting that.

Doobie Littlething smiles

Doobie: Sorry about that. It's called Awaited Embrace. First poseballs I could lay my hands on.

Twist: Yeh, right.

The three AVs stood looking around them. Asian windchimes made a constant musical accompaniment to the ambient sound of SL and the constant crashing of waves on the beach. Wooden steps led down to a pier, where a junk with a red-and-black striped sail was anchored. Torches flamed on the end of long uprights strategically placed to light the garden at night. Sunloungers with sunbathing and cuddle animations sprawled on the deck, and at the side of the house, a wooden bridge arched over a small stream to a tiny, sandy island shaded by leaning palms, where deckchairs were arranged around a campfire.

A path led round the side of the house to the back, where another landing stage providing docking for a red-sailed yacht anchored between the uprights of a tall Japanese gate. Hanging lanterns provided light for a circular table and half a dozen seats where food was set out for a picnic. More stairs led up to a raised deck, another Japanese gate, and a swinging bench seat with a view across the property. A screen of sand dunes hid the far side of the island from view. It was empty, as yet undeveloped.

Chas followed a wooden path around the edge of the dunes and climbed steps down to yet another deck. Slow-dance pose-balls were placed with a view through a third Japanese gate toward the spot on the horizon where the sun would set. He wondered with whom Maximillian Thrust might have danced in the red light of the setting sun, or whether they had been placed there in anticipation, or hope, of future romance.

Doobie: It's a stunning property.

Chas turned to see Doobie and Twist coming down the steps to join him.

Chas: What will happen to it when the tiers fall due again?

Doobie: If they remain unpaid, ownership will revert to the sim owners, and everything you see will automatically be returned to Thrust's inventory.

Twist: Which doesn't exist.

Doobie: No. Which, I guess, means that they will simply be deleted from the asset server. Lost forever. Like most things in SL, nothing lasts for very long. Someone else will buy the island, and six weeks from now you won't be able to recognise it.

Twist walked to the edge of the deck and stared out over the ocean. Distant islands had partially rezzed close to the horizon.

Twist: What I don't understand is how it was possible to actually "kill" Thrust's AV. I mean, I know we can do passing damage to avatars. But it's not usually permanent. And I've never heard of anyone actually being able to destroy one.

Doobie: No.

She paused.

Doobie: But clearly someone did.

Chas: How?

Twist: Well, if anyone in SL can tell us, it's Kuro.

Doobie: Who?

Twist: Gunslinger Kurosawa. He crafts some of the best weapons in SL. It's where we got Chas his handgun the other day.

◇◇◇

Kurosawa sat behind his desk, feet up in his favourite animation, glancing from time to time at his watch, as if he was impatient to be rid of them. Twist and Doobie sat in leather client chairs, and Chas stood with his back to the window. A green laser security beam moved disconcertingly about the office, and downstairs they could hear Kurosawa's guard dog barking.

Kurosawa had been giving the notion that a script might be able to destroy an AV some silent thought.

Kurosawa: I guess it would be possible. You hear rumours of such things. But I've never actually seen one that would do it.

Twist: How would it work, Kuro?

Gunslinger Kurosawa releases a long, thoughtful sigh.

Kurosawa: Well, like Doobie suggests, it'll be a script of some sort. Something pretty sophisticated. Way beyond my abilities as a programmer. The only way it could actually destroy the AV would be by hacking into the main server and deleting it. Cloning it and creating bullet wounds and blood, is just a bit of window dressing. A bit of fun for the programmer.

Chas: Is that possible? I mean, that someone could write a script that could hack into the mainframe?

Kurosawa: In theory, yes. In practice very difficult, but not beyond the bounds of possibility. In this world, my friend, almost anything is possible.

Twist: So if the script hacked into Linden Lab's main server to delete the AV, presumably it could also delete the whole account and any record of it.

Kurosawa: Sure. Once you've actually hacked your way in, you could write your script to do whatever you wanted.

Chas: Which would explain why there's no record of Maximillian Thrust ever existing.

Twist: It also means that whoever killed him in SL probably murdered him in RL. So we're looking for a killer in both worlds.

Doobie suddenly interrupted.

Doobie: Hey, guys. Fascinating though this is, I'm afraid I've gotta go. Rendezvous with a client. Seeya.

Her head tipped up to the top left of her screen as she selected an LM, and then she vanished.

◇◇◇

When they got back to the office, Twist jumped into the seat behind his desk and sat gazing idly at his screen. Chas slipped into the client chair opposite and crossed his legs. Each was lost in wordless contemplation of a question that neither was sure he was ready to address. It was Chas, finally, who broke the silence.

Chas: What are we going to do about this, Twist?

Twist O'Lemon shakes his head.

Twist: I don't know. What do you think?

Chas: I think if we were being sensible about it, we would pass on everything we know and leave it to the pros.

Twist: But?

Chas sighed beyond the screen.

Chas: Well, I can just hear us telling Laurel and Hardy that we are private investigators in Second Life, and that we think Arnold Smitts' AV was murdered in the virtual world before someone killed him in the real one.

Twist: Yeh, and that his AV was shot with a virtual gun that hacked into Linden's computer and erased his account. I've been sitting here myself trying to make any of it sound like the reasonable conclusion of a sane person. I mean, by the time they stopped laughing and asked us if we had any proof, what would we say? Yeh, sure, there's a body and a crime scene. Come with us into SL and we'll show you.

Chas: FSS would have us up for psychological evaluation before you could say, "What's your prim count?" And you know what? I'm not sure I'd pass.

Twist: So what are we going to do?

Chas: I think we need to follow up on this ourselves, Twist, until we come up with something a little less virtual, and a little more concrete. And, anyway, you wanted to be a private detective, didn't you?

Twist: Hahaha, yeh. Quite exciting, isn't it?

Chas: Scary, Twist. I think that's the word I'd use for it. I'd be happy if it was all a little less real and a little more virtual.

They continued to mull it over in silence until Twist introduced an abrupt change of subject.

Twist: So tell me about Doobie Littlething.

Chas: Nothing to tell, Twist. She's a dancer at Sinful Seductions.

Twist: More than a dancer, I'd say. She was pretty smart to track down Thrust's AV to that island.

Chas: She knows her way around SL, that's for sure. She's been in for three years. And she's certainly smart. Gave me a thrashing at chess yesterday.

Twist: You were playing chess? Was that before or after you took her to dinner?

Chas Chesnokov grins.

Chas: Why? Are you jealous, Twist?

Twist: How could I be jealous? I'm a guy, remember.

Twist paused for a moment.

Twist: She said she had a rendezvous with a client. What kind of business is she in?

Chas: The sex business. She's an escort.

Twist: Ah. Ok. Lots of girls in here are. Easy way of making money. Hard work, but risk free. Unlike RL.

Chas: Twist…How does it work?

Twist: What?

Chas: Sex in SL. I mean, I know you get these poseballs, and I've actually seen Doobie with a client. But that's just cartoons humping. I mean, there must be more to virtual sex than that, surely?

Twist O'Lemon smiles.

Twist: You want a demonstration?

Chas: Not with a man, thank you. But maybe you could show me how it works when we're back in RL.

Twist: Yeh, dream on.

Chas smiled but knew that in reality Janey would jump at the chance, even if Twist wouldn't. It was unfair to tease her.

Twist: By the way, are you still showing that three million dollars at the top of your screen?

Chas glanced up.

Chas: Yes.

Twist: Hummm. Maybe you should try logging out and logging in again.

It took Chas thirty seconds to transition through the log-out/log-in process. He checked his screen again.

Chas: It's still there.

Twist: Very strange. Well, keep an eye on it, Chas. I'm sure it's either a glitch or a mistake of some kind, but you don't really want to be sitting there with three million dollars' worth of unexplained cash in your account.

Chas was thoughtful.

Chas: No. No, I don't.

◇◇◇

By the time he logged off and became aware again of his real life surroundings, Michael saw that he had missed the sunset. It was dark out on the terrace as he wandered out with a glass of wine in his hand. Since opening that first bottle with Angela, he had decided that he should drink as much of it as he could before her late husband's family laid claim to it. Mora had bought it to drink after all, not as an investment.

He sipped on the pale pinot noir, a vintage from the Ambullneo winery near Santa Maria, and let the smooth, silky, oaken vanilla of it slide back over his tongue. On the peninsula, beyond Balboa Island, the ferris wheel and the Maritime Museum were all lit up, a tracery of neon light. The sky was almost as black and star-studded as those he had seen in Second Life, and the sound of the ocean mimicked the ambient atmosphere of the virtual world. A plane roared overhead, outbound from John Wayne Airport. Something you never heard in SL.

It was strange how quickly it had all got under his skin, how rapidly Chas had taken on a life of his own. But one thing, at least, that both Michael and Chas had in common, was a growing sense of unease about the real and virtual parallels in the murders of Arnold Smitts and Maximillian Thrust. Michael knew that they should tell the police what they had discovered. But he also knew that Janey was right. They would be laughed out of court. Literally.

His thoughts were disturbed by the telephone ringing in his office. He closed his eyes and tried to ignore it, as he had done several times while he was online. When it stopped, the silence was deafening, and he couldn't stand it any longer. He carried his glass back to his desk and sat down. A winking red light told him that there were several messages. He pressed a button to listen to the first of them, and was greeted by the velvet tones of Mr. Yuri of the State Bank of Southern California.

"Mr. Kapinsky, I just wanted to let you know that the bank has had a report back on the appraisal of your property. We're having to cut our losses, I'm afraid. In the current marketplace, the house has been valued at $2.75 million. So we will be selling to the first bidder who comes closest to that figure. Which, unfortunately, will still leave you owing us $433,000. I'd be obliged if you would call my secretary to arrange a meeting to discuss the current value of your stocks and shares, and any other assets you may possess. Have a good evening."

Michael closed his eyes again and felt his hands trembling. He didn't have the heart to listen to any more messages. But the phone was not about to give him any peace. Its shrill warble filled the office once more. He opened his eyes and snatched the receiver.

"Yes?"

"Michael, where have you been? Did you not get my messages? I've been trying to get hold of you all evening." Michael drew a long, silent breath. Sherri was just about the last person on earth he wanted to hear from right now.

"I've been busy, Sherri."

"We've had an offer for the house, Michael. The couple who were there the other day."

Hope flared momentarily in his heart. "Tell me."

"They've offered $2.6. But I think I can push them up another $100,000."

Michael felt as if he were spinning backwards through space. There was to be no last minute reprieve. "It's out of my hands, Sherri. The bank have valued it at $2.75 million. And they are going to be selling it without further reference to me." There was a long silence, in which he could feel her anger transmitting itself across the ether.

"You signed a three-month, exclusive contract with me, Michael. I have spent a lot of money on photographs, promotional material, and advertising. Now it turns out you don't really own the house at all. The bank does. You had no right to enter into that contract. I want compensation, do you understand? Expect to hear from my lawyers."

Michael heard the phone slam down at the other end of the line. He took a deep breath and poured another glass of wine, and thought that maybe tonight he would need to open a second bottle.

Chapter Twenty

It had been a long day. Michael had spent most of the afternoon at the home of a rape victim, photographing evidence. Blood and semen stains, a knife left behind by the attacker, the clear signs of a desperate struggle, that had taken place during an hour-long ordeal.

Although the perpetrator had been caught later in possession of items taken from his victim's suburban villa, rape was never easy to prove. And so began the long process of putting together the evidence that would ensure a conviction. It was all the motivation Michael ever needed to be meticulous in the execution of his job.

One by one he slid the selected prints into their plastic sleeves and clipped them into a folder, then returned to his cubicle to print out labels for each of them.

He always paused for a moment when he sat down, to take in the framed picture of Mora that he had placed on his desk. She gazed back at him from a moment captured in the past to a future where she no longer existed, and to the lover who mourned her. He felt caught by her eyes, a look in them he had always recognised as love, a hunger for him. With Mora he had never felt so wanted or so loved. And now he felt abandoned. And there was something buried deep inside him that he had never quite managed to expunge. Something he had tried many times to rationalise. Something he knew was neither fair, nor worthy of him. Something very much like anger with her for leaving him like this.

"Hey, kiddo."

He turned around as Janey slid into his cubicle and pulled up a seat beside him. She had a conspiratorial air about her, her face flushed a little with some secret excitement. She pushed her glasses back up her nose, peered over the cubicle wall to check if there was anyone nearby, then dropped down again and leaned toward him. She spoke in a stage whisper.

"Listen. That money in your account."

"What about it?"

"It's real."

Michael looked at her, a dead stillness in him. "How can you possibly know that?"

She glanced over her shoulder and huddled even closer. "Listen, you've got to promise me you'll tell nobody about this."

"Janey…"

"Promise, Mike."

"Okay, I promise."

She smiled. "I have a part-time job."

"Jesus, Janey, FSS will bump you if they find out."

"Well, duh! Why do you think I'm swearing you to secrecy?"

"Doing what?"

"Working for Linden Lab."

He looked at her in disbelief. "You're kidding me. Why?"

She sighed. "Well, I guess I needed a reason to justify spending all those hours in SL. To myself, I mean."

"Well, why do you?"

"Jesus, Mike, I'm lonely, you know? Last time anyone asked me out on a date was nearly two years ago. And I'm not getting any younger. I have friends in there, a social life, a reason to get out of bed in the morning."

He looked at her with pity welling in his heart. She deserved better.

"Don't look at me like that!"

"What's the job?"

"I'm an inworld accounts assistant. I set up accounts for people and deal with any problems that arise. And for that, I have access to the database."

"Hi, guys." A secretary from the administrator's office drifted by, clutching a handful of papers. Janey waited until she had gone.

"There was a six-month trial and assessment period before I got that access. I'm a trusted employee now." She drew a long breath. "The point is, Mike, I was able to get in to have a look at your account and see where that money came from."

"And?"

She shook her head. "Couldn't tell. But here's the thing..." She lowered her voice even further. "It's real, Mike. No mistake, no doubt. That is three million real dollars sitting in your account. And you can bet that someone, somewhere is going to come looking for it sometime real soon."

Michael could almost feel the blood draining from his face. Janey looked at him blankly for a moment, then he saw suspicion, followed by disbelief, dawning in her eyes, and he could no longer meet them.

"Michael, that money is still *in* your account, isn't it?"

He felt the beginnings of panic. "Not exactly."

"Well, either it is, or it isn't."

"It isn't." And then he added quickly, "But I can get it back."

"Mike!" She raised her voice almost to a shout, then became suddenly self-conscious and grabbed his arm. Her voice dipped again to barely a hiss. "What have you done?"

"The bank was going to take the house, Janey, and give me way less than the value of the loan and the payment arrears. I was going to end up in serious debt."

"You used that money to pay off your home loan?" Realisation washed over her like ice cold water.

"It's just temporary. Like a loan from SL, till the house sells. Then I'll pay it back."

She stared at him in wide-eyed disbelief. "Jesus, Mike! Three million dollars! You'd better just pray that whoever it belongs to doesn't want it back in a hurry."

◇◇◇

Michael picked up his car from the lot outside the Newport Beach Police Department, where it had soaked up the sun all day and still held its residual warmth. A cooling breeze was blowing now off the ocean, stirring the limp fronds of the palm trees that lined the road. The sky was turning puce in the west, where long strips of grey-pink cloud were gathering along the horizon. He sat holding the steering wheel with both hands and lowered his head on to his arms.

How could he have been so stupid!

He had done it on an impulse. In a moment of desperation, somehow convincing himself that the cash wasn't real. It was money that existed only in a virtual world, after all. How could it be? Until the transfer had gone through, and his debit account had been credited with $3,183,637 very real dollars. And he had felt a strange chill run through him. But the deed had been done. Whatever action he had taken then, that money would forever have shown up as having been in his bank account. Even if he had paid it straight back into Second Life. There was an electronic, forensic trail that led directly from one to the other.

And so he had simply closed his eyes to the consequences, telling himself that he would pay it back when the house was sold, and then find some means of explaining it away to the taxman when he came knocking at the door.

He had felt, for just a few moments, exultant as he walked out of the bank. The house was his. No more home loan, no more arrears. Mr. Yuri had, for once, been speechless. It had almost been worth it for that alone.

He lifted his head and peered through the gathering gloom into an uncertain future. He had hoped to hold off on a sale until he could realise the full value of the property. But he knew now that he would have to push Sherri for as quick a sale as possible, even if he didn't get the full market value, and put that money back into the SL account. He sat clutching at straws. Maybe whoever owned it had no idea where it was. Maybe no one would ever come looking for it. He sighed, shaking his head at his own naivety. And maybe pigs would fly.

He pulled out of the parking lot, turning right into Santa Barbara Drive and then left on to Jamboree, before taking another left at the next set of lights and heading up into the sprawling Fashion Island shopping mall.

The parking lot opposite Circuit City shimmered under the streetlamps in the evening heat as he pulled into a slot, and as he crossed to the escalators and rode up to the main mall level the last light was leached out of the sky by the fall of night. There were already queues outside P. F. Chang's China bistro. He pushed past the chattering crowds awaiting their table call, and into the California Pizza Kitchen, where they had his Cajun Pizza ready and waiting. It smelled mouth-wateringly delicious. Blackened chicken and spicy andouille sausage with a creole sauce, roasted red and yellow peppers and mozzarella cheese. But somehow tonight, he had no appetite for it, and knew it would sit on the kitchen counter getting cold as he opened another bottle of Mora's wine and fretted about his stupidity.

As he came back down the escalators he saw, across the car-park, two shadowy figures at the door of his SUV. One of them appeared to be bending down to peer inside, while the other walked around the back and tried to lift the tailgate.

"Hey!" MICHAEL shouted at the top of his voice, and he took the remaining stairs two at a time, nearly falling as he reached the foot of the escalator. He ran across the road, almost dropping his pizza as a car horn blasted and a vehicle swerved to avoid him in a screech of tyres. He ran between the potted palms and out across the asphalt. His SUV stood, where he had left it, all on its own between a set of angled white lines near the back of the lot. There was no one anywhere near it. He looked around, heart pumping, to see if he could spot the figures he had seen from the escalator. But there was nobody around. He turned as a car engine burst into life and its headlights laid down two conical beams across the tarmac. The vehicle pulled away, and

Michael saw that its occupants were a young man and his girl eating ice creams and laughing.

He walked the rest of the way to his SUV and made a quick tour around it. There didn't seem to be any damage. He unlocked it with his remote and slipped inside. He laid the pizza box on the passenger seat and let out a long sigh of relief, as a leather-gloved hand came around from behind his head and clamped itself over his mouth. Iron fingers almost crushed his jaw. He could smell the leather of the gloves, and he felt cold metal pressing into the side of his neck.

"Do not move a single, fucking muscle, you understand?" It wasn't the low rasp of the voice in his ear that stopped him from moving. He was paralysed by pure, naked fear.

The shadow of another hand came around from behind, only this time it wasn't leather he smelled. It was something medical. Something that made him think of hospitals. He only recognised it at the last moment. As a warm, damp, cloth was folded over his nose. Chloroform. Not very original, but very effective. He tried to hold his breath, tensing against the pressure of the hands from behind. But it wasn't long before the weight pushing down on his chest caused him to gasp for air, and he choked, and coughed, and saw the world fade away.

Chapter Twenty-One

He seemed to be tethered to something anchored at the bottom of the sea. He couldn't breathe, or move, but had the sensation of floating, as if in water. It was impossible to open his eyes. And as oxygen starvation increased, the pressure in his chest became almost unbearable. He tried to draw breath through his mouth, but something was stopping it. And then, as he thought despair might steal away all reason, he found himself sucking air in through his nasal passages. Long, thin columns of it that he dragged down into his lungs, almost gagging from the effort.

And it was as if the tether had been cut. He went spiralling upwards through the water. Up and up, endlessly it seemed, until at long last he broke the surface. He breathed out, but still couldn't draw air back through his mouth. He opened his eyes. Wide. But he couldn't see anything. He could feel the physical pounding of his heart against his ribs. The sound of it filled his head. The rushing of blood filled his ears.

And slowly, as comprehension took hold, he realised that it was consciousness whose surface he had broken, not water. He was perfectly dry, apart from the sweat that ran in rivulets down his face. He could feel it dripping from his chin. He couldn't see for the simple reason that it was dark. Profoundly dark. He was seated, his arms bound behind him, tied at the wrists to a chair. His ankles, too, were secured, cutting off circulation, biting into his flesh. He couldn't open his mouth because there was something taped across it, holding it firmly shut.

As his breathing became more regular, and his heartbeat less frantic, he tried to listen. But he could hear nothing. Not a sound other than the rasping of his own breath. Although he had the very strong sense that he was not alone. A smell, perhaps. Something in the air. The heat emanating from another body.

And then suddenly he was blinded. Cold, white light sent pain spiking through his brain. He screwed up his eyes against it, turning his head away as much as his bindings would allow. Hands grabbed his head roughly from behind, and forced him to look forward again. As his pupils contracted, the scene before him began to take form, like something rezzing in Second Life. An office desk. Polished mahogany. A desk lamp, its shade swivelled toward him, so that he received the full, reflected glare of its naked bulb. A man sitting in an executive leather chair, leaning forward, forearms planted on the desktop, staring intently at Michael. There was something lying flat on the desk in front of him, but Michael couldn't see what it was.

He tried to swallow, but his mouth and throat were so dry his tongue stuck to the roof of his mouth. For a moment he thought he was going to be sick and started to panic. The man nodded, and someone reached around to tear away the tape that sealed his mouth. He heard the sound of it ripping free of his flesh and the sharp sting of it as it tore hairs out of his skin. He gasped for air, and felt the threatened bile retreat to his stomach.

The man leaned forward into the light, so that Michael got a clear sight of him for the first time. He wore a plain dark suit, with a white shirt and red tie. He had ginger hair, gelled and scraped back across a broad skull. His skin was very pale, very un-Californian, and spattered with freckles. At a guess Michael would have put him at mid- to late-forties. But he was carrying a fair amount of weight and might have been older. He was clean-shaven, almost shiny-faced. His lips were exceptionally pale, and his green eyes were so cold that Michael could almost feel them on him like the tips of icy fingers.

Michael started to speak, but the man quickly raised a silencing finger to his lips. Then he waggled it backwards and forwards in front him. A tiny shake of his head.

"Just listen."

Michael nodded.

"You are a thief, Mr. Kapinsky."

Michael began to protest. But the man tilted his head to one side and raised a single eyebrow, and Michael shut up.

"You are a thief. *And* a liar. You stole more than three million dollars from our account, and if I'd let you, you would have denied it, wouldn't you?"

Michael assumed, because this had been couched as a question, that he was expected to reply. "Yes. Because I didn't steal it."

"See? A thief, *and* a liar. Just like I said." He raised his finger again to pre-empt any further attempt by Michael at denial. "We were most perplexed when that money suddenly disappeared from our Second Life account. Vanished without trace. You can imagine how we felt. Close to three and a quarter million is no trifling amount, Mr. Kapinsky. But just as well for us that human frailty is something we have always been able to exploit to our advantage. We are past masters in the art of bribery and corruption. In truth, it is such an easy path to tread. People are so…bribable. And…corrupt. So we had little trouble finding someone in San Francisco who would take a look for us into the Linden Lab database to tell us what had happened. As you can probably understand, we were unwilling to go through official channels. The fewer questions asked the better."

He leaned back a little now, folding his hands in front of him on the desk.

"And what did we find? We found that our account had been erased. No record of it ever existing. And our three million plus gone, as if simply vanished into thin air. Perplexing you might think. And you'd be right. We were very perplexed, and not a little vexed. But then our friend in San Francisco stumbled across an extraordinary coincidence. A sum of money corresponding exactly to our missing cash—right down to the last cent—had been paid into another account the same day that ours went missing."

His face softened into what was almost a smile.

"Now, I don't know about you, Mr. Kapinsky, but I'm not one who believes much in coincidence. No effect without cause." He leaned into the light again, lowering his voice as if sharing a confidence. "But here's the thing. Before we could even lift a finger to do anything about it, the money was gone again. And that account erased. Almost before our very eyes. Again, no record that it had ever existed, and so no name to hang it on. As you can imagine, we were more than perplexed by now."

He stabbed a finger toward a ceiling hidden by the dark.

"But wait. Fortune favoured us yet again. Because guess what? That self-same exact amount turned up in yet another account. The same day the second one vanished. And do you know whose account that was, Mr. Kapinsky?" But he raised his hand. "No, don't answer. We both know whose account it was. It was your account, Mr. Kapinsky."

He sat back again.

"Very clever. I have to confess to a certain admiration. From a purely professional standpoint. But from a personal one, Mr. Kapinsky, I have to tell you that I am extremely pissed off. In fact, I can't even begin to convey to you just how pissed off I am. But we'll come to that. Many things we will come to, very soon. But first things first."

He reached in front of him to the flat object lying on the desk and lifted its lid. As he turned it around, Michael saw that it was a laptop computer. The screen was lit up and displaying the Second Life welcome page. The SL eye/hand logo seemed to be mocking him now. The man nodded, and a shadow emerged from the dark, light catching the blade of a large hunting knife. Michael flinched as the hand that wielded it swooped to cut through the bindings that held his wrists and ankles.

The red-haired man rose from behind his desk and walked around to the front of it. He took a folded sheet of paper out from an inside pocket and smoothed it open on the desk beside the laptop.

"Quite simple, Mr. Kapinsky. Here you have the name of an AV. You log yourself in, and transfer our money into his account. Quite painless, and all over in sixty seconds."

Michael made no attempt to get to his feet, until rough hands grabbed him from behind and forced him into a standing position. He was breathing in short, sharp bursts, aware that there was only one possible way this could end. "I can't do it," he said.

And a fist came from nowhere, like bunched steel, driving itself into his diaphragm. The pain was nauseating, and completely robbed him of the power to breathe. He doubled over and dropped to his knees, before the same rough hands as before pulled him back to his feet.

"There is no such word as 'can't' in our lexicon, Mr. Kapinsky."

Michael shook his head, trying to find breath to fuel his voice. Finally he managed what was little more than a forced whisper. "I can't make the transfer because the money is no longer in my account."

All animation deserted the face of the man in front of him. It was as if he had laid eyes on the Gorgon and turned to stone. "Show me."

Michael was shoved forward to the computer. With shaking fingers he typed in his AV name and password, and there was Chas standing in the familiar surroundings of Twist's office. If only he could just be subsumed into the virtual. Become Chas, and escape this hell. The man with the red hair leaned toward the screen to check out the linden total at the top right. There were less than two hundred Lindens in Chas' account. He turned back toward Michael, who saw a blind fury in the cold green of his eyes, belied by the calm, even tone of his voice.

"You'd better put it back, then."

"I don't have it any more."

"You've spent it?" His voice became modulated by incredulity for the first time.

"I paid off my home loan."

The man leaned in toward him, till Michael could smell the stale garlic on his breath. "Then you'd better take out another, hadn't you?" He snatched the sheet of paper from the desk and stuffed it into the breast pocket of Michael's polo shirt. "I'll give you just twenty-four hours, Mr. Kapinsky. If you haven't paid the money into this AV's account by then, you will be seriously dead."

He turned around angrily and snapped the lid of the laptop shut, as light crashed through Michael's skull, blinding him again before darkness fell and pain vanished with consciousness.

Chapter Twenty-Two

The pain was the first thing to return. A thumping headache that felt like his head had been locked in a vice. From somewhere at the back of his skull he became aware of a different kind of pain. Sharp, persistent, throbbing. And even before he could open his eyes, he reached a hand around to the back of his neck and felt dried, sticky blood where it had run down from a wound in his scalp. Then came the awareness of an ache in his gut. A painful, muscular ache where a clenched fist had left its bruising. And then the stinging around his mouth where the tape that gagged him had been so unceremoniously ripped away.

Finally he opened his eyes, and even the light of the overhead street lamps hurt him.

He was completely disoriented, without the least idea of where he was, before slowly the familiarity of his SUV began to rez into his consciousness and he realised he was slumped in the driving seat. His nostrils were filled with the smell of stale food, and he turned his head to see his take-out pizza box on the passenger seat where he had left it. He checked the time. It was after nine. Somehow he had lost more than two hours.

The memory of what had transpired sometime during those lost hours was slowly finding form in his brain, and with it came a returning fear. A fear that impaled him, keeping him pinned back in his seat. Twenty-four hours to find more than three million dollars. Jesus! He didn't even want to think about it.

He peered through the windshield and for a moment was unable to place where he was. A tree-lined street. A car park. And then he saw, next to a covered passage leading to the marina, the familiar blue canopy of Offshore West, Inc, opposite his dentist's surgery. He turned his head and saw the windows of Stanley Armbruster's surgery and waiting room one floor up. And he realised in a moment of incongruous irrationality that he would no longer be able to afford Stanley's services. Not that it was likely to matter much. He would probably be dead by this time tomorrow.

He forced himself to sit up and felt his stomach heaving. He fumbled for the door handle and threw it open, leaning out to empty the bile that rose into his throat in a sudden rush. As he looked up, he saw a passing couple watching him with horrified fascination. The girl averted her eyes quickly. But the young man was embarrassed and felt somehow obliged to nod in Michael's direction. And Michael felt obliged to nod back. So the two men nodded acknowledgement of each other, and the girl tugged her lover's arm and pulled him off down the tunnel toward the marina.

Michael could see the lights of the waterfront restaurants, hear the sounds of diners laughing and talking, and he pulled the door of his SUV wearily shut. He felt completely dissociated from the world, dislocated and alone. He closed his eyes and wondered what the hell he was going to do.

◇◇◇

By the time he got back to the house in Dolphin Terrace, all his aches and pains had receded to a dull background discomfort. Foremost in his mind was a deep depression, closely followed by the fear that snapped constantly at his heels. He clicked the remote on his sun visor and the garage door lifted to allow him access. He drove in, cut the engine, and eased himself stiffly out of the vehicle, taking his pizza box with him. At the door leading to the utility room, he hit the switch to lower the garage door and went through to the house.

He felt for the light switch on the wall and nothing happened. The room remained in darkness. Michael cursed and felt his way down the steps into the kitchen, banging into the pots and pans that hung on hooks from the wall on his left. Mora's idea for keeping them easily accessible, but out of the kitchen. They clattered in the still of the house. There were more light switches at the foot of the steps. None of them brought light to his world. The house stayed stubbornly dark. And for the first time ever, Michael felt less than secure in his own home.

Faint, flitting moonlight, and the reflection of streetlights drifting up from Balboa Island below suffused the kitchen and living room with almost enough light for him to see by. He felt his way across to the black marble breakfast bar and laid down the pizza box. The fuses were at the other end of the house. For a moment he wondered how there had been light in the garage. And then he remembered that the electrician had wired the garage door and lights to a separate breaker box in the garage itself.

He waited by the breakfast bar and listened. There was no sound, not even the hum of the refrigerator. At the far end of the hall he could see that the lights were also out in the fish tank. The house was completely without power. An airplane passed overhead, its engines vibrating in the warm night air, and after it had passed, the same silence filled the house once more.

But in spite of that silence, Michael had the sense that he was not alone. He was not sure why. Was it some sixth sense? A faint, unfamiliar scent in the air, or some sound that he was not even conscious of hearing? He waited until his pupils were dilated enough to make full use of all the available light and began moving cautiously through the front hall. Normally light would be spilling into it from the courtyard, but that, too, was in darkness.

At the end of the hall he glanced to his left, toward the office. The door stood open, but the room was mired in the deepest shadow. There was no movement, no sound. The breaker box was in the bedroom at the far end of a corridor that ran behind glass the full length of the courtyard. He turned along it, passed the open door of his bedroom, pausing only briefly to listen, before carrying on down. Soft footsteps on thick-piled carpet. He climbed the three steps at the end of the corridor and moved away from what little light filtered down from the open skies above the courtyard, into even deeper shadow.

Now he knew that he smelled something. Something disconcertingly familiar. Some scent that hung in the air, a low note of something musky, almost sweet. There was someone here, of that he was certain. All his pain was forgotten as fear filled every available space in his body and mind, pushing everything else aside. And now he heard something, too. Someone breathing. A shallow, rapid breath. He held his own to listen more intently, and heard the soft scuff of a shoe on carpet.

He reached out to touch the wall, a guide to help him keep his bearings, and moved cautiously along it, inching toward the bedroom door. The breaker box was set into the wall just inside the doorway. He could tell that it was open, and as he felt for the door jamb he heard the click of a switch, and the house was suddenly flooded with light.

"Surprise!" Janey stood grinning at him, wearing a crimson basque and fishnet tights, her hair tied up in red, silk bows.

"Jesus Christ, Janey!" Michael's legs almost buckled under him. "What the hell are you doing!?"

Her face shone with amusement. "You wanted to know how sex worked in Second Life. I thought I'd dress up as Doobie Littlething and give you a real life demo."

"For fuck's sake! You just about gave me a heart attack!" He went storming off back along the hall. Janey teetered after him on perilously high heels.

"Oh, come on, Mike. It was a joke. Where's your sense of humour?"

He growled back at her over his shoulder. "Janey it wouldn't have been funny at the best of times, and this is not the best of times."

"Aw, hey Mike, it was a *little* funny, wasn't it?"

"No!" He spun around. "First of all it was a mock murder at your place. Now this. Where do you get off thinking scaring the shit out of people is funny, Janey?"

She frowned and peered at him more closely. "What have you done to your mouth?"

He turned into his bedroom and switched on the light above the mirror. A rectangular area of skin covering his mouth, an inch above and below and two inches on either side, was red and raised like a rash. He touched it and felt the sticky residue from the tape that had gagged him come away on his fingers. Then he heard Janey gasp.

"Oh, my God, Mike, what's happened to you? You've got blood all over your collar and the back of your neck."

He turned around and held out his open hands, heel to heel. "Yeh, and you might like to take a look at the rope burns on my wrists. I've probably got them on my ankles, too."

She looked at him in disbelief, for once at a loss for words. "I don't understand."

"I've been drugged, bound, gagged, beaten up, and threatened by a bunch of thugs who figure I stole their money."

Her hand flew to her mouth. "Oh, God, Mike. The three million?"

"Three million, one hundred and eighty-three thousand— and a few extra dollars thrown in."

"What did they say?"

"They said if I didn't pay it back within twenty-four hours they would kill me."

He pushed past her and out into the hall, heading for the kitchen.

"Well, pay them back, then."

"How? I used the money to pay off the debt on the house."

"Take out another loan."

Michael's laugh was entirely devoid of humour. "Janey, the reason the bank was about to foreclose was because I couldn't keep up the payments. They're not going to give me another loan when I still can't afford to pay it."

"Go to the cops, then."

"And tell them what? That I took money that wasn't mine and spent it. Besides, if I do go to the cops these people will probably kill me anyway. You weren't there, Janey. These were very serious people, and I have no doubt that they will very seriously kill me."

He took a wad of cotton wool from the medicine cabinet, ran it under cold water and started dabbing away the blood from his neck.

"Here, let me do that." Janey took the wad and began carefully washing away the blood from his skin and hair, working carefully through it to the cut on his head.

He winced. "Ouch."

"Hold still!" She poured disinfectant on to the wad and pressed it to his scalp.

He nearly went though the roof. "Jesus Christ, Janey! That hurts!"

But she continued to hold it firmly against him. "Don't be such a baby." Then, "So what *are* you going to do?"

"Somehow I've got to get the money back and make that transfer. Though I have this really bad feeling that they're going to kill me anyway, even after I've done it."

"Transfer?

"They want me to put the money into another SL account." He reached into his pocket and pulled out the crumpled sheet of paper that the man with the red hair had stuffed into it. "That's the AV name they want me to transfer it to."

She snatched the paper from him and looked at the name. "Balthazar Bee. Hah! They're not as smart at they think they are, Mike. They just made their first mistake. Come on."

By the time he looked around, she was already halfway along the hall, still teetering on her ridiculous heels, and he thought how absurd she looked in her outfit, breasts and butt bulging out of her basque, holes in her tights, and too much make-up smeared across lips and eyes. He knew that she had meant it that way. As a laugh, not a seduction. And as she wobbled past the fish tank, he found a wry smile creeping up on him unexpect-edly. In spite of everything. He was glad that she was here, that he wasn't facing this alone.

When he reached his office, she had already begun log-ging into Second Life. He stood behind her as Twist rezzed at the agency. Janey ignored her avatar and pulled up the Search window. She typed in Balthazar Bee. There was only one. The profile had no photograph and no description in the About window. But it did reveal that this particular AV had been born just six months previously. Janey navigated her cursor toward the Groups window and stopped dead.

"Jees," she whispered.

Michael leaned in to see, troubled still by the loss of his read-ing glasses. "What is it."

"There's only one Group, and guess what it is."

Michael's heart seemed to push up into his throat, pulsing there and almost stopping his breathing. "Virtual Realty," he read. "That's the Group Arnold Smitts used for his land transactions."

Janey turned to look at him, pale as a ghost. "Oh. My. God, Mike. You've stolen three million dollars from the mob."

Chapter Twenty-Three

What little moon there was seemed to have vanished. The night was black as ebony, the sky studded with tiny jewels of light that reached out to them from millions of years in the past. There was something about that vast, timeless cosmos that made Michael feel very small, and his troubles less than insignificant. But he knew that as the sun rose tomorrow and the first twelve hours of his twenty-four had passed, those troubles were going to loom very large in his mind and seem anything but insignificant.

Janey poured them each another glass of Syrah and set the bottle carefully back down on the stone tiles of the terrace. The silhouettes of tall palm trees bowed in the breeze against the lights of the island below, and a yacht under motor power chugged its way slowly up the channel, leaving shards of shattered light scattered in its wake.

"That money must have come out of Smitts' account when his AV was destroyed. Transferred to another account that transferred the money to you before it was erased."

Michael shook his head. "But why would anyone want to put it into my account? Didn't they know I was broke and liable to spend it?"

Janey laughed. "It must have been a mistake, Mike. The money must have been destined for someone else. Someone made a mistake when they were tapping in a name or a number, and it went to you instead."

Knowing that it must have been an error did nothing to improve Michael's mood. He sat clutching his glass, already partially anaesthetised by the wine, and felt himself slipping into an even deeper depression. "They're going to think I killed him."

"Who?"

"Smitts. If they think I engineered the theft of the money, they must think I killed him, too.

"Did you?

"Ha. Ha. Ha."

"Where were you the night of the murder, Mike?"

"Pole dancing at Minsky's."

"No, I'm serious. Where were you?"

He turned to look at her. "I was here."

"On your own?"

"Yes."

"Great alibi."

"I don't need an alibi, Janey."

"Well, if someone's setting you up for this, you might."

A chill ran through him, in spite of the warm night air. "You think I'm being set up?"

"I have no idea. It doesn't really matter, either way. Whether you're being set up or if it's all just some horrible mistake, you're in deep shit."

Michael slipped further down in his chair and took a long draught of his wine. "Thank you for those words of comfort."

They sat in silence, then, for a long time, before finally Michael turned and looked across at Janey in her ridiculous outfit. She was deeply lost in some distant contemplation. But he needed a change of subject, something to take his mind off the same thoughts that kept going round and around his head in never-ending circles.

"So tell me about SL sex."

"What?"

"That's what you came for, isn't it?"

Her head swivelled to look at him as if he were mad. Then she smiled and shook her head. "What do you want to know?"

"How it's done."

"Why?"

"Just curious, that's all."

"Jesus! Men! Doesn't matter what other kind of shit's going down, you only ever think of one thing. Figuring on trying it out on Doobie Littlething?"

"No, I am not."

"She's got a sexy AV."

"Janey, are you going to tell me, or are you going to tease me?"

She sat up. "Okay. But you know, it's really very simple. There are any number of shops that sell sex beds, sex rugs, stuff like that. And they all come with built-in animations. A menu appears on the screen and you can choose from a selection of animations. Making out, cuddling, sleeping, or having sex. The more it costs, usually, the bigger the choice. You can have missionary, blow-job, doggy, her on top, him on top, gay, lesbian, you name it. There are usually two poseballs. Three or more, if you're kinky." She grinned. "You just jump on to the poseball and your AV will be animated in the act of your choice."

"So it is just cartoons humping. Not much fun in that."

"Well, it's not so much what you do, as what you say while you're doing it. Sex in SL is just like sex in RL. Mostly in the mind. The best lovers conjure up the most vivid imagery and turn their partners on. Of course, the doing of it in SL would just be in your imagination and in the animation of your AV. While…well, while you masturbated in RL."

Michael blew air out through pressed lips as an expression of his distaste. "I think it might be more fun in the shower."

Janey laughed. "Only if there's someone else with you." They lapsed into another silence and Janey topped up their glasses from the last of the bottle. "What's wrong with me, Mike?"

He looked at her, surprised. "There's nothing wrong with you, Janey."

"So how come no one's interested?"

"I'm sure they are."

"I'm sure they're not. And if they are, they're pretty damned good at hiding it. The only guys interested in me seem to be in Second Life."

"But you're a guy in Second Life!"

She laughed. "That's my point. I've taken to frequenting the gay clubs. Seems the only way I can get myself a man. I've had some interesting experiences."

She turned and gazed off into an unfocused middle distance, and he took the opportunity to reappraise her. It wasn't that she was ugly. Just plain. And plenty of plain girls got themselves men. And it certainly wasn't that she lacked personality. But, he supposed, there was something innately asexual about her. She would always be your best friend, never your girlfriend, because somehow you would just never see her that way. She'd always only be one of the boys. He felt suddenly very sorry for her. He had lost Mora, but at least they'd had their time together. Janey had never, to his knowledge, had anyone. He said, "Any guy would be glad to have a girl like you, Janey." And in almost every respect he meant it.

She turned to look at him. He saw a hurt in her eyes as she went straight to the one respect in which he didn't mean it. "You?"

And he couldn't hold her gaze. "You know I'm still not over Mora. Not by a long way."

A small, sad smile crept across her face, and she turned her gaze back toward the cosmos and her future solitude.

Chapter Twenty-Four

The sun fell in long wedges across the cream shag of the bedroom carpet, zigzagging in broken patterns over the rumpled sheets of the bed. Michael felt the warmth of it on his naked leg and turned over to see from the beside clock that it was after nine.

He almost fell out of bed. The world had already started turning. He was losing time. He hurried barefoot across the carpet to the sliding doors of his wardrobe and stopped, leaning against the wall, giddy, almost faint. He was feeling the effects of his ordeal the night before. And the two bottles of wine that he and Janey had managed to consume between them were doing nothing to ameliorate the pain in his head. But a toxic mix of fear and adrenalin was urging him on in the cold light of day.

He selected a fresh pair of jeans and a cream polo shirt, and pulled on a pair of brown leather deck shoes. No time for a shower. He quickly brushed his teeth and dragged a comb through his hair. For a moment he stopped to take in the view from his bedroom window, across the reflecting pool, to the island and the peninsula beyond. It was that light that he loved so much. So clear, so luminous. Palm trees never still, even in the gentlest of breezes that blew in off the sea. He really was going to miss this place. If he ever lived to miss anything again.

In the kitchen, he stopped at the phone and pulled Sherri's number up from its memory. As it rang, he considered eating a cold slice of pizza from the box he had left untouched on the breakfast bar the night before. He flipped open the lid, and saw that there were only two slices left. For a moment he looked at it in puzzled astonishment. Surely he hadn't eaten the rest and forgotten? And then realisation dawned. Those bastards who had abducted him the night before. They'd eaten his pizza! Somehow it only seemed to add insult to injury and puffed him up with indignation. Sherri saved him from an outpouring of profanity.

"Yes, Michael." She had clearly seen that it was him from her caller ID and prepared her chilliest tone.

"Sherri, the house is mine. No mortgage. You get me three-and-a-half million for it by…" He thought about it for a moment. "…by the time the banks close tonight, and I'll give you fifteen percent." If he at least had a promise of the money, surely they wouldn't kill him?

He heard her excitement. "Can I have that in writing?"

"Twelve hours, Sherri." And he hung up. He didn't hold out much hope, but the more options he opened up, the better.

◇◇◇

Hal Bender sat across the desk from Michael and cocked a quizzical eyebrow in his direction.

"Three and a quarter *million*, Michael? Are you insane?"

Michael looked at him with a mixture of hatred and disdain. Only desperation had brought him here. Bender worked from his opulent home high on the hillside above Newport. His study overlooked the harbour, the obligatory view for the richest residents of this wealthy Southern California town. And it was from those very residents that Bender had made his money, investing their wealth, sometimes wisely, sometimes not. But never to his disadvantage.

"It's a pity Mora didn't ask you the same when you persuaded her to take out that home loan."

Bender pursed his lips. He had been Mora's financial adviser through good times and bad. Mostly bad. Michael had removed her remaining investments from his control after her death, but today had forced himself to swallow his pride to make the drive up the hill. If anyone knew how to raise three million fast, it was Hal Bender.

"It was always a risky investment, Michael. If it had paid off, it would have paid out big. Borrowing against the house was the only way she could raise the cash. And she was a bit desperate by then. In the end, it was her decision, not mine."

Michael bit back a retort.

"What do you want it for?"

"To pay off a debt."

Bender smiled. "Borrowing from Peter to pay Paul?"

"Something like that."

"How do things stand with the house?"

"It's mine. Good for collateral."

Bender raised his eyebrow again. This time in surprise. But if he was wondering how Michael had managed to pay off the loan, he wasn't going to ask. "When do you need it by?"

"Tonight."

This time both eyebrows pushed themselves up his forehead. "You're kidding!"

"I've never been more serious."

Bender shook his head. "I could probably get you the three and a quarter. But not by tonight. If you want that kind of money that fast you're going to have to go to people who don't ask too many questions. People who will charge you so much interest that you'll be in debt before the ink is even dry on the contract. People who will take your house off you without a qualm the minute the capital repayment is due, and take your kneecaps when you can't pay the interest."

Michael's mouth was so dry he found it hard to swallow. "So how would I get in touch with people like that?"

"Jesus, Michael, what kind of trouble are you in?

"Let's just say it's a matter of life and death. Literally." He paused, and the two men eyed each other in cautious silence. "So?"

"So what?"

"So how do I get in touch with people like that?"

Bender almost laughed, but in the end it came out more like a gasp. He shook his head. "Michael, I haven't the faintest idea."

◇◇◇

Michael walked down the steps from Bender's front door through a lush, semitropical garden and waited for the electronic buzz that would unlock the gate. The sun was rising now in the palest of blue skies, and he felt the heat of it on his skin. For a moment he closed his eyes, and when he opened them saw a black Lincoln saloon parked on the other side of the street. Two dark-suited gentlemen were making no attempt to conceal the fact that they were watching him. The driver smiled, raised his hand at the open window and gave him a small wave. His passenger puffed on a cigarette and fixed Michael in his gaze with dark, passive eyes.

Michael turned away, fear tightening across his chest, like the onset of cardiac arrest. It appeared they did not intend letting him out of their sight until the transfer was made. He walked to his SUV on legs that trembled beneath him and climbed into the driver's seat. There was nowhere to run. Nowhere to hide. It had become only too painfully clear to him that he was not going to be able to raise the money in time.

The only alternative was to try to find out who really killed Smitts, and why.

Chapter Twenty-Five

Stan Laurel looked up, surprised, as Janey laid a plastic cup of sweet, hot coffee on the desk in front of him. Michael settled himself in Hardy's seat on the other side of it and took a sip from his own. He peered at Laurel over the top of the detective's computer screen. Laurel's surprise turned to suspicion. "What are you two after?"

"Nothing," Janey said. "Just dropping off some files. We were getting some coffee from the machine and saw you sitting over here all on your lonesome, looking like a man who could do with some caffeine."

"Damned right I could. Been a helluva morning. That Brockman case? The guy who broke into the museum? Went to court this morning, and they kicked us into touch."

"Shit, why?" Janey perched on the edge of his desk.

"Someone forgot to read him his rights."

"No! Who?"

Laurel fixed his eyes on the screensaver in front of him and took a sip of his coffee, the cup trembling in bony fingers.

"Stanley, you didn't!"

He slapped his palm flat on the desk. "I was fucking sure I had. I always do. It's like breathing. You don't think about it."

Michael said, "So he walked?"

"He walked. And I am in deep shit."

"It's a shot of something stronger you want in that coffee, then."

"Huh! That's all I'd need. Caught drinking on the job. I'd be out the front door with a broken pension in my back pocket before you could say *do detectives think*."

Janey craned her neck casually to look at the file in front of him. "Still on the Mathews case?"

"That and twenty others."

Janey turned to Michael. "You remember that one, Mike? That's the one that gave me the idea for your welcome back party. Young woman shot in the chest. We were at the crime scene that afternoon. An apartment overlooking the marina."

"I remember." Michael brought back to mind the fleeting image of the girl spreadeagled on the bed, but he was having great difficulty containing his impatience or trying to sound natural. Time was slipping away, and they needed more information.

Janey turned back to Laurel. "So…any breaks on it?"

"Nothing. Not a dickie bird. Interesting background, though. Her daddy's Jack Mathews, the property developer. Owns that big island out in the bay. Rumour has it he's terminally ill, and she'd have got all his cash. There's a brother, too, but he and the old man don't get on. Cut out of the will completely, from all accounts."

"Good motive for murder, then," Janey said.

Laurel grunted. "Except that he was in New York at the time."

Michael said casually, "What about the Arnold Smitts case? Anything happening there?"

"Nah. Same story. Ollie's been looking after that one. Having trouble finding a motive. And you guys didn't come up with anything." He took another sip of his coffee. "Damn, that's good. Interesting coincidence, though."

"What's that?" Michael leaned back in the chair, affecting disinterest.

"Well, you know how he was into that Second Life shit—first Internet port of call for lost souls and losers?"

Janey shifted uncomfortably. "Yeh."

"And how his account had been erased from the computer database?"

Michael said, "Ollie did mention something about that."

Laurel slapped the back of his hand across the file in front of him. "Same shit."

"What, the Mathews girl was in SL, too?" Janey frowned.

"Sure was. And just like Smitts, no record of her account in the database."

"That's a helluva coincidence," Michael said.

"Well, yes and no. I mean, who knows how meticulous these Linden Lab people are at keeping records. The database could be a shambles for all we know. And Ollie did some research. Apparently there's nearly fourteen million people signed up for Second Life. That's almost half the population of the state of California. So it's not that big a coincidence if two random murder victims turn out to be Second Lifers."

Janey stood up, and as she turned, her hand caught Laurel's cup, and knocked the coffee into his lap. He leapt to his feet, cursing in shock and pain as it scalded him. "Jesus Christ!"

"Oh, hey, I'm so sorry, Stanley. Here let me take you to the washroom and wipe you down."

Laurel glared at her, wiping at himself with a paper tissue. "Well, there's an offer I can refuse. Jesus Christ, Janey! You're a clumsy fucking bitch, you know that. Goddamn!" And he went hurrying off toward the washroom.

Janey smirked across the desk at Michael. "Always spilling things, me." Then her smile faded. "That's fourteen million people worldwide, Mike. Not just in California. So I'd say it was more than a coincidence." She bent over Laurel's desk, ostensibly to mop up the pool of coffee that was dripping over the edge, and flipped open the Mathews file to squint at it. "What do we need to know?"

Michael stood up, hope returning with the prospect of something new to follow up. "Her AV name. Groups she was in. And the old man's address would be good."

Janey looked up at him and smiled conspiratorially, lowering her voice. "We gonna play real life detectives, too?"

"Whatever it takes, Janey."

She grinned. "Good. I always wanted to be a cop."

She swivelled the file toward her to take some quick notes, and the corner of it caught Laurel's computer mouse. The movement swiftly banished his screensaver to reveal a familiar scene. A busy shopping mall, with AV's moving back and forth viewing skins all along a back wall. In the foreground a tall, thin, good-looking avatar stood, head bowed, an *Away* sign attached to a tag revealing him to be Phat Botha. For a moment, Janey stared at it, confused. Then, "Jesus!" she whispered. "Look at this?"

Michael rounded the desk. He looked at the screen incomprehendingly. "It's Second Life," he said.

Janey's face split into a grin. She put her hand over the mouse, and Phat Botha sprang to life. "First Internet port of call for lost souls and losers, huh? The damn hypocrite's a Second-Lifer himself."

◇◇◇

The Mathews did not encourage visitors to their island. It was situated almost in the middle of the bay about halfway between Balboa and Lido islands. There was no bridge, no road, and they did not lay on water transport for casual visitors. Michael and Janey had to hire a boat from a rental outfit off Bayshore Drive and chug out across the channel, weaving between yachts at anchor and huge motor-driven cruisers that powered in and out of the harbour. Seagulls wheeled and cawed overhead, and Janey looked back at the two dark-suited figures who stood on the landing watching them go. She frowned.

"Who are these guys? Do you know them?"

Michael switched the tiller from one hand to the other and glanced back. He sighed. "I figure these are bastards who ate my pizza. They're keeping an eye on their three million."

Janey paled a little. "Oh, shit. Really?" Then she chuckled. "Well, I guess they must reckon they've lost you now, unless they can walk on water."

"They'll probably just wait for me at the four-by-four. They know I'm not going anywhere fast without it."

The Mathews mansion occupied around 80 percent of the island. A huge two-storey classical Italian stone-faced villa with colonnaded terraces. The back wall went straight down into the water. The sides and front were ringed by beautifully manicured lawns screened from the curiosity of passing boat-owners by columns of palm trees and tall flowering shrubs. Beyond the grass a white-painted wooden landing stage extended along the front of the property, big enough to berth two fifty-footers at the same time. A short floating pier ran out at right angles, with half a dozen small craft bobbing on the swell. The Stars and Stripes hung limp from a tall flagpost in the midday heat. The breeze from the ocean had dropped, and the air fibrillated in the heat, vibrating to the hum of myriad insects.

Michael steered their rental boat into a berth at the pier and Janey leapt out to tie it up to a metal ring set in the planking. A water-borne ambulance was tethered to the main landing stage, and several smaller boats clunked and creaked alongside it, straining gently at their moorings. As they walked along the pier to the landing stage, Michael and Janey saw a small crowd of people gathered on the front lawn. On the landing stage they passed a couple of medics wheeling a stretcher across the boards to the ambulance. A bulky figure lay prone on the gurney, covered over with a white sheet. The group on the lawn began to disperse. Michael caught sight of a short, elderly Latina woman in a black dress with white trim. The maid. He hurried after her.

"Excuse me."

She turned. Her face seemed strained. Her eyes bloodshot.

"I'm looking for Jack Mathews."

She nodded toward the stretcher being wheeled up the ramp to the water ambulance. "You just missed him."

Michael glanced back in dismay as Janey caught him up. "Wassup?"

"Looks like the late Mr. Mathews has just departed."

"Oh."

A young man had detached himself from the group heading for the house and was making his way back toward them. He was around Michael's age, wearing beautifully tailored grey slacks and an open-necked white shirt with short sleeves. His skin was smooth and evenly tanned, his light brown hair bleached in places by exposure to salt water. He had startlingly white teeth and eyes completely hidden behind a pair of large wrap-around sunglasses.

"Can I help you?" Even although he stood a good four feet away, Michael could smell the alcohol on his breath.

Michael said, "We're from the Orange County Forensic Science Service. We had been hoping to speak to Jack Mathews about the murder of his daughter."

"Well…" The young man pursed his lips thoughtfully. "You're timing could have been better."

"So I understand."

"Does that mean you have news of Jennifer's killer?"

"I'm afraid not."

"So what did you want to speak to him about?"

"I'm sorry, you are…?"

"Richard Mathews." He looked around and tossed a hand vaguely in the direction of the house. "Jack's son. Which I guess makes me the proprietor. If only by default."

Michael heard the bitterness in both his tone and his words.

Janey said, "We wouldn't have disturbed you at a time like this if we'd known."

But Richard Mathews didn't seem to be in mourning. "Do you want to tell me why you're here?"

"We were wondering about your sister's involvement in Second Life."

He stared at them implacably from behind his shades. "Second Life, huh? So I guess you know the whole sordid little story, then."

Yes," Michael said, having no idea what the story was or how sordid it might be.

Richard removed his glasses and squinted at them in the sunlight. "Well, I guess the money's beyond my reach now, anyway. At least for the moment. You'd better come in."

Michael and Janey exchanged glances as Richard Mathews led them up a short flight of steps to a portico leading to the main entrance. She shrugged and pulled a face, evidently no wiser than Michael. They followed the young heir to the Mathews fortune into a large salon furnished with eighteenth-century French antiques arranged around priceless Oriental rugs. He went straight to a glass drinks cabinet, and filled a crystal tumbler with pale Scottish malt.

"I won't offer you one. I know you people don't drink on duty." He turned toward them and took a slug of whisky. "He'd have been really pissed, you know, to think of me inheriting."

"Is there no other family?" Janey asked.

"My mother's been dead for years. My father doted on Jennifer and thought I was a drunk and a waster." He smiled. A small, bitter smile. "I didn't mean to be. It's not the way I started out. But it's funny how, in the end, you seem to live up to other people's expectations of you." He sucked in some more whisky. "I'll have to sell the place, of course. Just to pay the death duties. And I suppose the rest of the money will be sequestered until such time as legitimate inheritance can be proved."

Michael tried to maintain a neutral expression, so as not to betray his ignorance. "What money is that, Mr. Mathews?"

"The cash in Jennifer's Second Life account, of course. His goddamned tax-free lump sum that he didn't want anyone to know about. Least of all me." He moved toward the window, sipping his whisky, turning his back to them, perhaps to hide his anger and disappointment. But he couldn't keep it out of his voice. "She told me about it, you see. Rubbing my nose in it. There always was a spiteful side to her. Like father, like daughter. And no amount of expensive therapy could ever remove that nasty little character trait. She knew how pissed off I'd be. Daddy salting away money in a secret account for her so she wouldn't have to pay taxes on it. Very smart. And in a way, I can't blame him. You pay taxes on your money all your life. Several times over. And then they tax it again when you're dead." He turned back toward them, and they saw the fire of hurt and jealousy in his eyes. "But it should have been equal shares. We came from the same loins."

He drained his glass.

"So anyway, tell me. Because *she* didn't. Exactly how much did he manage to stash way in Linden dollars before she was murdered?"

Michael stared at him, the seeds of understanding beginning to sow themselves for the first time in his mind. "I have no idea."

"Well, you must know how much money there is in her account, surely?"

"There is no money, Mr. Mathews," Janey said. "In fact, there is no account. And not even a record of it."

◇◇◇

They headed in silence back across the channel to the boat rental yard, sunlight dancing on the swell of the dozens of boats, large and small, that plied in and out of the harbour. The breeze had got up again, and Michael felt the hot wind tugging at this shirt. He closed his eyes for a moment, turning his face up toward the sky to feel the sun on it.

"Hey, I'd be happier if you kept your eyes on the road, Mr. Driver."

Michael opened his eyes and looked at Janey. "Someone's bumping people off for their money, Janey. Secret money that's hidden away in Second Life accounts. Money that no one's ever going to report missing, because it shouldn't be there."

"Two swallows do not a summer make, Mr. Kapinsky."

"Eh?"

"Two murders, Mike. That's all."

"That we know about. There could be others."

"So what are you going to do?"

"I'm going to go back inworld and try to track down Jennifer Mathews' avatar."

"You think there might be another dead AV, like there was with Maximillian Thrust?"

"It's possible."

"And where would that lead us?"

"I've no idea. But what else am I going to do? Whoever killed them is still in there, as well as out here. Someone, somewhere, must know something. Do you have those notes we took on her account?"

She slipped a folded sheet of paper from her back pocket and handed it to him. He held the tiller steady with his thigh while he opened it up. Quick Thinker was the AV name she had used. And she had joined at least a dozen different Groups.

"I gotta go back to work," Janey said. "If it's a quiet afternoon I'll see what I can find out about Mathews' and Smitts' RLs. See if I can find anything to connect them, apart from SL."

Michael nodded. "Thanks, Janey." But he wasn't very sanguine. He glanced at the time. Eighteen hours of his twenty-four had already gone. Seconds, minutes, hours ticking away, slipping like sand through his fingers. If he didn't find this Second Life killer in the next six hours, he was as good as dead himself. He looked up and saw his two minders waiting for him on the landing stage. Dark suits and sunglasses, and murderous intent.

Chapter Twenty-Six

Chas logged into SL and rezzed in the offices of the Twist of Fate Detective Agency. There was something oddly reassuring about being back in the virtual world. A sense of escape, of safety, no matter how illusory that might be. The serenity of the fish that swam endlessly from one side of the fish tank to the other without ever needing fed was, in a way, comforting, as if for all its impermanence this world had also a sense of something enduring. And in the persona of Chas, he felt a greater sense of optimism. That there was more he could do in here than he ever could out there.

He checked his Friends List to see if Doobie was online and saw that she was. He sent her an IM.

> *Chas:* Hey, Doobs. I need some help.

Almost immediately he was offered a teleport to Bahia Tiki and Zen Beach Store. He accepted and rezzed on a wooden boardwalk laid between houses on a vast stretch of sandy beach. Doobie was standing, arms folded, looking at a wooden signboard outside a sprawling teak house with thatched roofs and a red cloth canopy over the main entrance. The sign read: P. Cana House (Dominican Republic). And underneath, a list of features. Fireplace. Mod and Copy. 103 prims. Adjustable Blinds. Lockable Door.

Doobie: What do you think?

Chas: What do I think about what?

Doobie: The house. Just 2300 Lindens. And a nice big deck area for sitting out on.

Chas: You're not thinking of buying it?

Doobie: Of course. Why not?

Chas: Well, what would you do with it?

Doobie: Live in it, of course. I'm fed up with my old place, and the land will support a few more prims. So this would make a nice change.

She turned toward a packing trunk half buried in the sand beside the sign. Text hovering above it read, *Barbados/P. Cana Furniture.*

Doobie: A full kit of furniture for another 2600. I'm sorely tempted.

Chas: I didn't know you had a house here.

Doobie: Lots of things you don't know about me, Chas Chesnokov.

He paused for a moment to look at her now that she had fully rezzed. She was wearing the tiniest of red bikinis, top and bottom connected by a series of gold chains. She stood on high heels that gave her an extraordinarily sexy, animated walk, stilettos clicking as if on terracotta tiles, even when she was walking on sand. Her dark, red-streaked hair tumbled luxuriantly across square shoulders, and her skin seemed shinier than he remembered, more tanned.

Doobie: Come and have a look inside. Tell me how I can help you while we're viewing it. Oh, and if I don't respond straight away it's 'cos my mouth's full of coffee. Hard to drink and type at the same time.

Chas: Damn, Doobie, I could murder a Starbucks right now! Didn't get my fix today.

Doobie: LOL. Wouldn't have taken you for the Starbucks type, Chas.

Chas: I'm an addict. Doobs. There's one on the island right down below where I live. I'm in there every morning. Free wifi now, too, for regulars. So no excuse ever to be offline.

He followed the sway of her hips up a short flight of wooden steps to the deck. Potted plants and multicoloured loungers peppered the terrace. Doobie went straight inside. Fronds and flowers grew in a circular plot of earth bounded by a stone wall, and a palm tree sprouted up and out through an open-roofed area of the entry hall.

Bamboo walls gave way to a bedroom off to the right and a dining room through wooden arches to the left. More arches led through to a long living room where settees and armchairs were gathered around a log fire burning in a stone hearth.

Doobie: What do you think?

Chas: It's nice. A bit dark, though. Be nicer if the wood was a lighter tone.

Doobie turned toward him.

Doobie: You're right, Chas. I probably wouldn't have thought of that till I'd bought the damned thing, and then got depressed once I was sitting in it. So what's happening?

Chas: I'm in trouble, Doobs. Big trouble.

Doobie: Connected to the murder of Maximillian Thrust?

Chas: Thrust was the AV of a real-life accountant called Arnold Smitts. He worked for the mob.

Doobie: Oh, my God, Chas.

Chas: He must have been laundering or hiding money for them. There was more than three million dollars in his account when it got erased. That money got transferred twice after that, the second time ending up by some mistake in my account. But his employers think I stole it.

Doobie: Just give them it back, then.

Chas: I can't. I used it to pay off my home loan.

There was a long silence.

Doobie: I keep wondering why the words fucking and stupid come to mind.

Chas: I know, I know, I know. I was in desperate trouble financially, Doobs. But the money's not lost. Just tied up in my house. Trouble is, they want it back by tonight, and there's no way I'm going to be able to do that.

Doobie: So what do you think they'll do?

Chas: Oh, they've made it perfectly clear what they'll do, Doobs. They're going to kill me.

Doobie: OMG!

Chas: But here's the thing. Smitts wasn't the only one to get bumped off for his money in Second Life. A young woman called Jennifer Mathews was murdered the day after Smitts. Her father had been using her account to hide money from the taxman. And it's gone, too.

Doobie: Not into your account again?

Chas: No, not this time. But I thought maybe if I could track down her AV, figure out what she maybe had in common with Maximillian Thrust, that might lead us to the SL killer.

Doobie: And therefore the RL killer.

Chas: Exactly.

Doobie: A bit of a long shot, Chas.

Chas: I know. But what else am I going to do? Will you help me, Doobs? There might be a dead AV lying somewhere, just like Thrust. Some clue that might help. I don't know. I'm clutching at straws here.

Doobie: What was her AV name?

Chas: Quick Thinker.

Doobie: Hmmm. Didn't think quickly enough, obviously. Let me take a look.

Chas: You can't. Her account was erased. Just like Arnold Smitts' account.

Doobie: You know what Groups she was in?

Chas: Some of them.

And he reeled off the ones that he and Janey had noted from the file.

Chas: DJ Badboy's Fans, MANO-SAV INC, Pink Parts, SL's Black Label Society, The BDSM Forum…

Doobie: That's interesting.

Chas: What is?

Doobie Littlething: The BDSM Forum. I know a number people who're into that. Let me see who's online right now, and I'll fire off a few IMs.

Chas: Sure.

While Doobie's animation override took her through a series of thoughtful poses as she composed and sent her IMs, Chas took the opportunity to explore the house. A long table of aged mahogany stood on a glowing orange carpet in the dining room, beneath three basket-woven lampshades. Windows with retractable blinds gave out on to views all along the front and side of the house. The bedroom had three picture windows and a large colourful bed beneath sloping thatch.

Chas glanced back to see if Doobie was looking. But she seemed engrossed, and he clicked on the bed hoping to see a menu for its sex animations. But none appeared. Hovering his mouse over it told him that it was a simple Barbados bed. Not a sex bed. He felt mildly disappointed. Janey had aroused his curiosity.

Doobie: We're in luck.

Chas went back through to the sitting room.

Doobie: One of the girls in the BDSM group knew her quite well. Apparently she used to dance at a joint called the Twisted Shemales Club.

Chas: Shemale?

Doobie Littlething sighs.

Doobie: She. Male. Transsexual, Chas.

Chas: But she wasn't a transsexual. Not as far as I know.

Doobie: Doesn't matter. Some people like to role-play in SL. Sometimes the more extreme the RP the better they like it. Easy enough for a girl to buy a penis and play out the role of a shemale. After all, it's the fantasy that counts, not the reality. Hang on…

He saw her head turn left and right, looking up and down the screen, following the movements of her cursor. Then,

Doobie: Okay, I've got me a teleport to the club. I'll TP you when I get there.

And she disappeared, this time in an explosion of coloured light radiating out from a central point. It had barely faded before Chas' TP invitation arrived. He accepted immediately, and was sucked into the time and space continuum of Second Life that delivered him seconds later into a sex mall immediately outside the Twisted Shemales Club. As the mall began to rez around him, he saw a store selling XXX DVDs under the heading *Boys will be Girls*. Another was called *Ass Hole*, opposite which a clothes store sold *Star Panties for large breasted women with dicks*. Outside the entrance to the club itself an enormous poster pasted to the wall displayed a voluptuous shemale bending over, baring her ass to the world. *Twisted Shemales Club open 24/7. We offer you a nice and friendly atmosphere, our girls are wonderful, and open-minded. Feel free to walk in and get to know us if you haven't already.*

Doobie had not waited for him, but gone straight inside. Chas followed, passing between two blue columns and a transparent veil that allowed him to pass right through it without hindrance. He found himself in a large, square room with a panelled ceiling and a dazzling, flashing dance floor that was liberally scattered with poseballs.

On the far side of the room, stools were set all along two low stages that flanked a central bar, and customers sat watching what appeared to be women sliding provocatively up and down gleaming dance poles. There were blue tip jars placed in front of each dancer, most of whom were in various stages of undress. Chas joined Doobie in front of one of the dancers and immediately received an IM from her.

> *Doobie:* LOLOL. I've had half a dozen propositions already. They're all so disappointed when I tell them I don't have a little package tucked away between my legs. This girl knew Quick, though.

Chas looked up at the dancer. Her name was Lashing Vollmar. She wore a long-sleeved black top that just covered her breasts and no more, the skimpiest pair of denim hotpants he had ever seen, and impossibly high-heeled red shoes. Her auburn hair was partially tied back in a knot behind her head, leaving strands of it to loop down on either side of her luminous orange sunglasses.

> *Doobie:* We might have to pay her something, though, to persuade her to come down and talk to us for a few minutes. You don't have any money, do you?
>
> *Chas:* I did have three million or so. But right now I'm down to my last two hundred.
>
> *Doobie:* Well, that should get five minutes of her time.

Chas paid his remaining two hundred Lindens into Lashing's tip jar and logged into a three-way IM with Doobie and the dancer. As he did, he glanced up and saw that Lashing had removed her top, and a pair of magnificent virtual breasts swung free as she slid down the pole and swivelled to face them.

> *Lashing:* Thanks, honey.
>
> Chas was unaccountably embarrassed.
>
> *Chas:* I didn't mean for you to take your top off.
>
> *Doobie:* LOLOL!
>
> *Lashing:* Well, it's five hundred if you want me to go all the way. You wanna see my cock?
>
> *Chas:* No! We want to talk.
>
> *Lashing:* Hahaha. Well, talking's expensive. Especially in a threesome. You guys are kinky!
>
> *Doobie:* How much?
>
> *Lashing:* Another five.

Doobie Littlething sighs.

Chas heard a cash register as Doobie paid another five hundred into Lashing's tip jar.

> *Doobie:* You owe me, Chas. Okay, girl. Tell us about Quick.
>
> *Lashing:* Well, I'm not really the one to ask.
>
> *Chas:* Jesus Christ! We just paid you seven hundred Lindens.
>
> *Lashing:* Okay, cutie pie, keep your shirt on! You're getting your money's worth, aren't you? Take a look.

Chas glanced up from the dialogue box and saw that Lashing was now wearing nothing except for a pair of black leather leggings, with cutaways around the crotch and calfs. Between her legs hung an enormous penis in full erection.

> *Chas:* OMG!
>
> *Doobie:* LOLOLOLOL! So who should we ask about Quick, Lashing?
>
> *Lashing:* A girl called Raika Spirit. Another of the dancers here.
>
> *Doobie:* A shemale?
>
> *Lashing:* Only in SL, dear. RL female. Just like Quick.
>
> *Chas:* Are most of the dancers really women?
>
> *Lashing:* Some of them. It's easier to get work, you see. Too much competition in the straight clubs. And in SL it's easy just to buy an add-on attachment.
>
> *Doobie:* What about you?
>
> *Lashing:* Oh, I'm the real deal, sweetheart. SL and RL. Why? You interested? I can give you an hour for fifteen hundred in one of our skyboxes.
>
> *Doobie:* Hahaha. No thanks, Lashing. Interesting thought, though.

Lashing Vollmar smiles sweetly and blows Doobie a soft kiss.

Chas opened up his search window and typed in the name of Raika Spirit.

> *Chas:* Raika is online. I'll IM her.
>
> *Lashing:* No, let me talk to her first. I don't want her thinking I've been shooting my mouth off. Hold…

Chas and Doobie watched for several minutes in silence as Lashing gyrated around her pole, thrusting her naked bottom in their direction, then spinning around and leaning back to raise her erection toward the ceiling. A large crowd was gathered around them now, everyone watching. None of the other dancers was yet revealing as much as Lashing.

> *Lashing:* Okay, Raika's not sure if she wants to talk to you. She and Quick are good friends.
>
> *Doobie:* Were, Lashing.
>
> *Lashing:* Were what?
>
> *Doobie:* Good friends. Quick is dead. SL and RL.
>
> *Lashing:* OMG! Hold…
>
> This time she was back to them much faster.
>
> *Lashing:* She's at home. Here's an LM
>
> Landmark windows appeared on both their screens.
>
> *Lashing:* But before you go…Tell me. What happened to Quick?
>
> *Chas:* She was murdered, Lashing.

Chapter Twenty-Seven

Raika Spirit lived in a rectangular Japanese house of windows and screens built around a central courtyard with a hot tub and flower garden. Eerily, it made Chas think of the house in Dolphin Terrace. But in all other respects it was quite different. Set in rolling parkland, thickly wooded by leafy, deciduous trees, it stood in the tranquility of an arboretum behind a brick wall and high hedges. It was breezy here, and everything bowed and dipped in the wind's soft caress. To access the garden they had to pass through an arched brick gate bearing the sign "Slow Down!!! Sim X-ing." Chas was aware of the slight jolt as they passed almost seamlessly from one sim to the next, and looked up to see Raika standing waiting for them at the top of the steps.

Raika: Come in.

She led them into the long east wing of the house, divided by screens into three open rooms. The door slid shut behind them. They passed a Buddha on a bookshelf, potted plants, and occasional chairs, and followed her into a corner room with windows looking out over the arboretum toward the ocean beyond. A long, low table with kneeling mats then led off into the central area of the house. There was a bottle of saki sitting on the table, and several china cups.

Raika stood for a moment, as if contemplating her next move, and Chas thought how attractive she looked. She had long, crinkly, red hair tied at the nape of her neck and tumbling in a mane down her back. She wore tight jeans and a cross-over cream sweater that revealed the swell of her breasts. Her face was thin, with an almost pointed chin, and she had the most penetrating amber eyes that blinked continuously behind long, long lashes.

She padded in bare feet across the carpet and sat on one of the kneeling stools.

Raika: Take a seat.

Chas knelt with his back to the window and saw, through a partially open screen door, water tumbling over a collection of large boulders in a square, marble hot tub. The sound of running water tinkled gently in the silence of the house.

Raika: Tell me it's not true.

Chas: I wish we could, Raika.

Raika: I can't believe it. She was my best friend in SL. I couldn't understand why I hadn't heard from her. We exchanged IMs every day. And when the grid was down, we would chat on Skype. What happened?

Chas: Somebody shot her, Raika. We think she was killed for a large amount of money that was in her SL account. Did you know anything about that?

Raika: No. I didn't know that much about her RL. Except that money didn't seem to be a problem. She had a huge house in SL, just off an island called Revere. She'd bought it, along with an enormous parcel of land. God knows what she was paying in tiers. We used to hang out there a lot when we weren't working. Fabulous beach. Views across the water to a little group of islands and a smoking volcano. It was cool, you know. People used to drop by. We would drink wine and chat.

Doobie: Where did you meet her?

Raika: At Twisted's. She'd been dancing there a while, and I was the new girl. The guys, you know, girls, whatever…they were a bit cliqué, know what I mean? Nice, but, well, you know, the third sex. So we real girls kinda stuck together. Quick took me under her wing. Took me shopping for clothes, skins, anims. She's basically responsible for the way I look now.

There was a long pause.

Raika: I…I still can't believe it. I could tell her anything, you know? And she never judged me. Jees, I mean, I had some pretty rough relationships in here, and she was always there to pick up my pieces. I don't know how I'll survive without her.

Chas: Did you ever hear her talk about a guy called Maximillian Thrust?

Raika: No, not that I can remember. One of her clients, maybe.

Doobie: Clients?

Raika: She did escort work, as well as dancing at Twisted's and a couple of straight clubs. Loved the whole virtual sex thing. Playing the slut. Know what I mean? She didn't do it for the money. She got such a kick out of it.

Chas: Did she have any boyfriends? Or any other special friends?

Raika: She had lots of friends. She was a popular girl. But she didn't seem interested in having any kind of serious relationship in here. No BFs that I knew of.

Chas: Did she ever give you the idea that she was scared of something, or that something was troubling her?

Raika: In RL?

Chas: Both.

Raika: Not really. She always seemed pretty fearless to me. Nothing fazed her, you know?

Doobie: Could you give us a Landmark for her house in Revere?

Raika: I'll take you there, if you like.

There was a pause.

Raika: Oh, God. I just looked in my Landmark folder and saw the LM. Quick's Place. I used to click on that so often. Every time I was down. Every time I was up, and needed to share. I guess this'll be the last time I go there. What'll happen to the house and all her stuff? I suppose it'll be returned to her Inventory when the tiers run out.

Doobie: There is no inventory Raika. The account's been erased. I guess all her things will just be deleted from the asset server.

Raika: Aw, shit. That's such a shame. She has lovely stuff, too.

She stood up.

Raika: I'll send you a TP.

◇◇◇

As in RL, Quick Thinker lived in a mansion, a huge house that filled an entire corner of an island in Emelia Bay, just off the coast of Revere. Water tumbled over the smooth boulders of an enormous waterfall into a small inlet behind the house. Acres of deck space, and a roof terrace covered an area the size of two tennis courts. The west-facing beach was punctuated by leaning palm trees and dotted with tables and chairs and loungers. A campfire sent smoke and sparks spiralling up into a clear sky. On the far corner of the parcel stood a blue helter-skelter tower with dance animations on its flat roof, and beyond it, the smoke from the volcano hung over the island like a dark, brooding cloud.

When Raika clicked on the wood-panelled front door, it turned transparent, and they were able to walk through it into a marble-floored sitting room where sofas and armchairs were grouped around a large open fire. Coloured light filtered in through a tall stained glass window above the mantel.

Reproductions of works by famous nineteenth- and twentieth-century impressionists hung on red and tan walls. In the hallway, a Roman-style bath sank into the marble had two poseballs set along one side of it, *lix m, lix f.* Which didn't take too much imagination to envision.

The hallway then opened into another sprawling lounge area, arched windows looking out over palm-shaded gardens. Here stood another open fire, and an oval frame on the wall above it showed an SL photo sequence of Quick herself.

Raika: That's her. OMG, I think I'm going to cry.

Chas watched the slide-show once through. The sequence contained half a dozen pictures, some portraits, some full-length poses, and one depicting her naked on a beach. She was tall, blond, and beautiful, like so many other women in SL. Chas had seen her corpse spreadeagled across the bed and knew that, in truth, she'd had short, brown hair and a broad, plain face. But, then, death had a habit of stealing beauty away from the features of its victims. Quick, he imagined, was how Jennifer would have liked to look.

A spiral staircase led up to a sumptuous bedroom, where a bed was raised high on three levels. Flames licked around the hearth of yet another open fire. Windows looked out over the sea, and patio doors opened on to the roof terrace. There was no sign of a corpse. Quick's dead AV was not here.

A touch on a tile set into the wall TP-ed them back downstairs.

Chas: Nothing here.

Raika: What were you hoping to find?

Doobie: A corpse.

Raika: I don't understand.

Chas: We're pretty sure that her AV was killed in SL before or after she was murdered in RL. There should still be a body somewhere.

Raika: Maybe in the Whorehouse.

Doobie: The what?

Raika Spirit laughs sadly.

Raika: It's what she called the place she took her clients. Just a small house, over on the main island. She did it up like your classic whorehouse. Red velvet. Black velour. Silk sheets, sex furniture, and more poseballs than you'd find in a sex shop. Wanna see it?

◇◇◇

They flew over to Revere, following Raika as she passed over the Lost Frontier sound stage and Emelia shopping plaza. Beyond two enormous trees whose spreading branches supported platforms and pavilions that overlooked the stage, they overflew an open-roofed art gallery and crossed a stream, landing finally beside a small, square, two-storey brownstone house with blacked-out windows. Raika led them around to the far side, where an ivy-covered wooden fence bordered the property. She clicked on the door and it slid open.

From the inside, the windows were clear, giving out views across the stream toward the gallery. Sex settees and lapdance armchairs filled the downstairs area. An item of furniture called

Sex Stand Behind Pleaser looked like some implement of torture. Floating green text above it read *Pump* and *Tie Down*. White shaggy rugs covered the floor, and a variety of poseballs offered every imaginable sexual position. A ramp led upstairs to where a large bed with black silk sheets and white pillows was pushed up against the wall.

Quick was stretched out across the bed, just as in real life, still attached to her poseball in the open-legged missionary position, a single black hole torn through her naked chest. Blood was spattered across the pillows, and the wall behind the bed. The sheets were soaked in it, as if it were still fresh and wet. Light slanting in through the windows was reflected white on red.

Raika gasped.

Raika: Oh, my God! Oh, my God! How is this possible? Oh, my poor Quick! I can't stay and look at this.

Chas: Just two minutes, Raika, please. I need you to tell me if there's anything here out of the ordinary. Anything here that shouldn't be. Anything that might give us a clue as to who did this.

Raika controlled her urge to flee and turned, looking around the room. In the end, she shook her head.

Raika: I'm sorry. I can hardly see for the tears in my RL eyes. It's just awful. But there's nothing…you know, that I can see. It just looks normal. Except for Quick. Can I go, please?

Doobie: Go, hon.

And Raika was gone in a twinkle of lights to nurse her SL grief and spill her RL tears. Chas and Doobie looked at the dead AV in silence for several minutes, before Chas ran off a series of snapshots, putting them in a folder in his Inventory, and copying them to Doobie.

They moved out, then, onto a long terrace, with views over a small lake to a collection of beach houses on the far side.

Dolphins frolicked in the water, and seagulls swooped overhead, their distant cawing carried on the wind.

Chas: It's a dead end, Doobs. Nothing to connect her to Thrust. And nothing in RL that we know of to connect her to Smitts.

Doobie: And apart from the body, nothing much here to go on, either.

Chas: Unless there's something that strikes you. You have a more experienced SL eye than me.

Doobie looked around again.

Doobie: Nothing immediately obvious.

Chas leaned on the rail and gazed at the water, hope deserting him as depression descended once more. He was no further forward. No nearer to securing the required three and a quarter million or to finding out who had murdered Smitts or Mathews.

Chas: I think I'll log out.

Doobie: What are you going to do?

Chas: I've no idea. But I've reached a dead end in here. And time is slipping away. Time that I can't afford to waste.

Doobie: You know, in a strange way, you have more time in here than you do out there. You could have three days in Second Life before your real life deadline runs out. And you can do a lot more in three days than in six hours.

Chas: I suppose…

Doobie: What you need to do is empty your mind so you can think more clearly. There's nothing much better for doing that than a game of chess.

And when he didn't respond…

Doobie: Would you like a game?

Chas sighed. He remembered all those games he had played with Mora. How he had lost himself in them, and how that single focus had created a perspective on the rest of his life that was somehow lacking now.

Chas: Yes, Doobs. I would.

Chapter Twenty-Eight

The air was suffused with the pink glow of sunset. They were well into their game and the sun seemed no lower on the horizon.

Chas: Does the sun ever set here?

Doobie: I'm not sure that it does. I know that night falls in other parts of the island, but on the chess terrace it has only ever been sunset while I have been here.

The circle of columns around them glowed warm in the reflected light from the water below, and each chessman was highlighted in amber. On Doobie's advice, Chas had zoomed back, adjusting his POV so that he was looking at the two of them facing each other across the chessboard, with the light of the dying sun shimmering on the moving surface of the ocean beyond.

Doobie had changed her outfit yet again. A long, black dress, sleeveless, with a dipping neckline. Her skin seemed to shine like tinted ivory, her hair piled high on her head. For a time Chas forgot the game and examined her. He had seen more glamorous AVs in his short time in SL. But there was something different about Doobie. There was almost beauty in her face, a serenity in her expression that he knew was more than animated pixels. In some way that he couldn't quite understand, her personality was colouring his perception of her appearance. He followed the line of her fine, full lips with his eyes. Her cupid's bow, the slight upturn of her nose, her liquid brown eyes. The tiny heart-shaped birthmark high on her cheek, below her right eye. And he thought that she was very lovely. And that if he had been a man on his own looking for a woman, he might have found her. He was a man on his own, certainly, but the only woman he had ever really loved was lost, and he doubted that he would ever find another.

Doobie: Chas…

Chas: Yes?

Doobie: It's your move.

He glanced down at the board and saw that she had shifted her knight to C6. But he barely had time to consider the consequences of her move.

Doobie: I sense a sadness in you, Chas.

He looked up. How could she sense anything across the ether? He had known her for such a very short time, and their exchanges had hardly been intimate.

Chas: How do you detect my sadness?

Doobie: It's in your tone.

Chas laughed.

Chas: I have a tone?

Doobie: Yes. We transmit so much about ourselves, in the way we construct a sentence, in the length of a pause, in the speed of a response. I have become sensitive to these things in SL. It is the only real way I have of gauging other people. We can seldom trust what they tell us: the man posing as the sensitive young lesbian; the night club gigolo who is really some decrepit old man. So we develop other means of divining the truth.

Chas: And what do you divine about me?

Doobie: That you are still a young man, perhaps in your thirties. That there has been some tragedy in your life, something I don't really think you have come to terms with. And there was something in an exchange you had with Twist that led me to believe that maybe you have just returned to work after a long absence. Perhaps an illness. That you are wealthier than most forensic photographers, but that you still have financial problems.

Chas was stunned to silence. That she had managed to infer so much about him from so little, it was almost frightening.

Doobie: Am I right?

Chas: You're pretty close. A good guesser, perhaps.

Chas Chesnokov smiles.

Chas: You know, I spent months in therapy, and I don't think my therapist could have summed me up that well. Actually, she's the reason I'm here. Group therapy sessions in SL.

Doobie: Was it a death? The tragedy. Did someone die?

Chas: My wife.

Doobie: Oh. When?

Chas: A little over six months ago.

Doobie: How?

Chas: A very short illness. Cancer. By the time they diagnosed it, the damned thing was too far gone for treatment. She barely lasted ten days. Long enough that I felt her suffering through every long, painful moment of it. But still not long enough to say goodbye. Not really. Not properly. I was still in shock when she went, as if she had been taken from me in an instant.

Doobie: So you're still saying goodbye.

Chas: I suppose I am.

Doobie: Because if ever you finish your farewells, then she really will be gone.

Chas was silent for several long moments. He had never thought of it that way. In all the hours of therapy he had undergone, it had never occurred to him that his problem could be that simple. Angela had only ever encouraged him to talk. And he must have repeated himself countless times, going over and over the same old ground.

Chas: I'm not sure I would know how to do that now, Doobie. After so long.

Doobie: You go to her grave, Chas, and you close your eyes, and you imagine her there in front of you. As clearly as if you could touch her. And in your mind you do. You reach out and feel her warm skin on your fingertips. You run them lightly down her cheek, and take her chin, turning it up a little toward you. And you lean in to kiss her. So softly. Conveying in that touch of your lips all the love you ever felt for her. Then you take her in your arms and hold her, and let the tears run down your cheeks. Don't be ashamed of them. And when you are ready, put your lips next to her ear and whisper, "goodbye darling." And let her go, Chas. Just let her go.

Somewhere on the far side of the screen, in a world beyond pixels and images, he felt real tears trickle down his cheeks. And it was some minutes before he found words again to work his fingers.

Chas: Sounds like you might be talking from experience, Doobie.

After a long silence new text appeared.

Doobie: They send our troops to some far-flung corners of

this RL world, Chas, and sometimes it's so damned hard
to figure out why. Young men, some of them barely old
enough to vote, many of them not old enough to drink.
Certainly without any understanding of the issues that led
the politicians to send them in the first place. So many
of them die without ever knowing why. A long way from
home and the people who loved them.

Chas: What happened?

Doobie: He wasn't even a combat soldier, Chas. Supplies
and inventory. But it meant he wasn't usually in the firing
line. So I didn't worry too much.

Chas: Were you married?

Doobie: Engaged. We were going to be married when he
finished his tour.

Doobie Littlething shakes her head.

Doobie: The irony is, it wasn't the enemy that killed him.
It was an accident. Damn chopper ferrying officers from
base camp to the airport. Came down with engine failure.
Eighteen young men. All gone. In that instant you talked
about. And I never did get over it. He had left me with
child, from his last home leave. And I thought, at least I
will always have a part of him.

Chas waited. He knew there was nothing he could say, no
question he could ask. Whatever she had to tell him would come
in her own time.

Doobie: I miscarried in the sixth month.

Chas: Oh, Doobs.

He wished he could reach out a hand to touch her. And for
the first time in this Second Life, he felt confined by it. Limited,
frustrated.

Doobie: I had no chance to say goodbye to either, until I knelt in the grass by his grave and held them both in my arms, and told them that one day I would be with them. And that although we were saying our goodbyes now, we would all be together again someday in the not too distant future. And then I let them go.

After another long silence Chas began typing.

Chas: People keep saying to me, Doobs, "You'll meet someone else". But I can't imagine it. How about you?

Doobie: No. Me neither. I never have, and I never will.

Chas: Never is a very long time.

Doobie Littlething smiles.

Doobie: It is.

Chas: So I guess you are an American, then?

Doobie: Oh, now you're starting to divine things about me.

Chas: You said, they send *our* troops.

Doobie: Well done, Mr. Detective.

Chas: And I guess since you seem to be online pretty much around the same time as me, you are West Coast rather than East? Pacific time zone?

Doobie Littlething smiles.

Doobie: It never ceases to amaze me how curious people are in Second Life about the real lives of others, but hardly ever wanting to reveal anything about themselves.

Chas: It's only human nature, Doobs. I suppose people are just people, whether in RL or SL. We're just the same.

Doobie: Not necessarily.

Chas: No?

Doobie: The real world has become so complex, Chas, that it's harder and harder for us to be ourselves, to express ourselves freely. SL removes the conventions. And here's the irony. In a world where the reality is virtual, and completely unreal, it is far easier for us to be our real selves. If you spend any time in here, you will come to see that.

They sat for a long time in silence then. Chas returned his attention to the chessboard and found himself running and re-running a sequence of moves around his head, each time arriving at the same conclusion. He moved his bishop.

Chas: Checkmate.

Doobie looked at the board, and studied it for several long minutes. Then she looked up, and Chas saw her animated smile peeling lips back across her teeth.

Doobie: You distracted me.

Chas: You distracted yourself.

Doobie: You cheated.

Chas: No. I beat you fair and square.

Doobie: Grrrr!

Chas: Hahaha. It's a long time since I beat anyone at chess.

Doobie: Who did you play, before you started playing against yourself?

Chas: Mora.

Doobie: Your wife?

Chas Chesnokov nods.

Chas: I think I beat her twice. But that was early on, just after I'd taught her.

Doobie: You taught her to play, and then let her beat you?

Chas: Oh, I didn't let her beat me. She just did. Time after time.

Doobie: A mere reflection of the innate superiority of women over men. The only reason you beat me today was because I was not giving the game my full attention.

Chas: Yeh, yeh, yeh. You realise that you will now have to number me amongst your potential suitors.

Doobie: Oh, will I? And why's that?

Chas: You told me, that last time, that you would never fall for a man who couldn't beat you at chess.

Doobie: Yes, well, it's a matter of respect, isn't it? But that, of course, would only apply if I was actually looking for a man. Which I'm not.

Chas: You don't need to. You have men all the time.

Doobie: For sex and money, yes. But anything else is strictly off limits. I'm not in the game for a relationship, Chas.

He felt himself unaccountably disappointed. Unaccountably, he reasoned, because how would it be possible to have a relationship in a world that only existed somewhere between the mind and a computer screen? Disappointed, because there was a big empty place inside of him that needed filled. And he liked her. Without rhyme or reason. He thought for a few moments.

Chas: Is it hard to buy a penis?

Doobie: LOL. Well, it's not hard when you buy it. Only when your lover touches it.

Chas: Ha. Ha. Ha. You know what I mean.

Doobie Littlething looks at Chas inquisitively.

Doobie: You really want to buy a penis? What for?

Chas: Just curious.

Doobie: Uh-huh? Sit tight. I'll send you a TP.

◇◇◇

Chas dropped down from a night sky into a winter landscape. Snowflakes fell all around, accumulating on the roofs of wooden ski lodges gathered around an area of ice sculptures and snow-men. People stood around in groups chatting. An IM *chinged* on his screen.

> *Doobie:* Inside.

Chas turned around to find himself facing the entrance to a sprawling stone-built store with a high, steeply pitched wooden roof. The doorway was flanked by giant posters. *What's Hot? THE X3 NIPPLES! ANAL TOYS.* And beyond it, a photograph of a couple making love above the legend, *Xcite! The Finest Sexual Equipment.* He waded through the snow to make his way inside.

Arched entrances opened into different areas of the store. Nonhumans. Boys. Girls. Upgrades. Chas walked past a fire smouldering in an open hearth and through the arch into the boys' store. The walls were lined with depictions of various versions of the Xcite penis, which advertised itself as *The Sculpted X3 Cock.* There were pierced penises and textured ones in different colours. Penises in cages and tied in ribbons. There were even penises that came ready-fitted with condoms and accompanying colour changes.

Doobie was idling impatiently beside a free-standing poster for a Male Starter Pack that boasted the inclusion of a Sculpted

Cock, X3 nipples, a HUD Control Panel, and an "Xcite Me' Club Shirt.

Doobie: For a mere 1200 Lindens, you too could be a real man. Actually this one's pretty good.

Chas: How do you know?

Doobie Littlething tuts.

Doobie: Use your imagination. Are you going to buy it or not?

Chas: I don't have any money.

He heard a cash register, and saw that Doobie had just paid him 1200 Lindens.

Doobie: You now owe me 2200, Chas. And since I have an investment to protect, I'm going to have to make sure we keep you safe from the mob. LOL.

Chas: Very funny.

Doobie: Go ahead and buy it.

She waited a moment.

Doobie: Done it?

Chas: Yes.

Doobie: Okay. I suppose I'd better show you how it works.

Chas: Here?

Doobie: LOL! No, of course not, you idiot. At my place. I'll TP you.

◇◇◇

Michael was suddenly transported from another world, another dimension, another persona, and found himself crashing back into RL with a start.

The phone was ringing.

He dragged his eyes away from the screen and the wall of sculpted cocks, to look at the info panel on the handset on his desk. It was Janey, calling from her cellphone. He had the sense that it had rung several times without impinging on his consciousness, so deep had he been in the character of Chas. He hesitated to answer it, drawn by a strange excitement and a curiosity about where this sexual interaction between Chas and Doobie was leading. But in the end, he decided that Janey wouldn't be calling unless she had something to tell him. He picked up the phone, but was greeted only by the dialling tone. She had rung off.

"Damn!"

Chapter Twenty-Nine

Doobie's home was located on a stretch of beach along an anonymous coastline, sea on one side, mountains rising on the other three to screen her from her neighbours. Wooden walkways criss-crossed the beach, leading to small, secluded areas—a tiny island below a waterfall, accessed by an arched bridge; a dead tree with a hanging swing seat surrounded by tall grasses and yellow flowers. Another waterfall was overlooked by a high platform with two chairs arranged for the view. And behind the house a two-tiered deck gave onto a private lagoon nestling between the hills.

The house itself was a two-storeyed mahogany beach house with a thatched roof, a plunge pool built into a wooden terrace. Palm trees leaned in from every angle.

Chas stood on the terrace and listened to the restful sound of bamboo windchimes stirring in the sea breeze, gazing out at a partially sunken sailing boat just offshore. The sound of the waves reached him on the same breeze.

Chas: This is wonderful. Why do you want a new house?

Doobie stood at the open door.

Doobie: When I bought this land, it was empty. Just the beach and the mountains. Everything here I bought or made. I created the little island, installed the waves, planted the trees and the grasses and the flowers, built the deck, created the waterfalls.

Chas: Wow! I wouldn't have known where to begin. It must have taken you ages.

Doobie: A couple of weeks.

Chas: Is that all?

Doobie: Well, when I'm not dancing or having sex, or shooting griefers, what else is there to do? Two weeks is a long time in SL.

Chas: So why do you want to change it?

Doobie: Because I'm bored. I like to be doing things. You'll find it's like that in here. As soon as anyone finishes something, they start again. Sometimes from scratch. You see, SL is really an escape, Chas. From an unhappy life. You need a reason to be here, a justification for the escape. So you never stop. Making, remaking, changing. It's the perfect excuse for wasting your life.

Chas turned to look at her. She stood in the doorway, arms folded, looking back at him. There was no change in her appearance, but suddenly her words filled her with bitterness and regret, and there seemed to him something sad in her expression. A reflection of those words.

She snapped out of her mood.

Doobie: Anyway, let's make a man of you.

He followed her inside, up a short flight of steps, and beyond a mesh screen to her bedroom. It was a simple room, with a bed, a shower, and a window that gave out onto a stunning view over the lagoon. Pictures hung on the wall: the sun setting with the sunken boat in the foreground; Doobie seminaked showering beneath one of her waterfalls; a gathering of friends around the campfire; a portrait of Doobie in camouflage and armour, holding her gun up close to her head, pointing it at the sky. Her head was dipped, and she was looking up dangerously from below her brows.

She turned to face him.

Doobie: Right. Strip off.

Chas: What?

Doobie: Come on. Don't be shy. I can't see you blushing from here.

Reluctantly, Chas removed all of his clothing, until he stood completely naked in front of the appraising eyes of his sexual mentor. He glanced at the vacant space between his legs, and felt oddly incomplete.

Doobie: Okay. Now you need to attach the penis to yourself.

Chas found the Xcite folder in his inventory and dragged it to himself. Suddenly a huge box, with a photograph of a giant penis on the side, attached itself to his head, and moved around as he did.

Doobie: LOLOLOLOL! ROFL!!! A huge penis on your head is not going to do the trick, Chas.

Chas: What happened?

Doobie: When I can stop laughing I might be able to tell you. I keep forgetting what a newbie you are. You have to open it first, Chas. LOL!!

Chas' embarrassment was acute, and he was glad that she couldn't see him blushing on the far side of the screen. But even as he detached the box from his head, he was starting to see the funny side of it. A window appeared on his screen. Doobie was offering him something. He clicked to accept, and a photograph of himself with a giant penis on his head rezzed on his monitor.

Chas: Hahahaha. Okay. I made a fool of myself. Start again, Chas.

He followed Doobie's instructions for rezzing his Xcite 3 Sculpted Cock, and an amazingly realistic penis appeared, hanging flaccid between his thighs. With Doobie's guidance, he found a control panel that allowed him to change the skin tone to match his own and bring a control HUD up on his screen. Suddenly his penis started growing to full erection.

Chas: What happened?

Doobie: I touched it. Just clicked on it with my mouse, and bingo, you are a man ready for action. LOL. Follow me.

She led him to the bed, and two poseballs appeared.

Doobie: Click on the blue.

He did, and found himself propelled on to the bed, lying naked on his back with his erection pointing toward the heavens. Doobie was lying curled into his side, stroking his chest. And somehow, in the time it had taken them to arrive in this position, she had become naked too.

Doobie: Have you ever had cyber sex, Chas?

Chas: You know I haven't.

Doobie: Then let me just take you through it. Slowly.

Suddenly they flipped positions and were sitting up on the bed, arms around each other, kissing.

Doobie: Feel my lips on yours, Chas. I open them a little, and you feel my tongue slipping into your mouth, searching for yours. Feel my hands on your back, pulling you closer to me, my breasts pressing into your chest.

Chas felt the shock of unexpected sexual excitement, and butterflies flew and battered about in his stomach.

Doobie: I can feel your excitement pushing against my thigh. Hot. Hard. Mmmmh. You taste good, Chas.

So this was how it worked. Chas tried his first line.

Chas: I open my mouth and feel your lips turn against mine. Warm and wet. And your tongue in my mouth sends a thrill right through me.

At first he felt strangely embarrassed, and then as his excitement grew, emboldened to the point where it didn't seem to matter any more. His imagination took over, his eyes half-closed, picturing every movement, feeling every touch. His sense of the woman he was with seemed so real, that he could almost believe she was there with him in the flesh. This was the first sex of any kind he'd had since Mora's death, and it was as if a floodgate had opened inside him. Feelings and emotions and desires that had been pent up for so long came flowing through him in an almost uncontrollable rush.

Step by step, Doobie somehow controlled their AVs through the physical stages of the sex act, to the point where he saw himself slipping inside her, and imagined it so powerfully that it seemed almost more than real. All the time her words provoked and inflamed him, his responses following almost involuntarily.

Until a *ching* broke his concentration and an IM appeared on his screen.

It was from Jamir Jones. The gecko. And Chas remembered with a start that he had taken Jamir and Roger's money, 500 Lindens, and done nothing to earn it. His sexual arousal rapidly faded as the image of the two geckos on the floor of Twist's office returned to him like a bad dream.

> *Jamir:* Hi, Chas. Just a quick IM, since we hadn't heard from you. Any news for us about Nevar Telling? Roger's very impatient, but I told him you would be on it.

Chas was flustered now.

Chas: Doobie, I'm sorry. I've got incoming from the geckos.

Doobie: What?!

> *Chas:* Hi, Jamir. I hope to have news for you very soon. I'm just on my way to Sandbox Island right this minute.
>
> *Jamir:* Oh. Good. I knew we could rely on you Chas. We'll be waiting to hear what happened. We'll not go offline until you get back to us.

Chas: Damn!

He detached himself from the poseball and stood up on the bed, his erection rapidly wilting from lack of continuous excitement.

Doobie: What is it?

Chas: I have to go to Sandbox Island, Doobs, to deal with a griefer.

Doobie stood up.

Doobie: Really! Well, I'd better come with you, then. It's a damned dangerous place.

Chapter Thirty

Chas stood on top of a giant ketchup bottle and surveyed the scene two hundred feet below him. A vast, sandy plain shimmered off into an unrezzed distance. Smoke rose from a disabled tank. Several armoured vehicles lay in a tangle, embracing in a death crash. A Second World War fighter plane was buried nose-first in the sand. The sounds of distant battlecries carried on the wind, and Chas could see figures diving and darting around each other in the airspace overhead, flashes of light and smoke accompanying the sounds of gunfire. This was Sandbox Island, and Doobie stood beside him in full armour, arms folded across her chest, smiling in anticipation. She was ready for action.

Doobie: Everything that happens here is just temporary. You can do almost anything. Build or rez whatever you like. The server scans every five hours and erases everything. So anything goes. Griefers come to try out new weapons on each other, experiment with revolving spam boxes that just keep duplicating until they bring a sim to its knees. Gangs come to fight it out. It's a dangerous and anarchic place, Chas. The SL equivalent of somewhere like Somalia. If this Nevar Telling character hangs out here, then he's a bad lot.

Chas: I thought you came here.

Doobie Littlething grins.

Doobie: Just for target practice.

Chas had filled her in on the background to the case, and she was looking forward, with what he thought was an almost unhealthy relish, to the idea of a confrontation with Telling.

Doobie: We'll overfly the island. You take the west side. I'll go east. Keep an eye on your radar. If Telling appears on it, IM me.

The giant ketchup bottle stood at the northern tip of Sandbox Island, and they took off, left and right to head south and scan for the griefer. It was less than a minute before Chas saw Nevar Telling's name appear on his radar, just seventy metres distant.

> *Chas:* Got him, Doobie.
> *Doobie:* TP me.

In an instant she was hovering beside him, swivelling through 360 degrees.

> *Doobie:* Down there. Next to that bombed-out building.

And she was gone again, leaving a trail of smoke in her wake. Chas went after her, but couldn't keep up. As he approached the building and dropped to the ground, he saw Doobie, gun drawn, facing up to a Neanderthal-looking man in jeans and a torn tee-shirt with two bloody bullet holes. The tag above his head betrayed him as Nevar Telling. He was barefoot, unshaven, and bald, a cigarette smoking in the corner of his mouth. His left arm was tattooed all the way up, and one of his eyes was pure red.

But just as Chas touched down, Telling took off. Straight up, like an arrow, spinning as he went. And Doobie went after him, a first shot ringing out, leaving a smoke trail soaring into the blue. Chas craned to try to follow them, but they were gone, and he could only assume that they were using some kind of accelerated flight HUD. There was no way he could ever have kept up with them. He looked around.

The building next to him was a ruin, walls pitted and pock-marked by gunfire. Wisps of white smoke rose from within, and a pile of rubber tires burned outside what had once been the entrance, belching thick black smoke into the air. Abandoned vehicles were scattered around, like the decaying remains of animal carcasses.

Chas was startled, suddenly, to notice an orange and green dragon perched on top of a smouldering gallows. The creature was looking at him, eyes blinking imperiously. The name tag revealed him to be Devil Davis.

Chas: Hello.

Devil: Hello.

Chas: Are you a friend of Nevar Telling?

Devil: Not telling. Never will. Why do you want to know, Mr. Private Detective?

Chas: Just wondered, since the two of you were down here together.

Devil: Doesn't mean anything.

Chas: No. Just wanted a chat with him, that's all.

Nevar: What about?

Chas wheeled around to find himself facing the Neanderthal Telling. His right arm was extended, a large, ugly-looking weapon two inches from Chas' face. His lips drew back to reveal a mouthful of broken and decayed teeth, in what was more a grimace than a smile. Chas glanced quickly around, but there was no sign of Doobie.

Nevar: Doesn't matter anyway. Gonna blow your fucking head off.

Chas braced himself for the shot. There was nothing else he could do. But in the blink of an eye, Telling was suddenly encased in one of Doobie's cages, closely meshed black metal holding him so tightly that movement was impossible.

Nevar: WTF!

Doobie dropped out of the sky beside them, grinning, her gun held up by her head.

Nevar: Fucking bitch. I'll de-rez this in sixty seconds, and you'll never catch me.

Doobie: Never say never, Nevar.

She turned to Chas.

Doobie: I'll let you have the pleasure of blowing the brainless head off this bloated bastard, Chas. But you only have about forty seconds left to ask your questions.

Nevar: Questions?! What fucking questions!?

Chas: About my clients Jamir Jones and Roger Showmun. You might remember threatening them from the wing of their jet plane the other day.

Nevar: Oh, them? What about it?

Doobie: You're running out of time, Chas.

Chas: Okay.

He clicked on the red gun HUD on his screen and drew his weapon.

Nevar: Jesus Christ, you're not seriously going to shoot me with that?

Chas: Well, maybe I won't. But I'm going to need your word that you'll leave Roger and Jamir alone in the future.

Nevar: Hey, anything, man. It was just words, you know? Nothing serious. I mean you shoot me with that, I'm a dead AV.

Doobie: What makes you think that?

Nevar: He's Chesnokov, right? Chas Chesnokov. That's what his tag says, unless he's some kind of replicant.

Chas: No, you're looking at the genuine article.

Nevar: Well, that's the Super Gun you got, right? Scripted to kill. Hack the computer and wipe me out.

Chas: I don't know what you're talking about. I just wanted to speak to you about the geckos.

Doobie: Hang on. What do you know about this Super Gun, Nevar?

Nevar Telling was scathing.

Nevar: Everyone knows about the Super Gun. It's a fucking legend, isn't it? Can kill an AV, kill an account. Ever since Wicked disappeared off-world about three months ago, there have been rumours about who had the weapon.

Doobie: Wicked?

Nevar: Wicked Wilson. Fucking genius. It was Wicked that wrote the script. Stuff of dreams, man. Or nightmares. But he's gone. History. No one knows what happened to him. Shot himself, maybe. LOLOLOL.

Chas: What makes you think I know anything about it?

Nevar: Common knowledge, pretty boy. You wuz talking to Gunslinger about it just yesterday. Word is, you know where the gun is. And for all I know, that's it clutched in your sticky little paw. So I ain't taking no chances.

The cage de-rezzed.

Chas: Don't move.

Nevar: Hey, man. You got it. I ain't going nowhere while you're pointing that thing at me.

Chas: I need your word that you're going to steer clear of Jamir and Roger in future.

Nevar: Man, if those geckos want to fly around my airspace, you tell them they can go right ahead. They got my full blessing.

Chas: Okay.

He waggled his gun.

Chas: Go.

Telling didn't need a second invitation. He took off like a bullet and spun off into the blue, vanishing completely within a matter of seconds.

Devil: Nice gun, Chas.

Chas turned toward the dragon.

Devil: Gunslinger's 1911A1 Custom, am I right?

Chas: Yes. You are.

Devil: Thought so. That asshole wouldn't know a Super Gun from a lollipop. LOL. Well, thanks for the entertainment. See you, guys.

And he flapped green, webbed wings and took off with a loud beating of the air.

Doobie stood looking thoughtful, and Chas wondered if it was the animation, or whether he was just superimposing that impression on to a blank AV. Either way, it was becoming clear to him that SL projected much more than met the eye.

Doobie: Methinks, Chas, that we should pay a return visit to your friend, Gunslinger Kurosawa.

◇◇◇

They stood in the yard, among the swirling papers and the smoke from the brazier, waiting for Gunslinger to show. He had told them in IM that he would meet them back at his place. A bunch of soldiers in army fatigues and dark glasses pushed past them and into the store, walkie-talkies humming and crackling, the sound of distant voices burbling across the airwaves. They lined up along the edge of the sandpit and took it in turns to fire at Bin Laden.

Chas was nearly finished with the IM he was leaving for Twist. He had written an account of the gecko case, telling her that they had paid a further 500 Lindens on learning that Nevar Telling wouldn't bother them again.

Doobie had been silent for several long minutes, engrossed in Search and IM, trying to piece together every scrap of information available in SL on the subject of Wicked Wilson. Finally she emerged from Busy mode, and swivelled toward Chas.

Doobie: Seems that Wilson was some kind of computer geek in RL. No one knew exactly who he was, but he was famous amongst the griefing community here in SL. A kind of genius vandal. The kind of malicious mind that would concoct the worst sort of computer virus and let it loose on an unsuspecting world. Until he disappeared, he had a store here that sold very sophisticated weaponry and tracking systems. It was a mecca for all the griefers in SL. And the military and police communities were also frequent customers.

Chas nodded toward the soldiers in Gunslinger's store.

Chas: You mean, like these guys?

Doobie: Yeh.

Chas: I didn't know there were cops and soldiers in SL.

Doobie: LOL. Oh, they're not real, Chas. Just muttonheads macho role-playing.

A diffusion of light burgeoned in the air above them, and Gunslinger Kurosawa dropped to one knee, then stood up and glanced at his watch.

Kurosawa: Hi, guys, what can I do for you?

Doobie: Well, for a start, you could keep your mouth shut in future.

Chas jumped in hastily.

Chas: What Doobie means, Kuro, is that somehow it was all over SL today that we were talking to you yesterday about the Super Gun.

Kurosawa: Yeh, well, you know, it's kinda hard to keep a secret in this place.

Doobie: Well, you managed to keep the secret of Wicked Wilson and his Super Gun pretty much to yourself yesterday.

Gunslinger Kurosawa shrugs.

Kurosawa: There was nothing secret about Wicked. Everyone knew about him.

Chas: And the Super Gun?

Kurosawa: A rumour. Nothing more.

Chas: So what happened to him?

Kurosawa: No one knows. It was a complete mystery. One day he was there, the next he was gone. And since no one knew his RL identity, there was no way to know what had happened. When the tiers ran out on his store, it got erased, and everything with it. Damned shame. There was some fine weaponry in there.

Doobie: So do you think Wilson would have been capable of writing the kind of script you described to us yesterday?

Kurosawa: If anyone could, it would have been Wicked.

Chas: And do you think this Super Gun might really exist?

Kurosawa: It's possible. We heard reports of AV's being zapped and replaced by cadaver clones. Nothing ever verified. But the rumour didn't go away.

Chas: Unlike Wicked Wilson.

He turned toward Doobie.

Chas: Do you think it's possible that someone killed him with his own gun, and that's what they're using now to wipe out wealthy AVs and steal the money from their accounts?

Kurosawa: I don't know how they would do that, Chas. There's no way to take something off another AV unless they give it to you.

◇◇◇

With the ringing of his phone, real life crashed back into Michael's consciousness for the second time that afternoon. He tore himself away from Chas and Kuro and Doobie, and saw that it was Angela calling. He picked up the handset.

"Hey, Angela. How are you doing?"

"Hey, Michael. Just a quick call to say I'm putting all my appointments on hold for the next few days. I'll reschedule when I get the chance. Sorry for the inconvenience."

"Is there a problem, Angela?"

"A bereavement, Michael. There's no accounting for death, and it's no respecter of diaries or schedules."

"I'm sorry to hear that, Angela. Don't give it a second thought, where I'm concerned."

"Okay, thanks, Michael. I'll be in touch."

It was only when she had rung off that he saw the red light winking on the handset to let him know there was a message. He hit the button and listened to the welcome message, before he heard Janey's voice, shrill, almost trembling with excitement.

"Michael, where are you, for God's sake? I think maybe I've cracked it. Found the link between Arnold Smitts and Jennifer Mathews, RL and SL. Staring us in the face the whole time. Even makes sense of the money being paid into your account." He heard her sigh of frustration. "Oh, God, typical that you're not there. There's someone we should really talk to together. But I don't think it can wait. Call me soon as you can."

Michael hit the recall button and listened as the phone rang four times before Janey's messaging service cut in. He hung up.

"Shit!"

Chapter Thirty-One

Chas and Doobie sat in the sofa chairs in Twist's office, watching the little train roll by. No giant dildos on it today.

Chas: It's so frustrating not knowing what it is that Twist has found out.

Doobie: It sounds promising, though.

But Chas was doubtful.

Chas: I can't figure how he could just stumble across something that connects all three of us—Smitts, Mathews, and me. And how can we all be connected SL and RL.

Doobie: Well, presumably he'll phone again.

Chas: I guess. Maybe I should have left a message and told her about the Super Gun.

There was a momentary pause.

Doobie: Her?

Chas held his breath for a moment. He had just let the cat out of the bag. Only, there didn't seem any point in keeping up the pretence any more.

Chas: Okay, you caught me. Twist isn't really a guy, Doobs.

Twist's a girl I work with at the FSS. Her name's Janey. Sorry about the deception. That's just who she is in SL.

Doobie: No problem, Chas. Actually, I was going to ask you to give me your RL ID anyway. I mean, I know what you do and where you work. But it would be useful to have a name.

Chas: Why?

Doobie Littlething sighs.

Doobie: I hate to put it to you this way, Chas, but if anything happens to you, don't you think there should be someone that knows the full story who can go to the police?

Chas: Well, thank you for that comforting thought, Doobs.

A silence hung in the air between them.

Doobie: Well?

Chas: I'll give you my name on one condition.

Doobie: What's that?

Chas: That you give me yours. After all, we almost had sex this afternoon. That makes us pretty intimate.

Doobie: I've had more than almost sex with lots of men, Chas, and I've never given any of them my RL name.

Chas: Yes, but none of them ever beat you at chess.

Doobie: That's true.

She appeared to think about that for some moments.

Doobie: Okay, you first.

Chas: Michael Kapinsky.

Doobie: And an address?

Chas: I live in Corona Del Mar, Newport Beach, California, Doobs. That's as much I'm telling you. Oh, and I'm ex-directory, so you won't find me in the phone book. Your turn.

Doobie: Gillian MacCormack.

Chas: Scottish?

Doobie: Irish. LOL. And French. What a mix, eh? And before you ask, you weren't far out in guessing what side of the country I live on.

Chas: California?

Doobie: Way up north. Little town called Auburn. Not far from Sacramento. And an easy drive to Napa and Sonoma.

Chas: You like your wines, then?

Doobie Littlething smiles.

Doobie: I've got a glass in my hand as we speak, Chas. But I'm going to have to finish it and go.

Chas: Oh. Commitments RL?

Doobie: Commitments SL. I'm due on stage for a couple of hours of pole dancing at Sinful Seductions. If I don't show I'll lose the job. But if you need me, just send an IM. Okay?

Chas: Sure.

And she was gone.

◇◇◇

Michael sat back and watched the sun starting to dip toward the west. In a few short hours, his time would be gone, wasted and lost. And he would be face-to-face with mob retribution.

He tried Janey's cellphone again and hung up when he got the answering service. Then he phoned the office. Someone told him that she'd gone home feeling sick. He frowned. It had to have been an excuse for getting her out of the office. But he phoned her home anyway.

"Hi, this is Janey. Either I'm not here right now, or I'm wa-ay too busy to talk to you. Leave a message, and if you're someone I like I might get back to you."

This time Michael decided to leave a message. "Janey, it's Michael. Where the hell are you? Call me. Whether you like me or not." He hung up, and sat gazing into space. This was frustrating. Why hadn't she called him back? He got up, wandered across his office, and stepped out on to the terrace. He took a deep breath. The way it seemed to him now, either Wicked Wilson was the murderer or he himself had been killed for his gun. But whoever had it was using it to kill AVs for the money in their accounts. Money that shouldn't have been there. Secret or stolen money. So it had to be somebody with access to that kind of information. But it still made no sense to him that the killer would have put three million into Chas' account, unless it really was just some kind of horrible mistake.

But, then, Janey had said she'd found a connection, something that linked Smitts, Mathews, *and* Chas. It seemed that the more he knew, the more baffling it all became.

A *ching* drew his attention to the computer, and he went back into his office to sit down at his desk. Chas was still lounging in Twist's office crossing and uncrossing his legs. There was an IM waiting for him.

◇◇◇

Chas opened up his dialogue box. The IM was from someone called Dionysus Winestock.

> *Dionysus:* Hi, I need your help to find out if my partner is cheating on me.

Chas sighed. He had enough problems of his own without worrying about taking on someone else's. But, then again, what else was he going to do while he waited for Janey to call? He was trapped in a frustrating limbo, somewhere between the real and the virtual worlds. He desperately felt that he should be doing something but had no idea what. And the illusion of safety in SL was far stronger than the very real fear that awaited him in RL. There was almost a comfort in it. An escape.

> *Chas:* What's the story, Dio?
>
> *Dionysus:* I need a good private eye.
>
> *Chas:* You're talking to one. How can I help you?
>
> *Dionysus:* Well, I fear my SL wife is messing around a bit. But you should know, straight off, that we are swingers.
>
> *Chas:* Swingers?
>
> *Dionysus:* Yeh. We swap partners for sex. Twosomes, threesomes, group sex, you name it. We're members of a swingers' club called Echangiste.
>
> *Chas:* So why are you worried about your wife messing about?
>
> *Dionysus:* I don't mind if she has sex, Chas. But the romance and lies, I can't handle. I just need to confirm my suspicions. There's another couple we know from the club. We're good friends. We've all had sex together. But I think she's having an affair with him.

If Chas could have scratched his head, he would. Sex was fine, but romance was taboo.

> *Chas:* Have you asked her outright?

Dionysus: I actually caught her at it by using a spy device. But she says it's all over now. I just need that confirmed. The guy's called Crompton Nightly. He and his SL wife, Tab, have an apartment at Shyland.

Chas: Is that where you think he and your wife are conducting their affair?

Dionysus: No. Too risky. I think they might be taking sex rooms at the club, and since I found her out, they might be using alternative AVs.

Chas: Any idea what their alts are called?

Dionysus: Not sure about Crom. But I'm almost certain she's going under the name of Icy Fizzle.

Chas: So what do you want us to do?

Dionysus: Get me proof. A photograph. Or better still, log some dialogue. I know that's hard if they only communicate in IM.

Chas: Well, can you get me an introduction to the club? What was it called…?

Dionysus: Echangiste. No. You'll have to join. And you have to be a couple to get membership.

Chas thought for a minute, focusing on everything he and Twist might need to know to get a foothold in the case.

Chas: Okay, listen, why don't you set up a notecard? Write down everything that might be useful for me to know. All the names. Where your wife logs in. Landmarks for the club and the homes of any of the other people involved. Drop the notecard onto my profile, and I'll take a look at it. I'll get back to you if we think there's anything we can do.

Dionysus Winestock sighs.

> *Dionysus:* Well, I guess that'll have to do. I'm kind of impatient to clear this up and move on. You know what I mean?
>
> *Chas:* Sure, Dio. I'll need to discuss this with my partner first, then we'll be in touch just as soon as we can.
>
> *Dionysus:* Okay. IM me. Bye.

Chas created a notecard himself and copied his dialogue with Dionysus into it to save for Twist. A couple of minutes later he received the notecard from Dionysus with the information he had requested. But before he had a chance to read it, a blue window flashed on and off to tell him that Twist O'Lemon was online. His heart skipped a beat.

Twist rezzed into the office, grey at first, before finding definition and turning toward Chas.

Twist: Hey.

Chas: Where the hell have you been, Twist? I've been calling and calling. Ever since you left that message.

Twist: Hey, calm down, Chas, I'm here now. What's been happening?

Chas: Nothing's been happening! I've been treading water till you got in touch.

Twist: No, I mean with the investigation in SL.

Chas: Nothing that can't wait, Twist.

Chas' impatience was very nearly palpable.

Chas: You said you'd found RL and SL connections between Smitts and Mathews.

Twist O'Lemon sighs.

Twist: Yeh. Turned out to be a total dead-end. Sorry, Chas. Didn't mean to get your hopes up like that.

Twist paused for several long seconds, during which Chas' dashed hopes were allowing despair to creep back in.

Twist: I'm just reading your IM about the geckos. Good work. You actually went to Sandbox Island? I hope you were well-armed.

Chas: You made sure I was.

Twist: LOL. So I did. Anyway, tell me what you found out about the Mathews girl in SL.

Chas: Not much, I'm afraid. She danced at a shemale club, as well as several straight clubs, and worked as an escort. She had a huge private house and a smaller place she called the Whorehouse. It's where she took her clients and where we found her dead AV.

Twist: Oh. You actually found her, then? Were there any clues as to what might have happened?

Chas: She'd been shot. Blood all over the place. But that was it. No trace of the killer. Nothing incriminating left behind that we could see.

Twist: We?

Chas: Yeh, me and Doobie.

Twist: Oh. Doobie. Right.

Chas: So what was it you found that made you think there was a link between Smitts and Mathews? And me, for that matter.

Twist stood going through his range of animated poses, but failed to respond. Chas waited. For nearly half a minute.

Chas: Twist? Are you still with me?

Twist: Sorry, Chas, I had incoming IMs. Anything else been happening while I was away?

Chas restrained an urge to shout. Twist seemed blissfully unconcerned by his predicament. He dragged the two notecards on the Dionysus case on to Twist's AV and waited until Twist had confirmed receipt.

Chas: That guy got in touch just before you logged in. Wants us to catch his old lady *in flagrante delicto.*

Twist: Just reading through it.

A pause.

Twist: Hahaha. Swingers in love. Almost a contradiction in terms. Let's go check it out.

Chas: The swingers' club?

Twist: Sure. I've never been to a swinger's club. Might be interesting.

Chas felt the tension in him ratcheting up several more notches. Not only had Twist's lead on the Smitts-Mathews connection fallen apart, but Twist himself now seemed quite unconcerned about his partner's increasingly unhappy predicament. He shook his head in frustration but had no idea what else to do. His pursuit of the killer in both RL and SL seemed to have come to a dead end. And so he responded with reluctant acquiescence and a deep inward sigh.

Chas: I guess.

Twist: Okay, TP from the LM and I'll see you there.

◇◇◇

The Echangiste Swingers Club was in Zurich City. Chas rezzed into a large, marble-floored hall just seconds before Twist.

Windows looked out into the city streets of old Zurich. There were two doors, but neither of them led anywhere except out again. In the centre of the floor stood a large box constructed from still shots of the interior of the club. Yellow text above it urged, *Please take a card for Club Echangiste information by touching this box.*

Chas clicked on the box and immediately received a notecard describing the purpose and facilities of the club.

CLUB ECHANGISTE (Swingers Club)—Sex with Elegance.

Club Echangiste is an exclusive, invitation-only club for open-minded, nonjudgemental men and women who enjoy their sexuality and want to explore intimate and group sex in a refined, elegant environment.

Here, you will find a romantic ballroom, "group activity" room, beautiful private rooms for couples or small groups, a 50's drive-in theater park with movies and TV, and a holodeck with twenty-five scenes. All well equipped with the best sex toys around!

A green pad on the floor read, *Teleport to Club Echangiste.* Chas right-clicked and selected Teleport. But it only turned him around, and left him standing where he was.

Twist: It must know, somehow, if you're a member of not.

Chas looked around. A constantly evolving slide-show on one wall depicted naked men and women in various sexual poses, but apart from the two exit doors, there didn't seem to be any way in or out of the club itself.

Chas: How are we going to get in, then?

Twist: This is just some kind of welcome lobby. I'll bet the club itself, and the various sex rooms and holodeck, are actually skyboxes.

Chas: Then there's no way of getting to them without an LM.

Twist: Of course there is. We'll fly. Do you have a flight feather?

Chas: What's that?

Twist: It's an attachment to help you fly straight up. Measures your altitude and lets you hover when you get there.

The offer of a flight feather appeared from Twist. Chas attached it invisibly to his left hand. Twist clicked on the main door and went out into the street. Chas followed.

Immediately opposite, a three-storey greystone building with a colonnaded arcade on the ground floor rose into a blue sky. Further along the street, a square building flew the Swiss flag, and open green lawns were bounded by tall office blocks. It was completely deserted. Chas looked up and saw that there were another four storeys above the lobby, and the building advertised itself as the Savoy Hotel. There was no sign of anything up in the sky.

Twist: Follow me.

And Twist took off, straight upwards, spiralling as he went. Chas put his arms at his side and followed, as instructed. The city fell away below him, and he had a view of the twin towers of the cathedral, a huge square building with a strange, domed construction on its roof. In the distance he saw the sea, before piercing the scattering of clouds overhead and rising at speed into the blue.

At three hundred metres, he flew past a square grey building floating in the sky, tall windows and a balcony running around all four sides. He nearly crashed into Twist, who had stopped and was hovering just above it.

Chas: There don't appear to be any doors. I don't see how we can get in.

Twist: Well, we don't need to get in. We can just take a look from here.

Twist O'Lemon grins.

Twist: An old griefer's trick for getting in and out of buildings.

Chas Chesnokov: I know. It was just about the first thing you showed me.

Twist: Exactly. So, let's take a peek inside.

Twist dropped down to land on the roof, and Chas did the same. He zoomed in on the side of the building and swivelled to swing his POV beyond the wall and into the club. Immediately he found himself looking into a large, high-ceilinged room, a thick patterned green carpet overlaid with Persian and Chinese rugs. Several beds, a sofa, and a profusion of sex poseballs were scattered around the room. Erotic paintings lined the walls, and in the centre of the room stood a large maroon circle with eight cushions around its edge. Eight naked Club Echangiste members, four men, four women, sat around a green bottle in the centre of the circle. With each spin of the bottle a new couple was paired off, and they got up and disappeared through a doorway to another room.

Chas carefully manipulated his POV to take him through to what was evidently the ballroom described in the blurb. It, too, was luxuriously carpeted. Flames flickered in an open fire, and there was the usual proliferation of poseballs, some of which were occupied by swingers grinding and grunting their way through various sex acts. Along one wall were teleporters to the other club rooms. The Traditional Suite, the Asian Suite, the Drive-In Theater, the Holodeck. He saw that from the inside all the windows were clear and realised that they might have been seen flying past. But everyone seemed too preoccupied to have noticed. He checked his radar and went into IM to talk to Twist.

Chas: Well, there's no sign of Icy or Crom in here.

Twist: There are more boxes above us. Let's go up.

Chas took his POV back outside and craned to look above them. He could see another, smaller building, about a hundred metres further up. Twist took off, and Chas soared after him. Again, they landed on the roof, and swivelled to peek inside. A black couple on an enormous bed were indulging in an oral sex act. Chas could hear the chatter of keyboards. So they were talking to one another, although they were too far away for the text of their conversation to register.

> *Twist:* Hahahaha. Didn't her mother teach her it was rude to speak with her mouth full?

But Chas was embarrassed to be spying on people's privacy like this.

> *Chas:* Come on, let's check out the other rooms.
>
> *Twist:* You go on, I'll catch you up. I'm enjoying the view from here.

Chas hesitated a moment. Twist was behaving very strangely. But then he pinned his arms to his side and soared upwards again, past another sex room and the holodeck, checking his radar as he flew. There were plenty of names appearing on it. But none of them was Icy Fizzle or Crompton Nightly. Finally, he arrived at the drive-in theatre, which was open to the skies and bounded by a low wall. There were two cinema screens and a red 1950s automobile. The place was deserted. The sun had sunk low on the far horizon, and night was falling fast.

Chas landed beside the car and looked around. There was nothing showing on either screen. He clicked on one, and a menu appeared, offering him a choice of half a dozen porn movies. He closed it again, wondering what drew people to a place like this. People's second lives seemed dominated by sexual obsession. Club Echangiste was the epitome of it. And then it struck him that, really, people's first lives were dominated by sex, too, but that here in the virtual world, there were fewer complications and no danger of disease. The worst that could happen was that you might pick up a computer virus.

While he waited for Twist, he opened up the Landmark folder in his Inventory, to start sorting his LMs into rational groupings—all the links that Doobie had given him to places he might one day explore. And he thought about how he and Doobs had very nearly consummated their relationship earlier before being subjected to coitus interruptus at the hands of two giant geckos. It was a thought that brought a smile to his face, in spite of everything.

He saw Twist appear on his radar, but no sign of him arriving at the drive-in. He turned through 360 degrees but still couldn't see him. For the first time, he felt a strange chill of apprehension. Something was wrong. He had felt uncomfortable ever since Twist had TPed into the office.

> *Twist:* I'm sorry, Chas. Didn't really mean it to end this way.

He turned around to find Twist standing behind him. How was it possible for an avatar to look evil? But there was something very menacing in Twist's proximity, a strange tilt of the head that caused his eyes to look up at him, narrowed and laden with threat.

> *Chas:* What are you talking about, Twist?
>
> *Twist:* You're too damned clever for your own good, Michael.

Twist made a swift movement, and there was gun in his hand. A large, silver revolver, beautifully engraved. Every fibre of Chas' conscious mind told him that he was looking down the barrel of the Super Gun. And yet he still found it impossible to believe.

> *Chas:* For Christ's sake, Janey! What are you doing?
>
> *Twist:* I'm afraid you serve no useful further purpose Chas. Time to die.

Chas knew he had a split second while Twist went into Mouselook to fire. He glanced at his open Inventory and the LMs that Doobie had given him. He double-clicked fast on the first one his mouse landed on and teleported out of the drive-in at the very moment Twist pulled the trigger. He heard the gunshot following him like an echo, but he was gone, intact, and rezzing suddenly into a strange new world.

Chapter Thirty-Two

He was on some kind of asteroid. It was dark, the skies filled with a million coloured stars, some of which streaked across his screen. Planets hung in the mist, green and molten amber, blue and red. Huge rocks tumbled through the night in slow motion. And slowly, as this bizarre world rezzed around him, he began to see people. Lots of them. His radar showed a long list of names. This was a busy place.

Blue chairs floated through the sky, avatars comfortably seated for a ride through the asteroid belt. Behind him was a blue globe, liquid patterns constantly changing, and sliding like oil over its shiny, smooth surface.

Yet more avatars lounged on cushions around a central circle, and beyond a collection of floating boulders that created a bridge to a neighbouring rock, citizens practised slow-motion tai-chi in perfect synchronisation.

He saw Twist's name appear on his radar and turned as his pursuer began to rez, still grey, and almost certainly still blind. Chas would have a few seconds before Twist would see him.

He started running. Straight across the floating rock bridge and into the serried ranks of the tai-chi practitioners. Almost before his eyes, a girl called Phacelia Jolles burst apart in an explosion of blood and flesh, an enormous hole torn through her middle. The avatar fell dead, blood oozing fast all around her. Chas turned to see Twist in pursuit, gun raised, ready to shoot again.

He swerved off to the right and ran across the smooth rock surface of the asteroid. Another AV, Thadeus Horchier, spun away, spraying blood through the sky. The report of the gun came almost immediately afterwards. Chas kept running, bumping and crashing his way through the crowds. He saw text appearing. Curses and cries of abuse.

He was almost at the end of the asteroid now. Nothing beyond it but empty space and a dark planet hanging ominously in the night. A young couple stood by two poseballs. *Orbital Kiss F* and *Orbital Kiss M*. The young man, Will Stacy, clicked on the *M* ball and vanished. Before the girl had a chance to click on the *F* ball, Chas stepped in and beat her to it.

Immediately he found himself floating through space in the arms of young Will. They were engaged in a long and passionate kiss. The young man had expected to be locked in the embrace of his girlfriend and was still muttering words of love.

Will: Mmmmh, darling. I've been wanting for this for so long.

And then came the moment of realisation.

Will: Jesus Christ! Who are you? Get off!!

A large ringed blue planet drifted by.

Will Stacy clicked to detach and was instantly disengaged from the animation, leaving Chas to float alone through the cosmos, embracing nothing but space vacuum. But only for a moment. Within seconds he was wrapped in the arms of Twist, running a hand over his butt, and making out in the shadow of the moon. Far below, he could see the chaos and confusion they had left behind on the asteroid. Dead and bleeding AVs. Panic among the space worshippers. But he knew that as long as he and Twist had their arms around each other he would be safe.

Twist: You caused me to terminate three innocent AVs, Chas. That is not good. And you can't escape from me, you know. I have a TP-tracker. I can follow you wherever you go.

Chas: I don't understand, Twist? Have you really killed all these people?

Twist: What do you think, Chas? How much sense does that make to you?

But Chas wasn't stopping to think. He needed to get away. Needed time to think elsewhere. The easiest way would be to log out. He clicked the Quit button, but nothing happened. He cursed to himself. His cursor had gone into egg-timer mode. The programme wasn't functioning properly. So he went instead to his Inventory and double-clicked another LM. In the blink of an eye, he was whisked from the arms of Twist, and hurled through the Second Life metaverse to rez on another continent, in another light zone.

◇◇◇

For a moment Chas was completely disoriented. At first everything was dark. Then luminous blue triangles appeared beneath his feet, moving away from him, like arrows pointing the way ahead.

A circle of blue contained him within a larger circle that burned a wide blue arc into black. Red light appeared suddenly on the horizon and sent sparkles glittering toward him across a flat, calm ocean. Behind him a large fishpond caught the light, and he saw a frog sitting on a waterlily looking at him.

Overhead loomed the shadow of a vast wheel-like construction with four arms extending to north, south, east, and west, where circular helipads were suspended in midair. Directly ahead of him, rezzing in the early dawn light, hung the neon blue legend, *ABBOTTS Aerodrome*. He was still set to Run, and so he ran, following the arrows beneath his feet.

They led him into a vast, circular hall where planes and helicopters were mounted on stands, an exhibition of flying machines, old and new. Tall windows all around looked out over the sea and the pink tinted clouds drifting in the from east.

Immediately ahead of him was an elevator that glowed with walls of blue neon. He ran inside and hit a luminous button on the side of the door. A menu appeared asking him to choose a level. Somewhere, once, he had read that people running away always go up and at some point run out of anywhere further to go. A glance at the panel told him he was currently on Level Two. So he chose Level One. He would break with convention.

As the doors slid shut, he saw Twist rezzing at the arrival point by the fishpond. But then, in a rush of sound, he descended in the elevator to be tipped out on to a walkway leading to the runway and hangar. He followed it through space to an elevator pod almost immediately above the runway. To his left, there were airplanes and helicopters parked along either side of the runway, a tall radio tower, and an orange hot-air balloon, tied down but inflated and ready for take-off.

To his right, beyond more stationary aircraft, a large, black hangar stood on the tarmac.

Text on the elevator pod told him to *Click Here*. He did, and was given a menu option to descend. He was immediately transported to the tarmac below, and started running toward the hangar. A piece of tarmac to his right lifted and burst into pieces. He turned to see Twist on the bridge above, aiming the Super Gun straight at him. He ducked behind a red single-engined biplane as its nose exploded in flames. Then he turned and ran again. Heading for the hangar. Looking around for help. But there wasn't a soul in sight.

At the end of the runway, a large passenger plane rezzed and slowly turned before heading down the tarmac, picking up speed for take-off. Its engines roared in the glowing dawn air and receded into the early morning mist. Chas ran on, past a teleporter terminal, and turned into the vast, echoing space of the hangar. It was filled with every imaginable type of flying machine and shrouded in a darkness that faded almost to black toward the back of the building.

Chas remembered seeing, somewhere on his screen, a box he could check to hide his avatar name. He found it in Preferences and checked it. Now he could hide without his telltale tag giving away his whereabouts. He would show up, he knew, on Twist's radar, but with luck it wouldn't be directional and Twist would take some time to find him. Time enough, perhaps, to figure how to log out.

He ran to the back of the hangar, into the gloom, and crouched down behind a twin-engined propeller plane from the 1950s. From here, he had a clear view out toward the front of the hangar, and the runway beyond. Another plane roared past, nose lifting as it headed up into the clearing sky.

A bare-chested figure ran into view, long red hair flowing out in its wake. Twist was little more than a silhouette against the morning sky. Chas watched as he stopped, looking around for Chas' tag. Twist's radar was telling him that Chas was here somewhere. But there was no tag hovering above Chas' head to betray his whereabouts.

Twist was still holding the Super Gun, but his arm was crooked at the elbow, and the barrel of the gun was pointing to the sky. He would need to go into mouselook again to fire. Chas ran his cursor along the top menu bar, looking for an alternative way to quit. His original command to log-out was still causing the egg-timer response. Somehow, his system had gone into a spin.

Twist was moving cautiously further into the hangar. He turned first one way, then the other. Chas imagined that he was checking distances on his radar and that he would very quickly pinpoint Chas' position. He had almost no time left. Then the drop-down menu under File showed him an alternative Quit option. He just prayed that this one would work. If not, he was cornered here. And the avatar Chas Chesnokov would almost certainly be erased from existence. He stood up and walked boldly out between the aircraft.

Twist swivelled toward him, evidently surprised by his sudden appearance. Twist O'Lemon's gun arm levelled out in front of him, the Super Gun pointing straight at Chas, sunlight casting pink reflections on its silver barrel. Twist's animated smile seemed almost grotesque.

Twist: Goodbye, Chas.

Chas: Goodbye, Twist.

Chas clicked on Quit and screwed his eyes tight shut. He heard the whooshing sound of log-out, almost at the same time as he heard the gunfire.

◇◇◇

Michael sat staring at the screen, breathing hard, perspiration gathered all across his forehead. Log-out had been successful. Chas had lived to fight another day. But that hardly made him feel any better. He had a sick sensation in the pit of his stomach and was aware of his heart punching his chest as if trying to escape. How was it possible? Janey?

He shook his head in disbelief and let himself tilt back in his seat, trying to control his breathing. There had to be some rational explanation. Something he was missing. He ran back through the events of the last fifteen or twenty minutes. Twist's strange, forgetful behaviour back at the office and at the Club Echangiste. His skilful avoidance of Chas' questions about what had made him believe there was some sort of link between Smitts, Mathews, and Michael.

And then he saw the answer, suddenly, clearly, in a moment of absolute revelation. Like that moment during a chess game when the route to checkmate becomes so obvious you wonder why you didn't see it from the very first move.

The thought took him back with vivid clarity to the drive-in porn theater above the Club Echangiste, his confrontation with Twist in the dying light. And Twist's words came back to him like bullets from the Super Gun, with almost the same devastating effect.

You're too damned clever for your own good, Michael.

Michael, Twist had called him. But Twist was Janey. And Janey *never* called him Michael. In all the years she had known him, he had been *Mike* to her.

The Twist O'Lemon who had just tried to kill him wasn't Janey. It was someone else operating Janey's avatar. And with that chilling thought came the realisation that if someone else was inside her AV, then Janey herself was either in grave danger, or…

He didn't even want to think about it. He snatched the phone and called her cellphone. *Hi, this is Janey…* He hung up and dialled her home number. *Hi, this is Janey…* He hit the End Call button and sent the handset careening across his desk.

He tipped back in his chair and cursed the heavens. "Damn you, Janey! Why didn't you call me back?" He stood up, his mind racing, blaming himself for not picking up the phone sooner the first time she called. He checked the time. It was almost six. It would take nearly half an hour to drive down the Coast Highway to Janey's place at Laguna Beach. But he didn't see any other option.

Early evening sunlight slanted through the birds of paradise growing along the front of his house as he backed out of the garage and saw, parked across the street, the same two mob minders who had been tracking him all day. They sat in their Lincoln, windows down, smoking, making no attempt to conceal themselves. In his rearview mirror, Michael saw the Lincoln pull away from the sidewalk to follow as he accelerated away along Dolphin Terrace. And as he swung out on to PCH south, in the dying light of the day, misgivings about Janey morphed into an almost unbearable sense of dread.

Chapter Thirty-Three

Traffic fumes rose infuriatingly into the cooling evening air, long lines of vehicles blocking the lanes of the Pacific Coast Highway as it came down the hill into Laguna Beach. The last of the rush-hour traffic.

Fading red light shimmered on the ocean as the sun began its inevitable descent toward Catalina, hidden tonight in a long line of purple haze on the far horizon. Traffic lights turned to green, and the lines of traffic began inching forward. Michael eased his way into the outside lane and pushed himself into the left-turn filter, patience finally giving out as the lights turned yet again to red. He flipped down his turn lights, and with a squeal of tyres, accelerated across the lane of oncoming traffic, turning into the narrow suburban street that would take him up the hill to Janey's bungalow. Behind him, he heard horns venting angrily at the car, three vehicles back, that had followed Michael's lead and jumped the lights for the left turn. He wondered, fleetingly, if the mobsters thought he was trying to lose them. But right now, he didn't care. The motor of his SUV screamed at high pitch as he accelerated hard, ignoring the give-way signs at cross-junctions, before finally turning into Janey's street, which ran at right-angles along the top of the hill.

Her car was parked below her house, a battered fawn-coloured Ford Focus, with its defiant bumper sticker, *Fermez la Bush!* Michael had no idea whether to read this as a good, or a bad omen. If she was at home, why wasn't she answering her phone?

He pulled in behind it and glanced back as his minders drew into the sidewalk on the other side of the street. He started up the steps, two at a time, to the veranda that ran along the front of the bungalow. Still breathing hard, he banged on the door with the heel of his fist then stood listening. But he could hear nothing except for the distant cry of the seagulls and the sound of someone mowing his lawn several houses along.

"Janey!" he shouted, and banged this time with the flat of his hand. But he didn't wait for the responding silence. He ran along the wooden deck and tried to peer into the living room window. The blinds were down, and the slats almost shut. With the sun sinking behind him, he couldn't see anything for reflected light. He ran back along the length of the house and around the side. A small gate opened into the back yard. Janey had never been one for spending time in the garden. Most of the yard was laid with concrete flagstones, weeds poking up between them. A small swimming pool had never been uncovered after the winter. A rusted grill still contained the ash of some long-forgotten barbecue. Bins lined up along the back wall were almost overflowing. French windows leading from the house to the patio stood open, and Chas paused, looking at them with a growing sense of misgiving. This did not look good.

Caution overtook him now, as he moved slowly from the patio to the interior of the house. He crossed a temperature threshold. The evening air outside was still warm, humming with the sound of spring insects. Inside the house it was cold and dark. He could hear the distant rumble of the air conditioning unit somewhere deep within and knew that no one in his right mind would leave doors wide open with the AC turned on.

He called out again. "Janey?" His voice cracked a little, and he became aware for the first time of his own fear. Still no reply. He was in her bedroom, her unmade bed a tangle of sheets and blankets, a smell of stale training shoes hanging in the cool air. Dirty clothes overflowed from a wicker laundry basket. He opened the door and moved through to the hall. The blinds everywhere were drawn, and the house stood in darkness, an odd sense of silence about the place. He glanced along the hall to the kitchen and then moved toward the front of the house and the main living room. This was where Janey had lain mock-dead on the floor the last time he had been here. But the room was empty, old beer bottles accumulating around the legs of her favourite armchair where she liked to curl up and read.

He began to relax a little. There was no one here, after all. And he began to wonder why her car was still parked out front. He moved back along the hall and pushed open the door to her den. The glow of her two computer monitors filled the room, and by their light he saw her lying on the floor by the wall, huddled like a child in the womb. A large, dark patch stained the creamy shag of the rug beneath her. Blood smeared the wall above her, and he could smell it in the chilled air.

"Jesus, Janey!" His voice came in a whisper that seemed to thunder around the room. He reached her in three paces and crouched to turn her over. There were two bullet holes in the centre of her chest, very close together. Most of the blood had leaked out through a single exit wound in her back. A dribble of dried blood had oozed from the corner of her mouth. Her lips were parted slightly, and her sightless eyes, still behind her thick-framed glasses, were wide and staring. She was cold, bloodless flesh as chilled as if it had come straight from the freezer.

There was a short trail of blood across the carpet as if she had not died immediately, but dragged herself to the wall and tried to stand up. Then slipped back down to her last resting place, where she had finally bled to death.

Her right hand was clutched tightly around something small and white. Rigor mortis had not yet set in, and carefully he prised her fingers apart to release what they held. It was a tiny plaster bust of a winged cherub, and he had a recollection, then, of noticing it on previous occasions, hanging from a picture hook on her wall. Janey was not a religious person, but she had been brought up a Catholic and had several religious mementoes around the house. For some reason she had made a determined effort to reach this particular piece, almost as if she knew she would die and wanted the comfort of it, or to ask for some kind of absolution for her sins.

He had blood now on his hands and shoes, and bile rising in his throat. The room blurred as tears filled his eyes, and he blinked furiously to clear them and stop himself from crying. As he stood up, something glinting on the carpet caught his eye, an eye trained by practice to notice the smallest detail at a crime scene.

He stepped over Janey's body and bent down to pick up a pair of broken reading glasses. And with a sudden start, he realised that they were his, missing from his desk at home for some days. One of Mora's final gifts. He straightened up, looking at them in disbelief. What on earth were they doing here? Had Janey taken them? And why?

And then it dawned on him. He was being set up. This was supposed to look like he had done it. He glanced at the blood on his hands and shoes, and thought about the trail of fresh fingerprints he had left throughout the house. There were shards of broken lens from his reading glasses lost in the pile of the carpet. Shards that would be recovered when the FSS team arrived to do their work. He turned toward the monitors, and saw, on one of them, the figure of Twist O'Lemon, standing in the hangar at Abbotts Aerodrome where he had last seen him. Only there was no longer a gun in his hand, and his arms hung at his sides, head tipped forward as if asleep in the standing position. Next to his name tag a fragment of text read, *Away*.

Someone had sat right here, manipulating Janey's AV, while Janey herself lay dead or dying on the floor. Someone who had shot her, then used Twist to try to erase Chas and blame it all on Michael.

Michael started looking around, panic rising now in his chest. There was very probably more incriminating evidence lying around. How could he explain any of this? And when they started to investigate, they would want to know how he had suddenly acquired more than three million dollars to pay off his home loan. If Janey's killer had succeeded in erasing Chas, then there would have been no trail leading back to his Second Life account. No way of accounting for it. Even so, he was still in big trouble.

His eye was drawn to something white lying beneath the computer desk. He stooped to pick it up. It was a bloodstained white handkerchief, his initials embroidered on it in blue. MK. Mora had ordered them each sets of embroidered handkerchiefs when they first got married. His and Hers. He always carried one with him. Somehow, someone with access to his house, had taken one. Along with his reading glasses. And God knew what else.

But his search for further evidence was cut short almost before it began by the sound of an approaching police siren. There was no doubt in his mind that the police were on their way here. He had been set up and stitched up so tightly he really couldn't see any way out.

As the sound of the siren grew louder, he went through to the kitchen and hurriedly washed the blood from his hands. He carefully wrapped his broken glasses in kitchen paper and slipped them into his shirt pocket. Then he took a deep breath, and walked to the front door as a police patrol car pulled up, lights flashing, immediately behind his SUV. He looked further along the street and saw that his minders had decided that discretion was the better part of valour, and had embarked on an exit strategy. Their black Lincoln was turning right at the far end of the street, on a one-way road that would take them all the way back down to PCH.

Michael ran down the steps, snapping on a pair of latex gloves from his pocket, as two uniformed officers climbed toward him. They met halfway. The older man was an officer Michael knew from way back, which meant he wouldn't have to explain himself.

"Hey, Mike. How did you get here so fast?"

"I was in Laguna on other business when they called, Sam." It was amazing, he thought, how easy it was to lie.

"You been inside?"

Michael nodded. He didn't need to look shocked, or grave, or pale. He was all of those things anyway. "It's Janey Amat, Sam. She's dead."

Sam stopped in his tracks, eyes wide, and stared at Michael in horror. "Jesus Christ, Mike! That plain little FSS girl you worked with?" Michael nodded. Suddenly that's what Janey had been reduced to. That plain little FSS girl that Mike Kapinsky worked with. "What happened?"

"She's been shot. You'd better call in a full team. I'm going to get my stuff from the trunk."

The younger officer said, "You'd better be careful there, sir. You got blood on your shoe."

"Yes, I know. I wasn't expecting…Well, you know. She was a friend. I had to establish she was dead."

Sam put a hand on his shoulder. "Tough break, Mike. Never good when it's someone you know."

Michael was nearly at the foot of the steps when he was struck by a thought. "Hey, Sam." He called back up the stairs. "Who called this in?"

Sam turned at the front door. "No idea, Mike. Anonymous tip-off." The two officers turned away again to move cautiously into the house, and Michael jumped into his SUV and started the motor. There was no sign of his mob minders. If they were doing a circuit, they hadn't come back around yet. This was his chance to lose them. He took the SUV through a quick three-point turn, and drove off at speed in the opposite direction from the one they had taken. He had to hold the steering wheel very tightly to keep his hands steady.

His twenty-four hours were up, and now he was on the run from both the mob and the police. He couldn't see any way for any of this to end, except in tears. Or worse.

Chapter Thirty-Four

The drive back along the Pacific Coast Highway to Corona del Mar passed in a blur. Michael was having to force himself to think clearly, which, given the events of the last twenty-four hours, was far from easy. Going back to Dolphin Terrace was no longer an option. The police would come looking for him at home sooner rather than later, and his misplaced minders would almost certainly come back to stake it out.

But he needed Internet access. The only person left in the world, it seemed, who could help him, was a Second Life avatar called Doobie Littlething.

He reached the junction where Jamboree crossed PCH heading down to the ocean and Balboa Island. There was the Starbucks on the island, where he regularly bought coffee. He would be able to log on to the Internet there. But parking was an issue. And then he remembered that there was another Starbucks about half a mile further on, still on PCH, just past the Porsche franchise. It had its own carpark. He accelerated across Jamboree as the lights changed.

Three minutes later he slotted his SUV between two compacts and carried his laptop into the Starbucks coffee shop. Frustratingly, it was busy, and he had to wait nearly ten minutes to get served with his usual caramel machiatto. He carried it quickly to a table at the window, freshly vacated by two teenage girls, and opened up his laptop. As he sipped on his coffee and waited for the system to load, he remembered that he didn't have the Second Life software on this computer.

He cursed aloud, then looked up self-consciously at the faces turning in his direction.

"Sorry." He blushed and lowered his head and tapped *Second Life* into the Google search engine to get a link to the website. It took several more minutes to download the software and go through all the disclaimers, before he was able to enter his avatar name and password. Finally, he was back in.

◇◇◇

Chas stood waiting for several seconds while Twist's office rezzed around him. He checked his Friends List and saw that Twist was still online, and his face stung from the shock of knowing that while Twist might still be around, the real life person who had created him was dead.

He let his eyes wander about the office. All the tiny details. The pictures on the wall, the friendship bear on the desk, the laptop computer with its joke welcome page for Third Life, the potted plants. Every item here had been bought or made, and placed by Janey. The world she had built. Her escape from a life that was disappointing her, to a place where she could re-make herself and take control. And Chas felt the pain of knowing he would never see her again. Never hear her laugh or tell her his troubles. In some strange way, by comparison, Mora's death seemed to have retreated to a distant place and time. To have gained a perspective he had never been able to find. And he reflected how, in just a few short days, he himself had changed almost beyond recognition. Become someone else.

But he had no time to dwell on it. Time had become a luxury. It was a commodity he could no longer afford. He saw, with relief, that Doobie was still online, and he opened up an IM.

> *Chas:* Hey Doobs!
> *Doobie:* How you doing, lover?

> *Chas:* Not good. I need to talk to you.
>
> *Doobie:* I'm still dancing, Chas. Come down to the club.

A teleport invitation to Sinful Seductions arrived almost immediately, and Chas clicked to accept.

The club was half empty when he arrived, and the few customers at tables or gathered around the stage rezzed slowly. Soft, sexy, jazz sax oozed around the auditorium, a bored-looking DJ sitting behind his desk, idling through piles of DVDs. There were only two dancers on stage, Doobie and another called Pennyweather Boozehound, a tall, willowy, blond with a small group of admirers urging her to take off more items of clothing as she gyrated around the pole for their pleasure.

Chas watched for a few moments, mesmerised. Doobie had already divested herself of her top and wore nothing more than the skimpiest pair of lace panties, stockings, garters, and the inevitable high heels. She was a sexy AV, and her dance animation showed her body off to best effect. She twisted and arched, and thrust in a sexually provocative manner, encouraging a string of lewd comments from a customer sitting on a stool immediately below her, leaning forward, his elbows on the stage, his upturned face just above a tip jar showing donations of almost 2000 Lindens. So she'd had a good afternoon's work.

The last donation, of 200, had been made by Biglurch Pinion, the customer still drooling lasciviously in front of her. He was a big-built man with impossibly wide shoulders and even more impossibly narrow hips. His features were gross, but clearly his RL creator had thought them attractive. He wore a tight, black tee-shirt, and even tighter jeans. There was a cigarette burning between the fingers of his left hand. He was passing comment in open chat, rather than discreetly in IM.

> *Biglurch:* Man, you got great jugs, woman. I'd just love to get my hands on those.

Doobie: Fifteen hundred an hour, Biglurch, and they're all yours.

Chas was alarmed. He didn't want Doobie tying herself up for an hour.

> *Chas:* Doobie, I've got to talk to you.
>
> *Doobie:* It'll have to wait, Chas. This guy's about to drop another 500 in my tip jar to make me take off my panties. And I don't want to disappoint either of us.
>
> *Chas:* Jesus Christ, Doobs!

Chas walked up to Biglurch.

Chas: Hey, Biglurch.

Biglurch: Hey, Chas.

Chas: Look, I don't want to spoil your fun or anything, but I really need to talk to this lady. Could you give us a few minutes?

Biglurch swivelled his head to glower at Chas.

Biglurch: Piss off! I've got an investment going here.

> *Doobie:* And so have I, Chas. You'll get me into trouble with the owner if you go bothering customers.
>
> *Chas:* This is important, Doobs!

Dennis: What's the problem here?

Chas turned to see an enormous gorilla of a man called Dennis Ember towering over him. His tag labelled him *Security*. A glorified SL name for a bouncer.

Chas: I just need to talk to Doobie for a few minutes

Biglurch: She's dancing for me, okay. I've got money in the jar.

Dennis turned to Biglurch.

Dennis: Is this AV bothering you, sir?

Biglurch: Yes, he fucking is.

Dennis: In that case, Mr. Chesnokov, I'm going to have to ask you to leave. Mr. Pinion is a VIP member here.

Chas: I don't care if he's the Sultan of Brunei.

Dennis: And I don't care for your tone. Goodbye.

Chas found himself spinning through space and time, until he landed with a thump on some anonymous piece of feature-less waste ground. He stood up and looked around, dazed and wondering what had happened.

> *Doobie:* You got ejected, you idiot! TP me.

Chas sent her a TP, and she arrived in a sprinkling of light several seconds later. She was still topless, but as she rezzed Chas was relieved to see that she had not yet removed her panties. She was fuming.

Doobie: Chas, I know you have big problems, but you're going to get me the sack here.

Chas: Doobie, Janey's been murdered. And whoever did it took over her AV and tried to erase me with the Super Gun.

Doobie stood still for a very long time, and the dialogue box remained inactive. Her silence spoke volumes more than anything she might have written in it. Then,

Doobie: What happened?

Chas: Someone shot her, then set it up to look like it was me. There was evidence planted all over the murder scene. I was the first there, so I didn't know if she was dead till I checked. And I got her blood on my hands and clothes, left my fingerprints everywhere. So now the cops are going to think that I killed her. And I'm not so sure I wouldn't be better off now in police custody, anyway. Because without that three million I'm a dead man.

Doobie: Whoa, whoa. Calm down. Let's take this slowly. Why would someone want to kill Janey?

Chas: I have no idea.

Doobie: She phoned you earlier, didn't she? All excited because she said she'd found something to link you and the victims all together.

Chas: Yes, but I don't know what that was.

Doobie: She was going to talk to someone, you said.

Chas: She never told me who.

Doobie: And there was nothing at the scene that might have given you some idea of what that link was, or who she might have been going to see?

Chas: No, nothing. Well, at least, not that I was aware of. She was murdered in her den. I didn't have time to go through her things before the cops got there.

And then, out of the blackness of his despair, came a pin-point of light, the tiniest fragment of hope. A recollection of the bloody trail on the carpet, the smears on the wall, the tiny plaster cherub clutched in Janey's blood-stained fingers. He hadn't been able to understand at the time why she would have made such a determined effort to pull it off the wall. But now comprehension came to him, as clear as day.

Chas: Jesus, Doobie. There was something. She left me a message. I just never realised it till now.

Doobie: What was it?

Chas: Oh, shit! RL! BRB.

◇◇◇

Michael dipped his head as the two police officers came through the door. They did not look immediately in his direction, but he knew they could not avoid seeing him on the way out. Cops always looked around, took in the lay of the land. It was their training and their instinct for self-preservation. He recognised one of them from the Newport Police Department, and knew that he would recognise him, too.

Michael leaned on his elbow, resting his head casually in his hand, and turned to look out of the window, attempting to hide as much of his face as possible. He listened to them order nonfat cafe lattes, then spoil the low-fat effect by asking for two traditional chocolate donuts. What was it with cops and donuts?

It was dark outside now, just the merest trace of light left in the western sky. All his options were rapidly running out, but if he was to confirm his revelation about the message left for him by Janey, there was only one course of action open to him.

"Hey, Mike, how are you doing buddy?" It was the NPD cop.

Michael turned around, feigning surprise. "Oh, hi. Didn't see you coming in." He nodded toward the bag of donuts. "I see you're still working on your waistline."

The cop laughed too heartily. "Don't tell the little lady; she's had me on a diet for months. Can't understand why I'm not losing weight." He put his fingers to his lips. "Our secret, huh?" He winked.

Michael smiled winningly. "Don't worry, it's safe with me."

He watched them go, his heart pulsing in his throat. But at least one thing was clear. There was no APB out on him. If there were suspicions about his involvement in Janey's murder, they hadn't yet surfaced from the crime scene. He turned back to his computer.

◇◇◇

Chas: Doobie, you still there?

Her AV was there, but she took several seconds to respond.

Doobie: Sorry, yeh. I was in an IM with my boss. I'm in the shit. What's happening?

Chas: I can't stay here. I'm going to have to move.

Doobie: Where are you?

Chas: I'm in a Starbucks. But I've been seen by a couple of cops. I'm going to transfer to another one over on Balboa Island. It'll take me about ten minutes. Maybe fifteen.

Doobie: Okay, IM me when you get back in. Oh, by the way, what was Janey's message?

But he had already logged out.

◇◇◇

From nowhere, it seemed, dark clouds had rolled in off the Pacific, pregnant with rain that was just beginning to fall in big, fat spots. Michael left the cover of Starbucks and ran for his car, his laptop clutched beneath his jacket. The rain was warm, like the air, and by the time he reached his SUV it was coming down from the heavens like stair-rods. He slipped into the driver's seat, breathless and soaking. On the far horizon, splinters of scarlet fractured the skyline, glowing pink around the edges of burgeoning black clouds.

He laid his laptop on the seat next to him and sat clutching the steering wheel, his eyes closed. He couldn't clear the picture of Janey lying dead on the floor of her den. It was as if it had been etched permanently on his retinas, like an image burned onto a computer monitor by too constant exposure.

He remembered the night she had come to his house to surprise him. Her mock seduction, which somehow, he felt, had really been a front for some more wishful intent. He remembered her laughter, her wicked sense of humour, jokes made so often at her own expense. And now she was dead. Because of him. Her blood staining the carpet of her den. Clutching fingers leaving smears of blood on the wall as she reached up to grasp the little plaster figurine. Her last act on this earth. Her last thought. A message for Mike.

And something else came back to him now, too. Something that had slipped by completely unnoticed. Although it must have lodged somewhere in his brain, as if waiting impatiently to be discovered and swept back into the flow of mainstream information where it might make more sense.

A throwaway line in their conversation with Jennifer Mathews' brother, Richard. His bitterness at learning from his sister that their father was salting away a tax-free inheritance for her in Second Life. *She told me about it, you see. Rubbing my nose in it. There always was a spiteful side to her. Like father, like daughter. And no amount of expensive therapy could ever remove that nasty little character trait.*

Michael flipped open his cellphone and pulled up a number from its memory. He clamped it to his ear and listened to it ring.

"Yeh?"

"Is that Stan or Ollie?"

"Stanley. Who wants to know?"

"It's Michael, Stan. Have you heard?"

He held his breath. This was the moment of truth. If word had got back about him from Laguna, then this conversation would be short-lived.

"Shit, yeh. About Plain Jane? Jesus, man, I can't believe it. I was talking to her just this afternoon."

Michael controlled his breathing. It seemed he wasn't in the frame just yet. "Stan, I need some information."

"About Janey?"

"No. About Arnold Smitts and Jennifer Mathews."

"Jesus, Mike! You and Janey both. She was bugging me for info this afternoon. What *are* you two, detectives all of a sudden?"

"Stan, it's important. It might explain why she's dead. What did she want to know?"

He could hear Laurel breathing heavily at the other end of the phone, wondering perhaps if he should tell him or not. "She wanted to know if Smitts and Mathews consulted with the same therapist. Seems like she'd been digging in the Smitts file and come up with a name."

"And *did* they?"

Laurel grunted. "What if they did? It wouldn't be unusual for two people in the same small town to be seeing the same therapist. This ain't LA."

"Who was it, Stan?"

But he knew, even before Laurel told him. "Some psychology consultant called Angela Monachino."

Michael closed his eyes and saw again the little plaster cherub clutched in Janey's hand. Only it wasn't, he knew now, a cherub. It was an angel. In her dying moments, even through all her pain and the certain knowledge of imminent death, she had found a way of telling him who had killed her.

"Mike? You still there, Mike? Hang on. There's some kinda weird shit coming in from Laguna Beach on the other line."

Michael snapped his cellphone shut. He could imagine only too well just exactly what that weird shit might be. Weird shit that was about to hit the fan.

He gripped the steering wheel even more tightly and cursed his frustration into the night. Angela had set him up right from the start. She had manipulated him into Second Life with the promise of continuing his therapy in her SL group. It must have been Angela who somehow contrived to transfer Smitts' millions into Chas' account. Though God only knew why.

Michael turned the key in the ignition. There would probably be alerts going out on every police radio in the next few minutes. And this was his last known whereabouts. He pulled out into the southbound stream of traffic on PCH and headed up to Jamboree, where he took a right. At the foot of the hill, he drove past the Cosmetic Care plastic surgery center on his left and the Newport Beach Yacht Club on his right, to cross the bridge over the channel to Balboa Island. He found a parking spot right across the street from Starbucks on Marine Avenue. Through the rain he could see that the coffee shop was nearly empty. Just a handful of customers sitting at tables in the window. He slipped his computer beneath his jacket again, and hurried across the road, the rain bouncing off the tarmac as he ran. By the time he pulled open the door and got himself in out of the rain, he was soaked to the skin and breathing hard.

The few customers there were in the place turned to look at him. Two middle-aged women in jogpants and training shoes, taking shelter, mid-jog, from the unexpected rain. A young woman with long hair tied back from a pale face, engrossed in a laptop. A middle-aged man in shorts and a yellow tee-shirt plastered to his chest and shoulders. He had clearly been drenched in the downpour, wet, dark hair swept back from his forehead. An elderly, silver-haired woman sitting in the corner, face buried in her MacBook. She dragged her eyes away from her screen for a moment to look up to give him a sympathetic smile.

The bearded barista smiled at him warmly across the counter. "How are you today, Michael? What can I get you? The usual?"

In truth, Michael didn't want another coffee. But he needed the excuse to be here. "Sure."

He carried his coffee to a free table and sat down to open up his laptop. He immediately received a warning that his battery was low. He muttered a mouthful of imprecations under his breath. He was going to have to be quick.

Chapter Thirty-Five

Twist's office was frustratingly slow to rez. Chas stood impatiently watching as hair sprouted from his bald head and clothes slowly took form on his grey body. Finally his skin morphed into tanned flesh. A *ching* alerted him to a waiting IM. It was from Doobie.

> *Doobie:* Hey, Chas, when you pick this up, drop me a line and I'll send you a TP.

Chas responded immediately.

> *Chas:* I'm back, Doobs. TP me now.

An invitation to join Doobie Littlething in Camelot appeared, and he clicked to accept.

He dropped from darkness on to a mosaic-patterned bridge with waterfalls tumbling on either side. Lush, green gardens rezzed all around, and he saw Doobie's name on his radar. But it took nearly thirty seconds for her to appear. She was wearing a cross-over blue top and tight black pants cut off just above the calf. Her hair was tied back in a ponytail, with a fringe falling loosely across her forehead.

> *Doobie:* Stay in IM, Chas. There are too many people around here. Follow me.

She set off across the bridge on to a wide plaza with an open log fire burning at the far side, and up steps leading toward a vast mansion that overlooked the gardens. Chas followed her on to the stairway.

> *Chas:* What is this place?
>
> *Doobie:* Oh, it's a kind of romantic garden and country house. I sometimes bring clients here for a dance before we go back to my place. It's not always all about sex. One or two like the romance fantasy thrown in as part of the deal.
>
> *Chas:* So why are you here now?
>
> *Doobie:* LOLOL. I was with a client, Chas. Dumped him as soon as I got your IM.
>
> *Chas:* Oh. Okay.

They passed between two suits of armour guarding the entrance to the mansion. Flaming torches burned on either side of the door, and a box on the step offered a free Tux for the discerning dancer. They entered a vast, baronial hall, its walls lined with renaissance portraits. Circular stairs led to an upper level where the floor was made of glass.

> *Doobie:* Click on a slow-dance poseball, and we can dance and talk undisturbed.

Doobie and Chas fell into a close embrace and swayed to the soft, romantic music plumbed into the Camelot sound channel. The entrance hall below them was disconcertingly visible beneath their feet, as if they were floating on air. In any other circumstance, Chas might have been seduced by the moment. But right now, romance was the furthest thing from his mind.

> *Doobie:* When we spoke a short time ago, you said you thought that Janey had left you message.

Chas: She did. Doobs, I know who the killer is. It's my therapist, Angela Monachino. It was her who got me to come into Second Life in the first place. And both Smitts and Mathews were patients of hers.

Doobie: So she has an AV in here?

Chas: Yes. Angel Catchpole. She appears as a witch. At least, she did in therapy.

Doobie: So it must have been her that transferred the money into your account.

Chas: I guess she must have. Although I can't think why. Somehow she has got hold of Wicked Wilson's Super Gun, and she is murdering wealthy clients for their money.

Doobie: That doesn't make sense, though, Chas. Why would she need to murder them? Enough, surely, just to kill the AV, erase the account, transferring the money to hers.

Chas: Unless the RL victims knew who had killed their SL AVs. Then she would have to cover her tracks.

Doobie: So Janey found out it was her?

Chas: Yes. The idiot must have gone and confronted her. Goddamnit! Why didn't she wait for me?

Doobie: So Angela killed her and tried to make it look like it was you?

Chas: The problem is going to be proving it, Doobs. There's no evidence. In fact, all the available evidence points at me. And how am I going to explain the three million plus in my account? Always assuming the mob don't kill me before I get the chance to explain anything.

Doobie: Shit!

Chas: What?

> *Doobie:* An IM from my boss at Sinful Seductions. There's a client asking for me back at the club. I'm in the bad books already because of you. If I don't go now she'll sack me.
>
> *Chas:* Jesus, Doobs, it's just a job!
>
> *Doobie:* No, it's not! It took me ages to get that job. You don't know how tough the competition for dancing work is in here these days. I'll go and deal with it, and IM you as soon as I'm free.

She detached herself from the poseball and vanished, leaving Chas dancing solo around the glass floor.

He jumped off his poseball and looked self-consciously about at the dancing couples who all seemed to be glancing in his direction. Had he just been jilted by a lover or offended the girl he was courting? The by-now familiar *ching* drew his attention to an incoming IM, and his heart very nearly stopped. It was from Angel. He hesitated to open it, feeling a strange cocktail of emotions. Anger, fear, apprehension, murderous intent.

> *Angel:* Hi, Chas. We need to talk.
>
> *Chas:* I thought you were indisposed due to a family bereavement.
>
> *Angel:* I didn't say it was family.

And Chas realised then that she had been talking about Janey, and he felt a surge of anger rise up through him like molten lava. But he resisted the urge to let it erupt. She didn't know he knew. And he wanted to keep it that way.

> *Chas:* Oh. Right. So what was it you wanted to talk about, Angel?
>
> *Angel:* Well, I'd rather do it face-to-face, Chas. There are some things I need to discuss with you.

> *Chas:* Where do you want to meet?
>
> *Angel:* Here at The Blackhouse, Chas. Where you came for your group therapy session. Do you still have the LM?
>
> *Chas:* Yes.
>
> *Angel:* Well, TP over. I'll be waiting for you in the main hall.

Chas stared at the dialogue box and felt tension tighten across his chest. She was going to kill him. What other reason could she have for luring him there? She'd failed to do it as Twist. Now the gloves were off. No more pretending. It would be crazy to go, he knew that. But he needed proof of some kind, some way of implicating his therapist—his extherapist—in the whole Goddamned mess. And at least he still had the element of surprise on his side. She had no reason to suspect that he knew about the Smitts and Mathews connection, or that she had killed Janey.

He went into his Inventory and attached all his weapons HUDS, so that he had an array of defensive and attacking firepower just a click away. He drew a deep breath, opened up his Landmarks folder, and double-clicked on The Blackhouse.

Chapter Thirty-Six

It was dark when he landed on the stretch of beach opposite The Blackhouse. The empty sandy wastes all around shimmered silver under the moonlight, and the big, square block of The Blackhouse itself stood out against a starry sky. Even from here he could see that there were lights inside, the flickering flames of dozens of torches lining the interior walls throwing dancing shadows out of huge windows into the night.

Chas waded through the water channel that separated him from the neighbouring parcel and approached the huge metal doors of The Blackhouse with caution. The red eyes of the carved devil heads glowed in the dark and seemed to be fixed upon him as he got nearer.

Just inside, the same pool of blood lay shimmering on the floor, shockingly vivid in the flitting half light of the torches, the same bloody claw marks leading off into darkness. He hesitated here. The last time he had come, they had watched him from the inside. Some concealed camera, perhaps. The devil eyes that held him in their gaze, transmitting his image to the hidden eyes within.

He knew that those eyes would be watching him now, aware of his approach. There was still time for him to TP away. Still time to log out of SL and go to the police, tell them what he knew, place himself at the mercy of the California justice system, and ask for police protection from the mob. But somehow the thought failed to inspire him with confidence. He needed to face Angel down, to force a confrontation himself. To get to the truth and survive to tell it.

He turned up the volume on his laptop, anxious to hear the least sound that might betray another presence, and advanced into the corridor that led around the side of the building to the main arena. It got darker here. And up ahead, where the passage curved away out of sight, he could see only the faintest of feeble flickering. But as he moved forward, the air became filled with the crackling of flames, which got louder as he passed successive torches, and he was guided by their light, finally, to the vast floorspace of the main hall, which opened up before him. He saw the stage on the far side, where he had sat for his group session. Moonlight fell in through all the windows and lay in silver slabs across the floor. The blood spill in the centre of the arena glimmered in the dead light of the moon, vapour rising from it like smoke. And there, with the mist swirling around her feet, blood on the floor reflecting on her pale witch's face, stood Angel, multiple shadows cavorting about her like demented ghosts. She held her oxblood book of spells in the crook of her arm, as before, and wore the same long, purple gown, its plunging neckline divided by her opal pendant. She wore a curious half-smile on her face, red lips almost black in this strange light, and her eyes burned in the glow of the torches.

Angel: Hello, Chas. I'm so glad you could make it.

Chas: What is it you wanted to speak about, Angel?

Angel: Well, I didn't want to talk in open chat, or even in IM. Nothing much seems very secure in SL these days. Too many people writing spy software, creating gadgets to follow an AV and record his conversation. Too many ways of being observed without knowing it. And most of the poor souls who inhabit this wonderful virtual world of ours haven't the least idea of what is really going on. They're all too busy shopping or having sex. And what a waste of an extraordinary technology that is.

She took several steps toward him, and he felt himself flinch, almost involuntarily.

Angel: I wanted this communication to take place between just you and me, Chas. I didn't want any chance of it being overheard. So I've prepared a notecard.

The offer of a notecard from Angel Catchpole appeared. He accepted it, and the notecard opened up. He looked at it for several seconds in some consternation. It was entitled *A Sorry Tale* and was completely blank.

Chas: I don't understand.

Angel: What's not to understand, Chas? Read it.

Chas: It's blank, Angel.

Angel: Nonsense. I'm looking at a copy of it right here.

A beep on his radar alerted Chas to another presence. He saw the name Dark Daley appear on his list.

Dark: I'm afraid he's right, Angel.

They both turned to see Dark descending the stairs from the upper level. He was, as before, bare-chested, his nipple ring glinting in the reflected moonlight. He wore black jeans and studded biker boots. His shock of brown hair seemed darker than Chas remembered it, shot through now with silver.

Angel: What are you doing here, Dark? You don't have an appointment.

Dark: I didn't think I'd need an appointment, Doctor Catchpole. I thought you might be interested, finally, to hear about my deepest, darkest fantasies. That's why I erased your little notecard. I can't let you go sharing too much with strangers.

Angel: What are you talking about, Dark? How could you do that?

Dark: It's easy when you know how, my little Angel. Easy, too, to kill when you get a taste for it. A simple transition from fantasy to reality. The act played out in the imagination to the act carried out in fact.

Chas was caught off-guard by the speed with which the Super Gun appeared in Dark's hand, his arm extended straight ahead of him, his head tipped slightly to one side, one eye closed to line up his target—Chas.

Dark: Just like this.

He swivelled through ninety degrees and fired three times. Each shot blew a ragged hole in Angel's AV. Chas felt something strike him, and his own AV staggered back. He glanced down to see blood and fragments of AV flesh on his shirt and pants.

Angel stood for a moment in what seemed like shocked disbelief. Most of her chest and stomach were gone. And then she simply folded up, almost dissolving in a bloody pile on the floor, her book of spells still clutched in the crook of her arm.

An IM flashed up in Chas' dialogue box.

> *Doobie:* Okay, Chas, I'm free now. TP me.

Chas awoke, startled, from his shock.

> *Chas:* Doobie, I was wrong. It's not Angel. It's one of her patients. Dark Daley. He's just killed her.
>
> *Doobie:* Jesus, Chas! Where are you? Get out of there, wherever you are!

Dark turned toward Chas, his mouth stretched open in grotesque facsimile of a smile.

Dark: Never could stand the bitch. Too fucking smug by half. And you, my friend, know way too much for your own good. Or mine.

A million thought fragments searched for a glimmer of light in the dark recesses of Chas' mind before one of them sent a blinding reflection arrowing back through his consciousness. The white cherub clutched in Janey's hand. Not Angel or Angela, but Angeloz. Luis LA Angeloz. The skinny half of Laurel and Hardy. Hadn't they seen his AV in Second Life? Phat Botha. Wasn't it possible he had a second account? An alt. Chas looked at Dark afresh, and the gun pointing straight at him. "Stanley?"

For a moment it seemed as if Dark had frozen. "What?"

And in that moment, Chas double-clicked the first LM his cursor landed on in his Inventory, and he teleported out of the Blackhouse before Dark could pull the trigger.

◇◇◇

As the grim brick and brownstone buildings rezzed around him, Chas realised he was back where most of his SL adventure had begun. In Crack Town, Carnal City, where Doobie had trapped and killed the griefer, Tommy Tattoo. He knew that Dark could only be a matter of seconds behind him. He clicked into Run mode and started running down the street. Past Dura's Play Lounge and Carnal Street Urban Building supplies, and Urban Grims offensive textures.

On the corner, a police car was pulled up on the sidewalk, and an officer was handcuffing a young thug against the wall. A scrawl of graffiti read *Fight apathy—or don't*. He heard the report of gunfire echoing along the street as the brick wall ahead of him splintered under the impact of a bullet. He glanced back. Dark was pursuing him at a run. He knew, from his brief experience how hard it was to hit a moving target. The secret would be to keep moving.

He passed a prostitute touting for business.

Becka Cale: Five hundred for an hour, Chas. What do you say?

But he didn't stop, even to turn her down.

He ran past the Bad Art store and turned left at the end of the street as another shot rang out. A butcher with a bloody white smock stood outside his store, a meat cleaver in his hand. He was holding up a string of sausages and grinning, as if he thought Chas might be interested in buying. Ahead, a single-decked bus was burning at the side of the road, and beyond it mist swirled around the headstones in the Carnal City cemetery.

Chas veered away from the cemetery gates and found himself in what seemed to be a dead-end yard. He panicked, aware that Dark was only just behind him. Then he spotted a narrow, concealed exit that led out between tall buildings, and he ran through it and into a maze of passages that zigzagged between meshed off courtyards. The walls were very nearly obliterated by graffiti. He passed *Strangled* and *Strangle* animations. Ahead was Le Baron 24-hour store, selling "kinky accessories and more".

Chas turned right, still afraid to look back. And suddenly the landscape seemed familiar. He ran straight up the street and turned left on to a bridge spanning a river of chemical green sludge. This was where Doobie had finally caught up with Tommy Tattoo. At the end of the street stood the Carnal City Police Department.

In a momentary but absolute failure of logic, Chas thought that he might find safety there. He glanced behind him to see Dark turning the corner, and when he turned back, found himself confronted by two bizarrely deformed AVs. Badwolf Lilliehook was a punk, with his right leg impossibly stretched and extended well above his head, his right arm growing out of his thigh. Ariel Kyle was a white-faced demon with a long, thin neck and both legs doubled over above her head. They looked like they had been pulled through a machine and mangled beyond any recognisable human shape.

Badwolf: Hi, Chas.

He sounded friendly enough. Chas stopped dead. Uncertain whether they posed any threat or not.

Chas: Hi. I guess you guys are into the deformed look.

Ariel: This is how we get off. Normal toon sex iz boring.

Almost before her words had registered onscreen she exploded, like a watermelon dropped from a great height. Blood spattered everywhere as the shot from the Super Gun echoed around the street.

Badwolf: Jesus Christ!

Chas took off again, running to the end of the street, straight for the precinct office of the Carnal City police.

A hooker in a short black skirt and thigh-length red boots called to him at the door as it slid open and he ran inside. But he didn't stop to read her text.

There was no one behind the desk. He ran past a wall of wanted posters and a map of Carnal city and turned through open steel doors into the cell area. Several role-playing prisoners lounged behind bars, drinking from beer cans. They looked up as he came in. Chas was panicking now. He was painting himself into a corner with no way out.

He ran down the hall and through the only door at the end of it, finding himself in a small, square interview room with scarred green walls. There was a plain black table with two chairs at either side of it. A blackboard on the wall was scrawled over in yellow chalk. *Witness. Photos. F/prints. Fluids. Weapons.* The door slammed shut behind him. He was trapped. He cursed himself. There was no way out.

An IM chinged into his dialogue box.

> *Doobie:* Chas, what's happening? Did you get out okay?
>
> *Chas:* I'm in deep shit, Doobs. In Carnal City.
>
> *Doobie:* TP me.
>
> *Chas:* No time.

He opened up his Inventory and clicked on the Landmark folder, then tried to turn at the sound of the door opening. The movement of his arrow key shut down his Inventory, and there was no time to open it again before he saw Dark standing in the doorway, the Super Gun pointing straight at him. It was all a question, he knew, of whether he could find the Quit key, before Dark clicked his mouse and fired the shot.

But there was no competition. Dark fired. Once. Twice. Three times. Chas felt the impact of the bullets. His AV reacted, thrown backwards as each one struck him, until the third propelled him against the wall. There was, of course, no pain. Just a sick feeling in the pit of his stomach, as his screen turned first red, then black, and his SL software crashed.

Chapter Thirty-Seven

Michael sat staring at his screen in disbelief. How could he have let it happen? Why hadn't he teleported out earlier, or simply quit?

Chas was gone, and with the erasure of his account, any chance of proving where the three million had come from. But Angel was gone, too. And in spite of everything that had pointed in her direction, any thoughts that he had harboured that Angela Monachino was the killer had been blown out of SL by three shots from the Super Gun. It could only have been Stan Laurel—Detective Luis LA Angeloz.

He slumped forward, elbows on the table, head in his hands, bereft of the least idea of what to do now. He found himself mourning for Chas. In some way that he barely understood, he had been born again in Chas. Rediscovered the emotions he had thought were dead inside him. Chas had shown him how to live again. How to be. How to feel. And now he was gone, leaving Michael all on his own to face murder charges and death threats. The killer had destroyed Chas and would almost certainly now come after Michael in RL, too.

And with that thought came the realisation that Angela was also in danger. Dark had only killed her AV. But Angela would know his true identity. Angeloz must have been one of her patients. While he might simply be content to let Michael be gunned down by the mob or sent to prison by the state, he would *have* to kill Angela. She knew too much.

"Sorry, Michael, I'm going to have to ask you to leave now. It's closing time." The bearded barista smiled at him apologetically over the counter. "You, too, ma'am."

Michael looked around, waking as if from a dream. The place was empty now, except for the elderly lady in the corner. Half the lights had been switched off, and the rain was still falling outside, battering off the metalled surface of the road with such force that the mist it created almost obliterated the far sidewalk.

His computer beeped loudly, and he looked down at the warning on his screen. BATTERY LEVEL CRITICAL. Almost before he had read it, the screen went blank and the machine whined, clicked, and fell silent. It had just shut itself down. No more juice. He closed its lid and stood up.

"Excuse me."

He turned to see the silver-haired woman in the corner slipping her MacBook into its carry-case and gathering together her belongings.

"Do you know if there is somewhere else around here that I can access the Internet? I haven't finished my business online, and it's rather important that I do."

Michael didn't want to be rude. But neither did he want to waste time directing her to an Internet cafe. He knew that somehow he had to get himself back home to get online. He needed to talk to Doobie. He needed another head to bounce all this off. "I'm sorry," he said. "I'm really not sure. I think there's a place somewhere over on the Lido. But you'll need to ask the barista."

◇◇◇

Collar up, laptop held to his chest, he ran through the almost tropical downpour to his SUV across the street and slipped into the driver's seat, rain streaming down his face. He tossed the computer aside and dug out his cellphone from an inside pocket. There was a good chance that Angela might still be alive. Her number was in the memory. He listened to it ring. And ring. And then the answering service cut in. He hung up, and had an ominous sense of foreboding. He needed to get into his house.

The engine coughed and spat, as if clearing rainwater from its throat, before roaring into life. He slipped the transmission into drive and swung a u-turn across the street, accelerating hard toward the bridge, and the long climb back up to PCH. He turned right at the lights, and right again into Irvine Terrace. In Ramona drive he reduced his speed to a crawl and turned off his lights as he veered right at the end of the street into Dolphin Terrace. Between the rain and the black, moonless night, he could barely see as he navigated west toward his house.

He was almost upon the patrol car before he saw it. It was parked right outside his gate, two uniformed officers only just visible through a fogged-up windshield in the halo of yellow light cast by the courtesy lamp above the rearview mirror. He cursed in a whisper, as if they might somehow be able to hear him, and swung right again into Patolita Drive, waiting until he was out of view before turning on his lights and accelerating back toward the highway. He was going to have to try to get in the back way.

◇◇◇

He parked in Bayside Drive and peered up through the rain and the dark to the line of houses along the top of the bluff, a hundred feet above him. Michael had never before tried to reach his house from here. Dolphin Terrace had been built precariously on the edge of the drop, and over the years several home owners had been forced to sink piles down to bedrock to underpin the foundations and stop their houses from sliding down the hill.

The gradient was just a little less than sheer and would have been almost impossible to climb had it not been so thickly planted with shrubs and bushes and small trees. Michael remembered when Mora had first had the house remodelled, the construction company had stripped the slope bare to facilitate the drilling. During a downpour not dissimilar to tonight's, Michael had spend a perilous two hours trying to position tarpaulins to prevent the soil from being washed away. The next day the architect had suggested a prolific planting from top to bottom to prevent further erosion.

Michael was glad of it now. For without these hand and footholds, he would never have been able to climb it. As it was the ascent was difficult and dangerous. Thorns and spikes tore at his face, and arms, and hands. His feet slithered in the mud, his hands straining to hold on to roots and branches made slick by the rain.

At one point he lost his grip, and slithered down ten or fifteen feet, before grasping a gnarled vine root to stop himself falling. A glance back down toward Bayside reminded him that it would have been a long way to fall. He scrambled up the slope to where he had slipped and forced himself on again toward the top.

It took him nearly fifteen minutes to get there. He heaved himself over the low boundary wall along the edge of the terrace, and fell in a gasping heap on to the tiles beyond it. He lay on his back for several minutes, rain pounding his body, washing him clean of mud and dirt and blood, and he closed his eyes, wishing that he could simply fall asleep and awaken in some sunny tomorrow, remembering all this as just a bad dream.

But instead, he made himself roll over, and got unsteadily to his feet. He found his keys and unlocked the door to his office, sliding it aside and stepping with relief into the warm, dry safety of the house. He knew that it would be fatal to turn on any lights, and so he hurried over to his desk and switched on his computer. He didn't care about the trail of mud he left on the white carpet, or the mess he made of his leather office chair.

He found the Second Life icon on his computer desktop and double-clicked it. Up came the welcome page. The cursor blinked at him from the window in which he would normally type his SL name. It was more in hope than expectation that he tapped out his username and password. An error message appeared almost immediately. LOGIN FAILED. PLEASE MAKE SURE THAT YOU HAVE THE CORRECT ACCOUNT NAME AND PASSWORD. He tried again. The same message. Chas really was dead, his account terminated. And he had no way of getting back into Second Life. There was no time to sit down and create a new AV. So he was on his own.

Angela was either already dead or in grave danger, and he had two possible courses of action. He could simply walk out into the street and tap on the window of the patrol car and throw himself on their mercy. But somehow he didn't think they would be very receptive. How could he possibly convince them in time that Angela really was in danger? He could picture himself being left to stew in an interview room somewhere, while the officers assigned to his case drank coffee and compared notes on his ludicrous story, commenting on how Michael had always seemed a bit strange. A murderous avatar and three million dollars of mob money in an account that had vanished? They would very probably laugh in his face.

No. If he could do anything for Angela, if it wasn't already too late, he would have to do it himself.

He made one final attempt to call her, only to get her messaging service again. Wearily, he hung up and stood to face the rain that still fell out there in the hot California night, and the long, treacherous descent in the mud back down to Bayside Terrace.

◇◇◇

There were two cars ahead of him in the line for the ferry. He watched its lights emerge from the mist of rain that fell across the channel. The ferryman, in baseball cap and oilskins, lifted the barrier and watched as his cargo drove off into the night. Then he waved vigourously at the waiting vehicles. He didn't want to be standing out in the rain any longer than necessary.

The trip across to the peninsula took less than five minutes. Everything was closed up on the other side. Jane's Corndogs stood brooding darkly on the corner as the cars in front of Michael drove with infuriating lack of urgency to the traffic lights on Balboa Boulevard. The neon glow of Bubbles Art Gallery reflected foggy blue in the deluge as the line of vehicles idled at the lights, waiting for them to turn green. As the other cars made a left, Michael accelerated straight through and up Palm

Street, turning hard right into the service lane providing vehicle access to the homes that ran along the boardwalk.

He had no idea which was Angela's. He had only ever approached it from the beach side. He made a guess at how far he'd come and pulled up outside a garage. There were no lights here, and as soon as he cut his engine, the world around him plunged into darkness. He waited a moment for his eyes to make the adjustment, before stepping out into the rain and peering through the dark to get his bearings. He crossed the lane and found a gate that opened into a narrow alleyway running all the way forward to the beach between two long, narrow houses. The gate at the beach end was locked, and he scrambled over it, feet sliding on the cross slats, to drop down on to the boardwalk. He was not sure why, but there seemed to be more ambient light here, and he saw that he was several houses short of Angela's. He ran fifty yards through the rain to reach it and stopped at the gate.

Rainwater was cascading from the Roman-tiled roof onto the first-floor balcony, then down on to the patio below. He could hear it drumming on the lid of the barbecue and on the glass tabletop of the beach dining set in the garden. The windows at the front were screened from the boardwalk by a profusion of desert plants and shrubs, spikes and fronds and cacti. But he could see that the blinds were all drawn and turned down. There were no lights anywhere in evidence.

He opened the gate, slightly surprised to find it unlocked and off the latch, and moved cautiously up the path to the house. Briefly he took refuge in the front porch, placing his hands on either side of his head to shield his eyes and peer in through the glass panes down one side of the door. But he could see nothing. He knocked and heard its empty, dead echo come back from within. No sound or sudden light returned with it to greet him.

Back out in the rain, he ran down the narrow passageway between Angela's house and the one next door, grey clapboard siding mired in darkness. He reached the side door about half way along. It was the door by which he had always entered and exited the house for his therapy sessions. The tradesman's entrance.

And there he stopped, standing stock still, with the rain running down his face. The door lay very slightly ajar, opening into the profound and impenetrable darkness of the interior. The wooden architrave of the doorframe was splintered and broken where it had been forced, and the lock broken.

Cautiously, he reached out a hand and pushed it inwards. It swung open with the faintest of creaks.

"Hello?" His voice sounded feeble and was swallowed up by the night. He tried again. More boldly this time. "Hello?" But as before, there was no response.

Chapter Thirty-Eight

Doobie couldn't concentrate. She hadn't heard from Chas in nearly an hour. At the urging of her boss at Sinful Seductions, and under the threat of dismissal if she refused, Doobie had agreed to entertain a customer in the privacy of her own home. Had she had the least idea of what else to do, she would have told her boss where to stick her job, and what she could do with her precious customer.

But as it was, she had reluctantly agreed, and lay now in the missionary position beneath a humping, grunting AV called Axel Corvale, who fancied himself as one of SL's great lovers. She had muted him, in order not to be distracted by his muttered sexual inanities, and had her head turned to one side, looking from the window out over the lagoon.

She thought about Chas and how she had lain with him in this very bed only a few hours earlier. Only then it had been different. He had awakened feelings in her that had been long dormant, and the little seed of regret he had sown in her during their unfulfilled lovemaking had grown to a terrible ache. An ache she knew she could never satisfy. A relationship she knew she could never realise.

She opened her Friends List to send him another IM and saw with a shock that stung her, that he was no longer on the list. There had to be some mistake. She closed the box and opened it again. Scrolled down the list and back again. He was gone.

In a panic she opened her Search window and tapped in his name. NOT FOUND was the response. Chas Chesnokov no longer existed in Second Life. She closed her eyes and knew with a terrible certainty what had happened. Which meant that Michael Kapinsky was now in grave RL danger. And she was trapped in this virtual world without any way of helping him. She thought about logging off and calling the police. But what could she tell them? It was an impossible story. And she had no idea where he might be, or who the killer was. An AV called Dark Daley. But beyond his SL name, she knew nothing about him.

She put the name into the Search Engine and brought up his Profile. It was blank, apart from the date he had been Born. Just four weeks ago. Which meant, in all probability, he was the second or third AV of someone else. Her mind was racing, and she forced herself to slow it down. To think her way through the problem as she would a game of chess.

What other information did she have?

She remembered the photographs Chas had taken at the Maximillian Thrust crime scene, at the house where she had discovered his body. She went into her Texture folder and pulled the pictures up on screen one by one. They brought back to her a vivid recollection of the shambles inside the house. Floors, ceilings, walls buckled and canted at odd angles. The detritus of a panicked battle that had ended in Thrust's murder. She looked at the body, wedged between two sections of dislodged floor, the blood pooling beneath it, and had a sudden thought.

The doors had been locked and there had been no furniture in the house with poseballs to latch on to. So how had the killer got in? She remembered very clearly, how she herself had got in and out, by shifting her POV to the inside and the outside, rezzing poseballs to latch on to. The oldest griefers' trick in SL. So the killer must have had to rez a poseball inside the house in order to get in. And in all the ensuing confusion and disruption, wasn't it just possible that the killer had lost sight of it, and might have forgotten to take it back again?

Doobie scrutinised every picture. There was no sign of a poseball, and the hope that had flared briefly died again, like a match that never quite caught. But there was only one way to be certain. And that was to go and look for herself.

She opened up her Landmark folder and found the LM she had taken inside Thrust's house. She double-clicked it and teleported out of her own home in a scattering of fairy dust, leaving her grunting client humping fresh air.

It took him a moment to realised she was gone, and even then he was unable to assimilate it. The hooker had run out on the virtual world's greatest lover.

Axel Corvale: Huh?!!

◇◇◇

Doobie rezzed inside Maximillian Thrust's Asian home, sunlight streaming across his tropical island paradise outside to slant in through the window and cast deep shadows amongst the chaos. Thrust was still there, where they had found him. Nothing had changed, and Doobie began a meticulous search of every hidden corner and crevice, switching POV when she could to look beneath sections of upturned floor. Nothing. It was still possible, she thought, that it was there somewhere, and that she just wasn't finding it. If Thrust had possessed terraforming rights for the island, then the very sand beneath the house could have been churned and deformed, hiding forever any poseball that might be down there.

But then, like that moment of revelation during a game of chess, when you see the route to checkmate with unparalleled clarity, she had an epiphany. The Land Window!

She clicked on the name of the land, written in blue across the top of the screen, and opened up the Land Window. Then she clicked on the Objects tab. The information that filled the window told her how many prims the land would support. There were 1265 primitives, with 681 still available. Then the crucial piece of information. Primitives Owned by Parcel Owner: 582. Doobie did the math. There were two prims unaccounted for.

At the foot of the Land Window was an option to refresh the list of object owners. Doobie clicked on it, and two names appeared. The first was Maximillian Thrust, who was the owner of objects accounting for 582 prims. The second was the owner of an object worth 2 prims. The missing poseball, Doobie was virtually sure. And her eyes opened wide in confusion and disbelief as she took on board the name, and knew now with an absolute certainty who the killer really was.

Chapter Thirty-Nine

Michael left the door open behind him as he moved step by careful step into the profound darkness that smothered the interior of Angela's house. He placed a hand against the wall to his right and used it to guide himself the seven or eight feet to the long hallway that transected the house lengthwise.

To the left, he knew, were the kitchen, bathroom, and utility rooms. To the right, a couple of bedrooms, Angela's office, and at the far end of the hall, the sitting room where she conducted her sessions with clients, blinds drawn against the glare of the beach and the ocean beyond. A narrow staircase led up to a guest apartment with its own kitchen and sitting room.

As he turned into the hall, he saw a faint glow of ghostly light spilling from the open door of what he knew to be the office. He waited for a moment, listening intently for the slightest sound. But the silence was so deep it was almost suffocating. All he could hear was the sound of the rain that still fell outside, the tattoo of it on the roof and the veranda. He started moving carefully down the hall, eyes now fully adjusted to the small amount of available light.

He pushed open the first door he reached and could just make out the dark shape of a bed, a wardrobe, a dresser. He reached inside for a light switch. But its dull click produced no light, and the apprehension in him rose like the acid reflux in his digestive system.

Further along the hall, he found a panel of switches, none of which brought light to his darkness, and he wondered what was powering the light source he saw emanating from the office. He was driven on now by a sense of dread, of a growing certainty that he was going to find Angela dead, and of wanting to get it over with. But there was, too, the very real sense that the killer might still be here. Waiting for him. The fact that there seemed to be power in the office put the thought in his head that perhaps someone had deliberately disabled the lighting circuits. Simple enough to throw a few switches in the fuse box.

He passed a second bedroom and hesitated for just a few seconds before moving into the ghost light from the office. The door was only partially open. He reached out to push it gently inwards to reveal an arc of computer monitors ranged around the inside curve of a long, semicircular office desk. Six of them. Each one illuminated by a scene from Second Life, an AV in each, heads dropped, arms hanging at their sides, all with the *Away* text next to their names.

Michael realised with a shock who each of them was, as his eyes jumped from screen to screen. Laffa Minit, Demetrius Smith, Tweedle Dum, Tweedle Dee, Dark Daley. All of Angel's patients from his group therapy session at The Blackhouse. The sixth and final screen displayed the Second Life welcome page that Michael had seen for the very first time at Arnold Smitts' home the night of his murder. There were keyboards in front of each monitor, and a single office chair on castors. Speakers set behind the screens hummed with the familiar ambient sound of the virtual world.

Michael stood rooted to the spot, mesmerised, confused, until a sound from along the hall filtered through the myriad thoughts that choked his brain and reignited his fear. It was just a small sound, as if the leg of a chair had scraped on a carpet. But it crashed into his thoughts like the discordant percussion of a Peking opera. He wheeled around toward the source of it, eyes straining in the gloom. He listened carefully to try to catch it again. Nothing. But there was somebody there. Of that he was certain.

He resisted an urge to turn tail and run. The adrenalin pumping through his body was readying him for fight or flight. But he had come too far to run away now, into the arms of the mob who would kill him or the police who wouldn't believe him. And so he prepared himself for the fight, tensed and ready, as he inched forward toward the sitting room.

Double doors stood wide. An electric clock display on the far wall cast the only light around the room and confirmed Michael's worst fears that someone had deliberately disabled the lights. The drapes on the side windows were drawn against the night, thick velvet curtains that fell luxuriantly to gather on the carpet. And as he passed them, he caught a tiny movement out of the corner of his eye. He turned in time to see the faintest reflection of light catching the blade as it plunged into his neck.

The pain of it seared through his body, the knife cutting through sinew and muscle, missing vital arteries, but penetrating deep into the flesh of his left shoulder. He felt a disabling weakness surge through his body, and his legs buckled under him. As he fell to the floor, his head hit the carpet with a sickening thud. He felt the blade sliding out of the wound it had made, followed by a rush of his blood, warm and sticky, spreading over his neck and shoulder, soaking into the floor. A sense of panic almost crippled him entirely. It felt like his very life was flowing out of him.

A dark figure emerged from the folds of the drapes and stepped over him, moving across the room to switch on a table lamp. The sudden light hurt like hell, and Michael screwed up his eyes against it. He put a hand to his neck and felt his blood wet on his fingers. He rolled over on to his side, opening his eyes to peer into the light to get a look at his attacker.

"Get up, Michael."

The shock of hearing her voice made his eyes open wide. He struggled to his knees, clutching at his shoulder, steadying himself against the wall with his other hand. "Angela?"

"Surprised?"

"I don't understand."

"Well, I wouldn't expect you to. For a clever man you're pretty stupid, Michael. Weak. Driven by your emotions rather than your intelligence. Which made you perfect, really, for what I had in mind."

She slid open a drawer in her writing bureau and brought out a small handgun. She waved it at him, casually, almost relaxed.

"I said get up."

So Detective Luis Angeloz was not, after all, Dark Daley or any of the others. They were all Angela. With a great effort of will, Michael managed to get to his feet. He felt the blood oozing between his fingers, and the pain was spreading down his back and across his chest. He felt giddy and took several staggering steps forward before dropping again to his knees. A bloody hand stopped him falling on his face.

"Good. That's going to look very convincing. You see, after I heard the side door being forced I grabbed the nearest weapon I could find. A kitchen knife. When you attacked me I stabbed you with it. But you were only wounded and came after me. I ran in here, where I took my gun from the bureau and… well, I think you can guess the rest." She sat down, perched on the edge of an armchair, and he saw how pale she was. For for all her superficial confidence, there was a tremor in her voice. "Oh, and you should know. When you broke into my house you triggered a silent alarm system. The police are on their way, even as we speak. Too bad they won't get here on time. You'll be dead, and I will be distraught. Attacked by one of my own patients. Of course, I'll tell them I didn't realise it was you until after I'd shot you. Not that it would have made any difference. You don't stop defending yourself from an attacker just because you know who he is."

"You killed Janey."

"The stupid girl came here trying to pass herself off as a police-woman. Asking questions about patients any detective would know I couldn't answer. And in any case, I knew who she was. You'd talked about her often enough during our sessions."

"Did I?" Michael had no recollection. He could only ever remember talking about Mora. All those hours of self-indulgent grief were a distant blur now.

"So she had to go, I'm afraid."

"But why, Angela? What's it all about?"

She sighed and looked at her watch. "Well, I suppose we have a few minutes. I can wait until we hear the siren before I shoot you. That way I won't have to sit too long with you bleeding on my floor."

"Jesus, Angela! You're a cold-blooded bitch!"

Her smile was strained. "Yes. I suppose I am." She drew a deep breath. "Where to begin…With Roger Bloom, I guess. A patient. Very interested when I told him my idea of starting group therapy sessions in Second Life. I'd already been in for a while by that time. Knew what I was doing and how I wanted to set things up. Turned out Roger was a real expert on the subject. Had his own software company in RL, created and scripted weapons systems in SL."

"Wicked Wilson."

Angela cocked an eyebrow. "Yes…You got further down that road than I expected. Well, Roger just couldn't resist telling me how clever he was. Always in therapy, so it was confidential. Like the confessional. Plus, I think, he wanted into my panties. He tried so hard to impress me. Which made him very malleable. So, anyway, he told me he'd created and scripted a weapon that would not only kill an AV, but wipe any record of its account off the database. And—this was the really clever bit—transfer any money out of that account into his own. An untraceable transaction. But the truth is, he never saw its financial potential, Michael. He was a mischief-maker. Enjoyed the sheer act of fucking with people's lives. A great big kid. I saw immediately how damned lucrative it could be. I mean, let's face it, you don't practise psychotherapy in Newport Beach without having a lot of very wealthy clients. If I could drop the idea, in casual conversation, that an SL account was an ideal place to hide money from the taxman, a business partner, a spouse, then persuade them to join my virtual group therapy…"

She stood up and wandered toward him. Michael's breath was becoming stertorous, as he continued to lose blood.

"A simple matter, to kill their AVs with an alt of my own, and suddenly all that secret money is in my account. Money that none of them could report missing, since it was there illicitly." She looked at him. "You're not going to pass out on me before I finish my story, are you? I've been just dying to tell someone. And I know you're just dying to hear it."

"You killed Wicked Wilson for his gun?"

"It was easy, Michael. I invited him over for drinks. Played on his fantasies. He'd shown me how it was possible to amend the script to pay the money into any account he chose. I persuaded him to give me a demonstration. We went online. On two different computers. But what he could never have guessed was that I'd slip a little sedative into his bourbon. And when he drifted off into his happy slumber, I took control of his AV, transferred the gun to mine, and amended the script to pay into my account. Then shot him. Simple.

"When he came round, I told him that the grid had shut down for maintenance, and that he had drunk way too much. I offered to drive him home in his car. When we got there, I shot him for real. Walked around the corner and got a taxi home. The Super Gun was mine." She smiled. "And that's when I hit on the really clever bit of my plan. When I persuaded a wealthy client to join group therapy in SL, I used the group to introduce the idea of hiding money in the account. Which was easy, because each and every one of the group was me. A small investment. Six computers, six AVs. Each one, in many ways, the personification of some part of me that I'd always had to keep under wraps.

"If was such fun, Michael. Hard for you to imagine. Being able to tell these poor little rich fucks exactly what I thought of them. All those hours of having to keep a lid on my private thoughts, finally given an outlet through Laffa, and Demetrius, and Dark, and the Tweedles. I could say anything through them. And I did. As you found out."

"So you killed your patients in RL after you killed them in SL."

"Good God, no. No need. Until Arnold Smitts, damn him! I had no idea he worked for the mob until I killed his AV, and ended up with three million in my account. Which was much more than I'd ever bargained for. He called me. Told me everything, without the least idea that it was me who had done it to him. He was terrified his employers would think he had ripped them off. But I knew that if these people started digging, there was a chance the money trail could lead back to me.

"Of course, none of the money ever paid directly into my account. I had created Green Goddess, another AV, especially for that, and to do the killing. Even so, I needed to divert attention as far away from me as possible. I had to go to Smitts place and kill him to stop him telling anyone else about his connection with me. Then I set you up to be the recipient of the mob money. Amended the script before I shot Green and sent the cash winging its way into your account. So now the trail led to you, rather than me."

"And Jennifer Mathews?"

"A spoiled brat. But smart, Michael. Way too smart. She started getting suspicious. And when her AV got killed and the money her father had put into her account just vanished, she came to see me, asking some very awkward questions. And with the whole Smitts thing having just blown up in my face, I couldn't afford to have her pointing any fingers at me."

Michael fell over on to his side. He was getting very faint now. He heard her words, but was having trouble making sense of them any more.

"It was fun shooting myself to put you off the scent, and letting Dark do the dirty work. But I knew the hero in you would think I was in danger and come charging in like a knight in shining armour. It took you a while, though. I was waiting almost two hours for you to show. Almost began to doubt you."

She took several steps back.

"Get up now, Michael. It's time."

"I can't."

"Get up!" Her voice became shrill.

Michael rolled over on to his knees and grabbed the edge of her writing bureau, trying to get himself to his feet. But his legs wouldn't hold him. He was too far gone now to feel fear any more. But he knew he was going to die, and something in him was resigned to it.

In the distance he heard the sound of the police siren and knew that it was his death knell. She would have to do the deed before they arrived. And he speculated, as he had many times during the past months, on whether there really was an afterlife. And if there was, if he might meet Mora there again. There was comfort in the thought, even although deep down he couldn't really bring himself to believe it.

He looked up as she raised her arm to point the gun directly at him, and he closed his eyes to brace himself for the impact of the bullets.

He heard the shots. Three of them. But felt nothing, and he wondered if death really came that quickly. He opened his eyes in time to see Angela stagger backwards, blood pulsing from three closely grouped wounds in the centre of her chest. She sat down abruptly in the armchair where he had sat so many times in the dark talking about Mora. Her arm fell away to the side, the handgun slipping from her fingers to hit the floor with a thump. Her eyes were wide, startled, staring off into some unseen distance. And Michael knew that she was dead.

He slid down to the floor and rolled over, propping himself on one elbow, and saw Angela's killer standing in the doorway, the gun that shot her still raised.

He frowned, confused, and thought that maybe he really was dead after all. Angela's killer was the elderly, silver-haired lady from the Starbucks coffee shop on Balboa Island. Her hand was trembling as she lowered the gun. "When I bought this, I took a course in care and maintenance," she said. "It included eight lessons in loading, targeting, and firing. I never ever thought I would actually shoot someone with it."

"Who are you?" Michael's voice was barely a whisper.

The sound of it seemed to awaken her, as if she was just emerging from some daydream, or maybe a nightmare. She hurried over to kneel down beside him.

"Oh, my dear, that looks bad."

He looked up into her pale blue eyes and saw her concern.

"Who are you?" he asked again.

For a moment she avoided his gaze, before turning her eyes directly to meet his. "I'm Doobie," she said. "I thought maybe you might need some help."

Chapter Forty

The Orange County Superior court in Santa Ana stood back from the road in Civic Center Drive, behind a screen of trees and bushes. A modern building of concrete and glass. Reflecting that, the courtroom itself seemed to lack the gravitas of many older courts—buildings which owed more in architecture and design to the influence of the Europeans.

But the hearing itself had been grave enough. The subjects under discussion—fraud, theft, and murder. Being decided here was what culpability, if any, could be placed at the door of Michael Kapinsky for the murder of Janey Amat, and the subsequent shooting of Angela Monachino. As well as whether there were sufficient grounds to charge him in connection with the theft of more than three million dollars.

Michael had been dreading it. After five weeks of recuperation from his stabbing, he had finally been deemed fit enough to go before a judge, and the stress of it seemed to make his shoulder ache all the more.

Now, as his legal team walked him from the courtroom, he could barely believe that, finally, it was over. He was still shaking. His legs felt weak. His attorney, Jack Sandler, slipped a triumphant arm through his and leaned in to whisper, "It's finished, Michael. Relax. You're home free."

But not entirely. The judge had ordered that as soon as the sale of Michael's property in Dolphin Terrace was completed,

$3,183,637 of the proceeds were to be sequestered pending an inquiry into where the money had come from and into Arnold Smitts' connections to the mob. The good news was that no one, either officially or unofficially, believed that Michael had stolen it. So he was off the mob hook as well.

The only thing, it seemed, that everyone agreed upon was how foolish he had been. And the judge had not been slow to pass comment on the subject.

Gillian MacCormack sat in the hall outside the courtroom, a sixty-seven-year-old lady in a grey tweed suit, sandwiched between a young lady lawyer sharply dressed in black and an older, male assistant. She stood up, filled with trepidation, as Michael emerged, pale and relieved. And for a moment their eyes met.

She had told police that when she and Michael exchanged RL names in SL, she had taken the first available flight from Sacramento to John Wayne airport, Orange County, a mere fifteen-minute taxi ride away from Newport Beach. Her instinct had been that he was in imminent danger and might need her help. Which had turned out to be extremely prescient. Of more concern now, it seemed, than even the shooting of Angela Monachino was how she had managed to smuggle a gun on board her airplane. To the consternation of the federal aviation authorities and Homeland Security, she had told them quite simply that she had wrapped it in a pair of camisole knickers and packed it in her check-in bag. Her lawyer made the point, quite validly, that she was unlikely to have been able to access the hold and retrieve the gun during the flight.

An enquiry had, however, been launched and was likely to take several months to complete.

She held Michael's gaze for a few brief moments. She was very petite, with a remarkably smooth and unlined, elfin face, and the bluest of blue eyes that seemed to penetrate his very soul. Her luxuriant silver hair was tied back in a ponytail. They had barely spoken in the weeks since the shooting. And although he owed her his life, his overwhelming emotion on each occasion they had met, was embarrassment. And humiliation at the recollection of the confidences they had exchanged, the intimacies they had shared. He was not sure he could ever forgive her the deception. She was, after all, thirty-five years his senior.

He didn't linger, or meet her eyes for more than a few seconds, acknowledging her only with the merest of nods, before allowing his legal team to steer him away toward the door and the Californian sunshine that split the sidewalks outside.

But even as he felt the warmth of it on his skin and turned his face toward the sky, he felt an ache of regret deep within. For the fundamental truth was that he missed Doobie Littlething.

Gillian MacCormack's attorney took her by the elbow and led her toward the courtroom. In a sense her situation was the graver of the two. It was she who had pulled the trigger, she who had taken a life. And the court would decide today whether or not she was to face charges of manslaughter.

Chapter Forty-One

All the doors in the house were open. A warm breeze blew through it from the ocean. Michael sat on the terrace staring at the chess board on which he had so often done battle with Mora. Every piece stood in its starting square, ebony facing ivory in an eternal stand-off. And he knew that he would never move these chessmen again.

He looked up as a squat, square man in blue overalls appeared at the open door. "You want me to pack that now, sir?"

Michael nodded and got up to let the removal man wrap and box the chessmen and board and free up the table and chairs to be taken out front to the truck. Virtually everything was gone now. The boxes packed all those weeks ago. The furniture. He had donated a lot of it to charity. After all, it would take much less to furnish the small apartment he had taken for rent further along the coast. He would still have his beloved sea-view and a small balcony where he could sit out and read, but a single man required less space and less baggage.

He had decided not to go back east. He had got too used to the sunshine. It would be hard to return to the cold, grey winters of New England.

He wandered now through the empty house that he and Mora had once animated, and knew that finally he had reached a place in his life where he felt able to move on. He had quit his job, and had no idea what the future might bring. But there would be no more looking back.

"You want us to pack up your computer stuff?"

Michael turned to find another removal man regarding him quizzically. "No, that's alright. I'll be packing it in the trunk to take to the apartment myself."

"Okay, sir. Well, that's us finished for now. Have a good day."

"Sure. You, too."

When they had gone, he went through to his office. There was no chair. So he lifted his computer and monitor carefully down to the floor and squatted in front of it with the keyboard in his lap. He would check his email one last time before dismantling it all. There were a couple of mails from his lawyer, another from the bank, one from Sherri, who was holding him to his promise of fifteen percent. In the end she had sold the property for just under four million, so she had earned her fee.

He dealt with them all, and was about to shut down, when his eye fell upon the Second Life icon on his desktop. It sent a tiny shard of regret deep into his heart.

He had said goodbye to his lawyers outside the courthouse in Santa Ana, and then stood for several minutes before deciding to go back in. The public benches were almost empty when he slipped into the back of the courtroom to listen to the proceedings. Gillian MacCormack had been sitting with her back to him, unaware of his presence. Legal arguments on both sides were presented to a judge who knew she was just going through the motions. No one had wanted to charge this genteel sixty-seven-year-old with anything, never mind manslaughter. After all, her timely intervention had saved a man's life. And so, in the end, the judge had found that there was no case to answer, and she was free to go.

Michael had hurried out again, even before Gillian had got to her feet. She had never known he was there.

Now, on an impulse, he opened up his browser and went to the Second Life website. There he created a new account, able once more to choose the name of Chas Chesnokov, since there was no record that it had ever existed.

He opened up the Second Life software and logged in with his old user name and password, and rezzed into Orientation Island as the basic AV he had been on his first sojourn into the virtual world. He looked around at the familiar landmarks, the volcano, the learning islands interlinked by bridges. And watched the newbies wandering around bumping into each other, waving their arms in the air, falling into the water. He clicked on his blank Lindens total at the top of his screen and bought himself twenty dollars' worth. Then went on a spending spree.

Body Doubles, and Naughty Island. A Brad Pitt body shape; Gabriel skin, Golden Tan with Facial Hair 4; Paris Blue Eyes; a shock of blond hair, Untamed in Golden Bay Multitonal III. And then a clothes mall. Rusted green cargos, white shirt and cream sweater, black grunge boots. Within twenty minutes he had remade Chas in his original image. There would have been no way to tell the difference. And in some strange way that he could never have quantified, Michael felt whole again. Chas had pulled him back from the brink once. Perhaps he would do it again.

◇◇◇

Chas rezzed into Twist's office. For a moment he was almost overcome with melancholy. This was the place Janey had made. This was the persona she had wanted to be. And now she was gone. When the tiers expired, so would her office, and everything in it. But it occurred to Chas that he could keep the name, set up his own agency in her memory, maybe even live out the fantasy for her. But, then, he knew that he was unlikely to stay here. Like other parts of his life, it was time to leave it behind and move on. This was just a last stroll down memory lane.

He went into the Search window and found Midsomer Isle. A final visit.

◇◇◇

The sun was setting, just as it always had been. Trees and ferns and bushes swayed in the sea breezes, and roses rezzed all around the entry columns. Chas looked at the empty chairs and the chessmen awaiting some avatar to come along and move them, and felt a pang of regret. Without Doobie he would never have survived, in either SL or RL. He remembered the confidences they had exchanged right here on this circular terrace overlooking the sea, the meal they had shared, and their first dance among the hidden columns somewhere further up the mountain.

He wandered across the terrace to the sweep of the retaining wall and looked out at the dying sunlight coruscating across the water, light reflecting all the way to the horizon and the setting sun.

Doobie: Hello, Chas.

Chas swivelled around.

Chas: Doobie!

She was wearing a black evening gown with a deep-cut neckline, her hair piled up on her head and hanging down in ringlets at the sides. She wore opal bangles on her wrists, and an opal pendant on a silver chain that fell between her breasts. And he thought she looked quite beautiful.

Doobie: I was down at Puck's Hideaway and saw you appear on my radar.

Chas: I heard they decided not to bring any charges.

Doobie: No.

There was a long, awkward silence.

Chas: I guess…I never did say thank you.

Doobie: What for?

Chas: Saving my life.

Doobie Littlething smiles.

Chas: There was something I've been meaning to ask you.

He hesitated.

Doobie: Yes?

Chas: That stuff about your husband being killed. And the baby…

Doobie: It wasn't a lie, if that's what you're thinking. It just happened a very long time ago. In the sixties. They were fighting in Vietnam then. Who knows why.

Chas: And you never married?

Doobie: No. I never wanted to. It was like I was dead for a long time. Just like you after Mora. And then Second Life, for me, was like being born again. A chance to go back and do the things I'd never done, be the person I'd never been. In a way, it gave me back my life, gave me a second chance.

Now they stood looking at each other. Neither certain of what to say next. And the silence hung. And hung. For what seemed like an eternity. Until finally it was Doobie who found words.

Doobie: I missed you, Chas.

Chas: I missed you, too.

Another silence, then,

Doobie: We were good together.

Chas: We were.

Doobie: We could be again.

She took a step toward him, then seemed to think better of it. She stopped.

Doobie: Does it matter how many years there are between us? We are who we are.

They heard the sound of the wind in the trees. SL ambience swelled and faded. Somewhere a bell sounded. Or it might have been windchimes.

Chas: Would you like a game of chess?

Doobie: I'd love a game.

Chas right-clicked on the nearest seat and sat at the table. Doobie sat opposite him. He looked up.

Chas Chesnokov smiles.

Chas: Your move, Doobs.

To receive a free catalog of Poisoned Pen Press titles, please contact us in one of the following ways:

Phone: 1-800-421-3976
Facsimile: 1-480-949-1707
Email: info@poisonedpenpress.com
Website: www.poisonedpenpress.com

Poisoned Pen Press
6962 E. First Ave. Ste. 103
Scottsdale, AZ 85251